NO FUTURE

DOCTOR WHO – THE NEW ADVENTURES

Also available:

NO FUTURE

Paul Cornell

First published in Great Britain in 1994 by
Doctor Who Books
an imprint of Virgin Publishing Ltd
332 Ladbroke Grove
London W10 5AH

ISBN 0 426 20409 3

Cover illustration by Pete Walbank

Phototypeset by Intype, London
Printed and bound in Great Britain by
Cox & Wyman Ltd, Reading, Berks

With thanks to:

Miles Booy, Keith Topping – Criticism and structural advice.
Penny List – Moral support.
Alan Barnes, Jon Head, Nick Pegg, Gary Russell – Research.
Andrew Martin – It was his joke originally.
John Freeman – An idea.
The MSCT – Fraternity.

Action by HAVOC

And to all my friends, for their love and patience.
And thanks to Mum and Dad, for Bread and Butter and Honey.

For
Kini Brooks
and
Karen Dunn

Prologue

The Brigadier glanced at the clipboard the clerical officer had handed him, signed twice and handed it back, not missing a step as he marched along the corridor. Captain Pike, new from the USAF, was at his shoulder.

'How many men do we have available?' the Brigadier asked.

'Number One Platoon of A Company. They just got here, sir. Number Four Platoon's on the way, we're pulling the other two platoons off leave as fast as possible, some of those guys are in Peru – '

'Fifty-eight men. Not many, eh Captain?'

'Never is, sir.'

Lethbridge-Stewart strode into the control room, glancing at the scientists with an assured smile. The UNIT troops saluted, and he returned the gesture. 'Now listen to me. The situation's under control, we're about to make our move. I want all non-essential personnel to retire to an area of safety.'

'There is no area of safety!' The female scientist in charge of the facility stood up, pointing to the screen that dominated one end of the room. 'Those things are boosting the reactor power over all the safety margins. This place could be a potential H-bomb. We're staring a criticality in the face – '

'That's what we aim to prevent, Miss Allen. Evacuate these people, Captain.' Ignoring the noises of protest around him, the Brigadier glanced up at the screen.

Cybermen. Six of them, standing motionless as their computer did something strange to the reactor controls.

1

They'd marched in, accessed the location of the reactor and just walked into the high radiation zone. He hadn't seen the creatures in six years, not since 1970. He only raised an eyebrow.

'Any suggestions, Mister Benton?'

The burly RSM stepped forward, pulling a communications link from his ear. 'Orbital says the sky's clear, sir. They might have come alone.'

'Or they're too stealthy for us. We can't assume that they haven't got support. Tell orbital to concentrate on finding a landing site. The buggers are probably down the sewers again.'

'We could do with the Doctor, eh sir?'

'We could indeed . . .' The Brigadier tapped his swagger stick in one palm, thinking. When the familiar noise rose in the next room, he turned, surprised. A murmur of relief and excitement shuffled through the men. They all knew what the wheezing, groaning sound signified.

Pike frowned. 'What does it mean, sir?'

'It means we are not alone, Captain.'

The Doctor strode into the room, scooping his hat from his head. Behind him were an elegantly slim woman with short dark hair, and a muscular one in a futuristic suit of body armour.

'Doctor! I see you've regenerated again!'

'The life I lead, Brigadier. These are Benny and Ace. What's the situation?'

The Brigadier was about to speak, but Ace interrupted, her eyes fixed on the screen. 'Six armoured, close group. Cybermen . . .' The last word was said with a little upward curl of the lip, like the creatures reminded her of something funny. Something long ago. 'One shot, so what?'

Pike ran his hand back through his hair, grinning. 'Ah, you know what you're talking about here?'

'Yeah. Got any gold?'

The Captain pulled two clips from a webbing pouch. '9mm Goldheads for the sub-machine-gun. Made for us in Belgium.'

'Good. But not that good.' Ace spoke into her wrist. 'Six flechettes, gold tips.'

'Flechettes? Don't talk to me about flechettes! They don't – '

'Captain Pike!' the Brigadier barked, gesturing his subordinate back to the control console.

'They're here for a reason . . .' The Doctor was pacing, glancing up at the screen, his hands knotted behind his back. 'But what? Why do they want a release of radiation?'

'Well, as an attack, obviously – '

'No! They have much more advanced weapons. It's more subtle than that . . .'

Pike slapped the console. 'Listen, sir, I don't know this guy, but I do know we've got about ten minutes before this situation goes right out of our control and – '

'That gives us five minutes to think, Captain. Find me a systems manual, would you?' The Brigadier bent closer to watch the Doctor scribbling on a pad. Benny, hugging herself, had wandered up to look at the figures also. She gave Lethbridge-Stewart a quick smile of encouragement.

Pike retreated to where Ace was checking the tabs on her armour. 'What d'you think?'

'Slice and dice. For God's sake, I used to take those things out without ordinance. With me or not?'

Pike glanced over his shoulder. 'Well – '

Ace reached up and took his earlobe between her fingers. There was electricity in her hands. 'With.'

Pike nodded. 'Yeah. Let's do it.'

'Tell me that in five minutes.'

The UNIT man checked the clip on his sub-machine-gun and followed Ace from the room. Nobody saw them leave.

Benny clicked her fingers. 'Look at them. Look how slowly they're moving . . .'

Benton nodded. 'That's the Cybermen for you.'

'But they could do this in a few seconds, couldn't they, if they control the reactor? Never mind a criticality, they could just let radioactive material into the atmos-

3

phere by bypassing the safety features. They're having you on, Brigadier!'

'I hardly intend to call their bluff, Miss –'

'No!' The Doctor leapt up from his scribblings. 'That's it! You've cleared an area already, complete with air corridor! They want a mass landing site!'

'So they're not planning on going critical?' the Brigadier looked almost relieved.

'Not unless the stalemate's broken. Then they'll probably sacrifice themselves. Ace –' he turned his head and saw that his companion had gone. 'Where is she?'

'I saw her just –' Benton began.

'Look!' Benny was pointing up at the screen. On it, two figures in protective clothing had tumbled into the reactor control area.

'Ace!' the Doctor shouted. 'Don't !'

Three Cybermen flew backwards clutching at their chest units, Pike rolling and firing his sub-machine-gun as Ace made a firm gesture with one hand. One of the creatures leapt forwards, slamming a fist into the alien equipment. Ace made another gesture, and its head silently burst into a bloom of green fluid. The remaining two raised their hands in a deadly pointing gesture, but Ace sent one spinning with clicks of her fingers, miniature explosions ripping its armour into shreds. Pike rammed his gun into the other's face and blew it off.

Lights on the reactor head were winking quickly.

'Doctor?' the Brigadier grabbed the Time Lord's shoulder.

'Ace . . .' The Doctor was staring. 'I can't . . .'

'Doctor, what's happening?' Benny grabbed him by his lapels. 'Talk to us!'

On the screen, Ace and Pike slammed their fists together in triumph.

'It's too –' The Doctor took a deep breath.

White light. The control room wall exploded and everything flashed into liquid death.

GAME OVER

The man in the hood leant back from his dark console, his finger tapping the screen in thought.

'Rewind the simulation.' The picture whizzed backwards, the humans running and jumping back to a certain point. 'There.'

Ace and Pike slammed their fists together. Inside the face-plate of the bulky radiation suit, ripped at the sleeves from where her flechettes had pierced it, Ace's grin could just be seen.

The hooded watcher tapped his finger against her image, smiling to himself. 'Right. Now . . .'

Chuckling, he stood up from the console. Would that what he'd seen had been real. But no . . . no, that would be far too quick.

There was plenty of time for the game. The Doctor's suffering had hardly begun.

In a room in a space-time machine in the space-time Vortex, Ace woke up, completely at ease and sane, at one with the world as a warrior.

That was what they didn't understand, she thought. They didn't understand that you could enjoy explosions and violence and murder and still be sane.

The woman in the red dress was standing at the end of her bed.

She pointed at Ace.

And she was laughing.

1

England's Dreaming

London lay under the haze of a June evening. Buildings let go of the heat they'd sucked in all day, and that breath let the streets cool slowly. The sky was summer orange, a shining blank that had all the lights of the city in it. It was refreshing after the day's sort of blank, bleached-out and dry. Car noises and sudden shouts and the low background whirr of air-conditioning blended with the clatter of footsteps on pavements, and all the business of a city was in place. Empty. Ready.

To feel it now was good, to finally understand how it felt. Bernice Summerfield, Ph.d. (Fictional) and Member of the Academy of Martian Studies (In Her Dreams) was enjoying England in 1976. Last time it had been fiction, but this was history and, yes, she still thought those two were different. This summer was like, well, like the first summer, like waking up from some sort of winter decade. She needed summer now, and she was willing to believe that this one was real. Benny was an archaeologist from the future, the latest companion of the adventurer in time and space known as the Doctor. Recently the Doctor's craft, the TARDIS, had been plunged into a series of adventures in bizarre parallel worlds, where nothing was what it seemed. It had come over almost as an ordeal, some kind of sadistic test. Getting back to reality, especially in her favourite historical period, was like a holiday. Two weeks ago the Doctor had dashed out of the TARDIS, leaving Benny with only a series of notes. Some of the requests contained in those, or perhaps they were better described as orders, had caused her slight pause.

6

Sweating in her duffle-coat, she walked quickly through the narrow backstreets of Soho, muttering words under her breath. Merging with an existent subculture was always hard, but 'deep cover' the Doctor had said, and you couldn't get much deeper than this. She stopped in an alley behind an old theatre, and glanced up at the sign nailed above the stage door.

The Chelsea Club. Spray-painted, of course, the wooden plank just about covering the gleeful bosoms that the club used to advertise.

Benny felt sick. She could have spent the summer punting or wine-tasting or something. She squared her shoulders, cleared her throat and tried an experimental scale. She hadn't really sung seriously since the Academy's production of Carousel.

'Step one. Remove duffle-coat.' She did so. Under the coat was a ripped-up leather dress with a hand-sewn swirl of lace at the hem. It was still not something that Benny would have wanted to be buried in. It matched the black swirls of face paint that she wore. 'Now, repeat after me. I do want to be anarchy. Oh yes I do.'

The stage door opened, and Danny Pain poked his head out. 'Benny! Where have you been since the sound check?'

'Walking off my nerves.' Benny tripped up the steps. 'Just stopped off for a pint of vodka or two. Anywhere I can leave my duffle-coat?'

The Doctor paced up to the wall of his cell and put his fingers on the mortar between the bricks.

'Solid. No ventilation ducts. No passages. No escape.' He lowered the hand. 'And why should there be? I'm not writing it, this time ... I don't know what's going to happen ...'

'Talking to yourself?' The soldier who had appeared outside the bars had identified himself as Major Bryan Carpenter when the Doctor had been brought in that morning. He was tall and thin, and had a scar down his

7

left cheek. 'Now, let's go back to the beginning. How did you get here?'

'In a van. You objected to me walking into the UNIT office in Kensington and asking for information – '

'I meant where is your craft, where did you land?'

'Trafalgar Square.'

Carpenter shook his head and sighed. 'I'm allowed under UN Resolution 2245 to use ultimate force on hostile extraterrestrials. You are not officially a person, Doctor, if that is what you're called . . .'

'So you can do what you like to me? Very neat. Very nasty. This organization seems to have changed in the last six months, or the last few years, depending on how you look at it. But who's doing the looking . . .?' The Doctor was gazing into the distance, his voice despairing.

'Philosophy will get you nowhere.'

The Doctor's eyes snapped back to Carpenter's, and the soldier took a step away from the bars. For a moment, some great anger had ignited inside the little man. It was gone just as quickly. 'I'm the Doctor. Look at the records. I used to be UNIT's scientific adviser.'

'So some of the men say.' A new figure had appeared at the cell doorway beside Carpenter, a dark-haired soldier with a laughter-lined face and a New York accent. 'They all know about the Doctor, but here's the problem. You don't look like him.'

'I change my appearance. Frequently. I can do that, you see, I'm an alien.'

'And these medical tests prove that . . .' The new arrival held up a sheaf of papers to the light. 'Got two of those, huh?'

'Captain Pike!' Carpenter interrupted. 'I'm conducting an interrogation. As senior officer – '

'Well, excuse me sir, but as Alien Liaison Officer, I have ultimate responsibility for captured ETs. Looking at these test results, I think he's had enough questioning for today.'

Carpenter met Pike's level gaze. 'I won't forget this, Captain.'

'No sir. Have a nice day, sir.' Pike leaned against the bars of the cell, sighing as Carpenter's footsteps receded down the concrete corridor. 'He doesn't know that the guys here call him Karen.'

'Karen?'

'Karen Carpenter. Hey, you must be an alien. Now, we're going to get you to some more comfortable secure accommodation as soon as we can. These SAS basements aren't too hot on the conveniences.'

The Doctor smiled ruefully. 'So you're the good soldier. As opposed to the bad one. I tell you everything because he's gone away. What's your first memory?'

Pike rubbed his chin, surprised. 'Ah . . . standing on a beach. I'm wearing a newspaper hat, and I got a Twinkie in my hand. Or maybe that's just because I saw that in some photos my Dad had, I'm not sure. Why do you ask?'

'Curiosity.'

'Gets cats killed.'

'I have more than nine lives. Is there nothing in those files about me?'

Pike leafed through his papers. 'A doctor John Smith was put on the payroll five years ago, and seems to have been active in the Big Bug Era as they call it here. Is that you? He didn't cash a lot of his pay cheques. He was involved in the death of some psychic guy . . .'

'Involved? I wouldn't call it that.'

'Hey, I just read what I got here. The last time any serving officer saw him was a few months ago, just before I transferred from the USAF.'

'That's in Scotland, Tulloch Moor. Or in Whitehall. The Zygons.'

'Yeah, yeah, those bugs. Thing is, we've had computer hackers in lately, we've had a major terrorist scare all summer, we've had Black Alert up every other week – '

'Terrorists?'

'Black Star. A development of the Angry Brigade. They're anarchists, you know, they want to deprive the country of the Queen, parliament, garbage collectors, you name it. Anything civic is their bag. We're being co-opted in the fight against, 'cos our tracking technology's a few steps up on regular issue.'

'How bad's the situation?'

'Well, life goes on, but we've had major bombs in Harrods, Hamleys, the Albert Hall, the Science Museum . . . the list goes on. They're at the top of everybody's hit list. And now you show up without a pass – '

'It's in my other jacket,' the Doctor said as he glanced down at his white safari suit. 'I thought I could do with a change.'

'And you expect us to believe that you're the Doctor. Well, hey, you might be, but UNIT's had several purges in the last six months. A lot of top brass have been shuffled out. How do we know you're not this guy . . .' Pike flicked through the file again. 'The Master?'

'The Master's dead. I killed him. There's one officer who'll identify me immediately. Call Geneva and ask for – '

'Brigadier Lethbridge-Stewart!' Carpenter clicked his heels behind Pike, who snapped to his feet and saluted.

The Brigadier stepped up to the cell and frowned. He looked the Doctor up and down. He was just as he should be, the Doctor realized thankfully, 46, but looking younger. Straight back, neat moustache, absolute confidence.

'The Autons, the Axons . . . Omega. Tell them who I am, Brigadier.'

'I'm sorry,' the Brigadier glanced at Pike. 'But I've never seen this man before in my life. Find out all you can.'

And he strode away before the Doctor could say another word.

The lights flicked up like a torch coming on, and flickered again, strobing over the band as they wandered on-stage to gathering cries and shouts. The air was humming with the amps, a great noise ready to happen.

Benny gripped the microphone to steady herself, and watched the lights wash over the faces of the audience. Their hair was cut, and they had taken in their breath, about to roar. Somewhere out there was Ace. She was probably laughing, or hurting somebody. Bloody demon that she was, bloody thing round Benny's neck.

Benny made herself say the words. In saying them, she discovered that she wasn't treating this as a game any more.

'Hello. We're Plasticine. This is Oxford Street.'

And the noise began.

Ace was leaning on a wall at the back of the club, one hand steady on a bar rail to stop herself being pulled into the mass. Her jacket hid the body armour she'd taken to wearing, and the expression in her eyes was secret behind her mirrorshades. She was watching Benny's pretend band play. The crowd were grabbing each other, staring rabidly into each other's eyes as they threw body into body, or slammed their ribs together, or clutched throats and strangled. They wore ripped-up leather and the thin straps and chains of bondage. They were really young, and they had their hair bleached and their faces made up like little dolls. Raving little dolls, dolls that bucked and slapped to the music as the lights and driving guitar filled them with energy.

A boy dived at her, hands outstretched to pull her into the crowd. She slapped him back. He spun away, surprised and hurt.

With a series of short concussions, the song stopped. Benny staggered back from the microphone, looking like she'd been shot.

'Don't spit at me,' she told the audience, in a voice that Ace was sure was taking the piss out of her, a voice full of pretend violence. 'I don't like it.'

The problem with Benny was that she thought she knew something about Ace. She thought she'd been told secrets, and the first thing she'd done with them was to go straight to the Doctor. That might, Ace told herself, have been the plan all along, to see how trustworthy this civilian was now. Might have been. Anyway, Ace'd acted like it hurt, and maybe it did.

She glanced between the shadowy figures on the stage, watched as the white light swept over them. Benny had hopped back to the bassist, a wrinkle-faced man whose hair was a bit too long, and who wore a silk scarf under his leathers. Behind them sat a bald drummer with a tattooed chest. On the other side of the stage, his cropped hair in every direction, his black T-shirt slit across the nipples, the other guitarist stared at the audience challengingly.

At the side of the bare stage, around the corner by the sound desk, a fat man was standing. He wore a grey suit and a skinny tie, and his hair was cut in a pudding bowl. He was smiling gleefully, rubbing his hands together. Ah. Profit. Every now and then he whispered to a thin man in a black polo-neck who stood beside him. The thin man was saying something, and had his fingers stuck in his ears. He glanced out into the audience and for a moment he seemed to connect with Ace. He took a step back into the shadows.

For the first time that night, Ace smiled.

'All right,' said Benny. 'This is Revolution Tomorrow.'

Pretending to be a punk. Typical Benny. How crap could you get?

The Doctor sat on the floor of his cell, his legs crossed, his eyes closed. He was thinking about reality, about control. The cell was almost a comfort to him.

In a different universe, the Silurians took over the world. And that universe was unstable, it wouldn't have lasted. So, with a bit of a delay to allow Benny and Ace their finer feelings, he'd switched it off. He didn't regret it, there had to be somebody who did things like t..at, otherwise the cosmos would drown in an ocean of good intentions that had come to bad ends. He'd told them something pseudoscientific, something they'd accept that explained why there was only one universe, why there were no alternatives. Ace had said that was rubbish. Natural alternatives did spring up from time to time, places like Morgaine's continuum, and of course Ace

12

would now love to be living in one of them. But what had scared him was the difference. The Silurian Earth had been made, created. Something had given Morka the power to kill his third incarnation. Something had resurrected the Garvond. Something was showing him all sorts of alternatives. But why?

He'd tried to right the world enough times, to be Time's Champion. Plotting, putting a mattress where he was going to fall. He'd felt his handwriting stretching across the universe, tripped over his lines, sometimes grasped a word or phrase that was suddenly, obviously, going to save him. And at the same time as Ace and Benny started to question why he needed them – why, why did people need to be told about things like love, when it was always too late, always no good – suddenly he was an extra again, blundering into the scenery in somebody else's script. He hadn't felt like that since his trial, since he saw what he was going to become and decided to stop it. Lost again. At least he remembered how to improvise.

The flower expanded in his mind once more, and he felt his scalp, remembering the feathers. Huitzilin had seemed designed to punish him. The spirit that haunted assassins, that goaded him for his naivety in the face of political reality. 'Pleased to meet you,' the Doctor murmured, remembering the contours of Huitzilin's mind inside his. 'Hope you catch my name . . .' Twenty thousand hearts. Run to the temple and shout for them to stop. Sing for me. The phrases seemed to be the lost lines of whatever manuscript he'd been preparing here, scraps of paper on the breeze. It was as if the Left-Handed Hummingbird was still laughing at him.

The healer becomes the warrior. True. That was the horror of it. Daleks, Cybermen, the Master. Every time he tried to stop, there was another monster to kill. He couldn't retire, couldn't just ignore it all and become that healer again. Ace had stabbed him, tried to stab him through one of his hearts. She'd been controlled, of course, but where had that impulse come from? None of the issues that adventure had churned up had been resolved.

13

At his most strung-out, when he thought he was going to vanish into the Hummingbird, he'd asked Ace to kill him. The Huitzilin inside him had wanted her to try that. He was certain that, somewhere inside her, Ace remembered his request.

And then the Land of Fiction, the most terrible and wonderful place, the place with no law to stop the monsters. Perhaps these days he should have felt at home there, written and rewritten, no will of his own. At least Benny hadn't left him then, as he thought she might. Without her . . . without Ace. No. There were more important matters than his own pain.

While he was going through these other worlds, the real one was in danger. Earth, as the Master of the Land of Fiction knew it, was a place occupied by alien invaders. That had happened in 1976. Which was why he came here. Trying to find whoever was behind all this.

There was a sound outside the cell. The light on the surveillance camera in the corridor had gone out.

The guard outside the cell crumpled and fell, making a tiny gasp. A dark figure rushed to the bars.

'Doc?'

'Who are you?' The Doctor stood up.

'A friend. Take this.' The figure slid a card through the electronic lock on the cell, and handed it to the Doctor. 'If you're careful, you can use this to open every door between here and the exit. This is only a temporary safe-house, there's no electronic security.'

The Doctor swung open the cell door and stepped out, looking at the man suspiciously. He was dressed in a black stealth suit, with a balaclava covering his features. 'Why are you doing this?'

'The Brig's acting really strangely. Some of us think he's been compromised. I'll meet you at the Valiant Trooper, six o'clock tomorrow.'

The Doctor stepped quickly into the corridor, and glanced back. The man was binding the guard's hands in adhesive tape. 'What about you?'

'I don't have to escape, do I?'

14

The Doctor nodded and ran.

The building was an old Edwardian tenement, and the Doctor quickly found his way up to the ground floor. An open door cast a triangle of light across the top of the cellar stairs, and the sounds of a television came from the room. Some soldiers were talking.

'You don't get harder than Daleks, mate. Hit one straight on with a frag grenade, it just keeps going.'

'Leave it out, the closest you've got to a Dalek is a casing in the training unit. You zap any Zygons?'

'You were here then? Before my time.'

'Yeah . . .' The Doctor detected a sigh in the voice of the second soldier. 'Before a lot of people's time these days . . .'

The Doctor crept up to the door. Across the landing, there was a glass partition with an electronic lock. The stairwell room had obviously been turned into a rough guardroom. He took a deep breath, and walked straight past the door.

'What was that?'

'RSM?'

'He'd have popped his head in, you know him.'

The Doctor had reached the partition, and swiped the card through the lock. A soldier appeared in the doorway, yelled and snapped his rifle up to shoulder height.

The Doctor jumped through the door and slammed it.

Two bullets hit the glass, smashing circles around the Doctor's body. He was running again, as the soldier hit an alarm.

Rounding a corner, the Doctor turned away from a running line of soldiers, ran up two flights of servants' stairs, thinking of not thinking, of randomly going where they wouldn't expect.

Another corner, straight into two troopers, sending them sprawling. 'That way!' he bellowed, pointing behind him, and they glanced that way, turned, glimpsed him hurdling out of a window.

They ran to it, looked down at the street below, past the fire-escape beside the window. The street was empty.

Then they looked up.

The Doctor was standing on the next flight of the metal structure. He smashed the window, hopped inside, bounced across three bunk-beds, opened the door. In the corridor, he heard running feet above and below, the alarm still obscuring everything.

Disguise, escape, distraction? The Doctor glanced about the corridor, and saw a fire extinguisher. He grabbed it and ran at the door, watched the door opening, caught two troopers running through it with a spray of foam at head height, then sprayed down as they scattered, sending the ones behind sprawling as he hopped between them.

He dodged grabs, shouted back at shouts and burst through into a central circular stairwell. With a polished banister. Throwing aside the cylinder, he jumped onto the banister and slid.

Gunshots buffeted the landings around him, sending plaster flying in chunks. He crouched into a ball. The noise was deafening, shouts and shots and alarms, and he yelled a piercing yell, clutched his chest, fell from the banister three feet before the end, deadfell onto his back, sprung back to his feet again past two soldiers who had run forward from their post to capture him.

Ten metres to the front door.

They were sprinting after him.

He slammed into the door, swiped the card through the lock, the door clicked open, he burst through it, missing a grab for his collar by inches.

Down the steps, into the street.

Big street, part of a square with a tiny triangle of trees in the middle. The warmth of the summer night air slammed into the Doctor's lungs as he sprinted, low orange light blinding him as it shone off car bonnets and parched stone.

Captain Pike was running with his men, catching up to the Doctor with every stride.

And then he stopped and shouted: 'Ready, Aim –'

Five troopers snapped into aiming posture. They had a clear line of fire.

The Doctor jumped in front of a taxi as it pulled away from the hotel opposite. Its driver gasped and swung, screeching to a stop.

'Hold your fire!' Pike yelled.

The Doctor dived into the back seat of the car.

'Drive!' he shouted. 'They're Russians!'

The taxi accelerated round the corner with a screech, the door swinging open.

'Russians my arse,' laughed the driver in a Londonderry accent. 'You're one of our boys, aren't you?'

'Trafalgar Square . . .' murmured the Doctor in his best brogue. 'And do you know a pub called the Valiant Trooper?'

'Thanks, goodnight!' Benny kicked over the mike stand and stalked off, to cheering and yelling. Individual voices piped up over the mob, and a thumping of boots on floorboards began. Shrill screams shone out as the lights clumped down to darkness.

'They're calling for you,' Kit grinned his bad teeth at her, rubbing his hair with a towel. 'What do we do for the encore, eh?'

'There is no encore,' Danny murmured, resting his chin on Kit's shoulder. 'We don't know any more songs.'

'Aw, come on mate, we could jam Paint It Black or something . . .'

Danny turned and carefully punched the white brick of the wall. He drew blood, and peered at his knuckle petulantly. 'Be real, shall we? I don't know it. I wouldn't learn it. It's crap.'

Cob raised his hands in a strangling gesture. 'Lads, Benny, listen. I didn't want to tell you this, but there's a guy at the mixing desk . . . Macoustra let him in, I dunno who he is. He's recording us tonight.'

Danny shrugged. 'So? I've got a mate in the audience doing a bootleg.'

'Yeah, but this guy's recording us for real. We've got to do an encore.'

'Who says we got to? Let them feel it, Cobby.'

Benny smoothed back her fringe with one hand. Her hair was wet with exertion. There were times when she regretted getting rid of her dreadlocks. Indeed, there were times when she wished she had a frying-pan handy. 'It's all right. I'll go back and explain, okay?'

She hopped on-stage again, surprising the lighting gantry, who quickly fixed a spotlight on her. A surprised roar came from the audience. This was too soon, she wasn't playing the game. And then they were suddenly silent, expecting her to sing alone. Benny was grateful for B1057: Essentials Of Rock Culture. 'We're very sorry,' she looked down at her shoes. 'But we've had a talk about it, and we don't know any more songs. I know a little poetry if anybody would, erm, dig that?'

Roar. Bad roar. Some laughter. A fire extinguisher narrowly missed her head and hit the back curtain, to general applause. 'I'll take that as a No. Thank you and good night.'

The audience howled as the house lights went up.

'That,' grinned Danny, as he heard the first crashes and splinters erupt from the auditorium, 'was such an intelligent thing to do.'

Benny gave him a hard stare. 'I'd better go and find my duffle-coat,' she muttered.

It took an hour for the trouble to subside, and for the audience to leave the building. Benny took an occasional glance out from the curtain, and saw things and people thrown. Not a lot of person-person stuff, though. Property damage and grappling. A bigger dance. Nobody should be proud of causing it, though. Power corrupts and all that. She made a mental note to chastise herself severely at some point in the future.

When the band were finally able to emerge, the club was a mess. Cob went over to his drums and started to lovingly pack them away.

'I am glad,' Benny opined, 'that we were paid cash in advance.'

The floor was covered in stains, many of them bloody, and the fading wallpaper had been ripped in great sheets from the walls. The sound engineer was shaking his head in horror at the speaker stack which had been kicked in. The wall beside the stage had been sprayed with a huge black star, unseen in the frenzy. 'Black Star bastards. Mr Macoustra isn't going to like this,' he called over his shoulder.

'What you worrying about, mate?' asked Kit. 'Bouncers handled it. Bit of a minor incident.'

'Minor incident?' Danny smiled. 'It was a riot. With terrorist overtones. I just called the inkies and said I was a punter. I told them I got my arm smashed up. I might be sueing us. Then I called them back as me, and said that we had no comment to make. Should set us up nicely for the Roundhouse next week. It's at times like these, my brothers, that I wish we had a manager.'

'It seems silly to me,' Benny sighed. 'Why can't they just enjoy the music?'

'I loved it!' shouted a voice from the back of the hall. Ace was leaning against the wall, toying with her back-stage pass. 'Thought that was good.'

'Did you?' Benny smiled. 'Which songs did you like?'

'Not the songs. The scrap.' Ace wandered forward. 'Taking care of business. You're Danny Plain, aren't you? The one who's gonna save the world?'

'Yeah,' Danny nodded without a blink. 'Who're you?'

'My sister, Ace.' Benny whispered.

'Dorothy Moose,' Ace interrupted. 'You play very well.'

'Do I? Try not to.'

'Our surname is not actually Moose,' Benny told him. 'We're Summerfields.'

'She's a Summerfield, I'm a Moose, our Dad was a real bastard.'

Kit was looking at Ace approvingly. 'I'm interested, even if Danny isn't. You look like you're from the future.'

'Yeah, I am,' Ace sighed. 'That's how I know you don't get off with me. You're really ugly.'

'Oh, for God's sake,' Benny turned quickly away. 'These are my friends, and I don't think you should – '

'Well who's gonna stop me? Are you?'

'No, what I'll do is go away, actually. I'll just walk away and leave you here.'

'Yeah, like that's an experience I'm not used to.'

'Does everything we do have to come back to that?'

'Stop it,' muttered Cob, having hopped down from the stage. He had a worried look on his face. 'Guy backstage wants to talk. He's important. Priory Records. Robert Bertram.'

'The Man, the very Man!' Danny grinned evilly. 'The man who's organizing that fascist charity peace concert on the twenty-second. Well, you can tell him to – '

'Wait a few moments while we catch our breath,' Benny raised her hand. 'And then we'd be delighted to see him.'

Robert Bertram welcomed Benny and the band with open arms, pumping her hand between two of his. He was a chubby man, with a jolly face and an infectious grin. The man, Ace thought, in the grey suit. He hadn't been around for the riot. 'Charmed, charmed. I must say, I've been watching you for quite a few gigs now – '

'This is the first one in a proper club,' Cob broke in. 'And the others were without Benny.'

'Why yes, yes, that's the real difference. Since things are happening so fast these days, I thought I'd see if we could talk about a contract. So many A&R men outside the door, but I know Mr Macoustra well enough to get in. Nothing huge, you understand, Priory's very new, and you'd be the first punk band anybody's taken on. We'd just sign you for one album and see what happens. How does that suit you?'

Benny looked around at Kit's and Cob's grins and nodded. 'We say yes.'

'We say no!' Danny yelled, appalled. 'This is Robert Bertram, Benny, the famous man, the one who says he's going to sail round the world or something. He owns lots of things. Some very big businesses. He believes in money.' He looked around at the rest of the band, wringing the air in disbelief. 'This is the man who persuaded Doorstep to lose Jack Hail!'

'I pointed out that he and the band were moving in different musical directions . . .' murmured Bertram. 'They were moving towards music, he was moving away. Now, we already have product, if you want it. We've been using our new technology to catch the gig. It's a huge opportunity for you.'

Benny counted to ten mentally, and looked Danny in the eye. 'If we don't sign to Priory, I'll leave,' she stated. 'I am, as you would say, Danny, a bit pissed off.'

'I'll leave too,' Kit added. Everybody ignored him. There was silence.

'Ah well, if you feel like that about it.' Danny slumped against the wall. 'Nah, what the hell, let's sign, we can always give the money to the kids, right?'

'I think it's rather early to be talking in terms of children.' Benny tapped his nose lightly. 'But thank you.'

'Well then,' Bertram rubbed his hands together again. 'I believe that the drinks are on me!'

Ace had been watching this little game from a distance, and now she hung back as the group headed for the door. She was watching Bertram's shoulders, watching the way the little man hunched.

At some time in his life, he'd ducked a bullet or two.

He held the door of the club open for her, so she slowed down.

'And you are?' Bertram said as she reached the exit.

'Ace.'

'Why yes . . .' he smiled, his bright eyes meeting hers. 'Of course you are.'

They got the Bear And Staff for last orders, and Bertram bought a round before dashing off. He told Benny that the band ought to come and see him in the morning to discuss the deal.

Ace had kept watching him, and he'd given her a couple of the most genuinely friendly grins she'd ever seen. It was like finding a veteran in a kindergarten. There was some shared experience there. When he'd left, things got boring.

'What are your influences?' she asked Danny. He'd bought an orange juice, and was looking blankly at the wallpaper. Benny and the rest of the band were sitting at another table, giving him space to sulk.

'I'm very influenced by television.'

'Tom Verlaine and that lot? Hey, I once saw – '

'Not the band,' Danny deadpanned. 'The medium. You're very young for your age, aren't you?'

Ace ignored that. 'Why aren't you drinking?'

'Why are you?'

'Cos it makes me feel vulnerable.'

'It makes me feel very bad. Like being signed to Priory Records will make me feel bad. Money's a drug, and I don't take any drugs 'cos it's a crap Jefferson Airplane thing to do, right? It just gets you into stuff you wouldn't dream of if you were straight.'

'We're very alike.'

'Nah, if you're trying to get off with me, don't. I don't do that either. Besides, I prefer your sister.'

'I mean that you cover things up, the way I used to have to. Great battle mask, Danny. You ever seen someone take a scalp?'

'No, go on, tell me you have.'

'I saw it done to a boy. He was still alive, he was shouting for me to stop it happening. I couldn't, I was doing other stuff. I don't feel guilty about this, nothing I could do. But he had his face mushed down into the mud in the next second, and the blade was just stuck into his head behind his ear, and whipped across. The top of the skull comes off with it, if the blade's sharp enough, and this one was, for reasons that I won't go into. His brain burst out, and then the man with the blade was away.'

'Where was this then, the wild west?'

Ace paused, wondering if she should say that it had

22

happened on Palmeras, right after she'd lost Maire. Another planet. No.

'Nowhere you know.'

'You're pissed.'

'I haven't drunk much yet.'

'Nah, but you're pissed anyway.' Danny got up and walked towards Benny's table. Ace glanced after him, expressionless. She drained her glass in one. A moment later she was out of the door.

Danny looked back as she left. 'Thank Christ she's gone.'

'Don't say that.' Benny sighed. 'She's been through a lot.'

'She really your sister?'

Benny let her gaze fix on his for a moment. 'Yes. We're a very close family. Sometimes.'

'That mouth of hers'll get her in trouble,' Kit said, thumping down his empty Guinness glass. 'Bird like that with a mouth, not needed on voyage thank you very much.'

'Bird?' Danny grinned.

'A slang term for a woman.' Benny told him.

'I knew that. You, Kit, are one of the Flaxton Boys. You should be on Follyfoot, with these attitudes of yours. Your hair has grown into your brain.'

'Yeah? Piss off.'

'Witty, so witty . . .'

'We are not,' Benny held up her hand, ' a band that splits up before we sign a deal, are we?'

'No,' Cob muttered. 'We're not. Punk is going to be big, bigger than the Bay City Rollers. We need to be in on it, not mucking about.'

'Punk? What an awful word,' Danny sighed. 'Anarchy is more important than the music, Cob. We need to use this to let people know what's going on, about the change that's happening in the world.' For a moment, Benny saw Danny's defences drop totally, watched as his hands met in an urgent spire above the table. His voice lost a bit of the distant snarl that she'd grown so used to in the last few days. 'It's important. It's the only important thing that we do.'

'Bollocks!' spluttered Kit. 'All this punk stuff is just Dr Feelgood at twice the speed. The Teds were doing this years back. Bands need real musicians, they always will.'

'Kit,' Cob told Benny, 'has been playing in pub bands for seven years.'

'But I thought you said you were just learning the bass?' Danny frowned.

'Yeah mate, I used to be a drummer! I just moved up the watchyercallit, the evolutionary scale a bit, eh Cobby? While Daniel was at university!'

'Didn't go to university, thank you. It was art school. And I dropped out.'

'I'm sure you did,' murmured Benny consolingly. 'Now, it's getting late, and we've got a big day ahead of us tomorrow, so who's going to walk me home? Not you, Kit.' She finished off her whisky.

Danny sighed and looked up at the ceiling. 'I suppose it'll have to be me.'

The night was warm, an orange moon sitting above London. Benny was pleased at how close her ideas of the place had been to the truth, but some things jarred: the rubbish, the fumes, everything that was destroying the environment. She'd forgotten about those. When she first arrived in this era, a week ago, she'd almost expected to meet Harold Wilson, George Best and Madonna in the street. In that respect, she'd probably have been better off staying in the Land of Fiction.

Danny was hopping from foot to foot, in and out of the gutter, kicking a can along in front of him.

'Where are we going, then?' he asked.

'Trafalgar Square.'

'Catching a night bus, are we?'

'Well, I am. Aren't you going home?'

'Yeah, 'course I am, it's just the way I speak! Listen, if you thought I was trying it on, you're wrong!'

Benny was amazed by the force of Danny's response.

She stopped walking. 'Wait a minute. I was hoping you'd have a bit of a walk with me, because I like you and I think your punk act's quite fun . . .'

'It's not – '

'Hush. It would help if you could get over the idea that I'm afraid of you. Take my arm.' She stuck the limb out at an angle. 'Now, we're going to have a pleasant evening's wander, we're not going to worry about each other, and I'll try and forget that you've got external gonads, okay?'

'Yeah . . .' Danny nodded, and took Benny's arm, incredibly gently. 'But it really isn't an act. Is it all right if . . . can I tell you about punk?'

'By all means.' Benny smiled at the boy. God, he was only about seventeen. They probably had some kind of law here against escorting somebody who still had acne.

'I saw the Pistols at the Free Trade Hall two weeks back,' Danny began, stumbling over his words in the rush to get them out. 'I was staying with a mate up in Manchester. They were everything, the whole bit on the spot. The crowd had just got rid of fashion, right, 'cos it's all so much crap. We were all just people, from all over the place, and Johnny wasn't singing about love or how much he wanted to shag somebody, and nobody was being hassled. I got talking with this bloke called Stephen, and he was saying how much he wanted to start a band. I told him I'd already started one. Met Kit from an advert in Melody Maker, a while back, 'cos I saw Eddie And The Hotrods and thought yeah, well, they haven't quite got the idea but we need a bassist who can play. And I knew Cob from way back, he hangs about my squat. He's just learning. We played some pubs, and I found out how sick being up in front made me, 'cos I can't even do that properly, right? So we put that ad in the NME, and got you, 'cos you were just ready, dressed right, the attitude, the age and being a woman and all that. It's all so different, it's not like all that rock and roll crap. You've got stuff to teach us, right?'

Benny was suddenly very sad. 'If you knew how I felt

sometimes . . .' She cut the thought off. 'Tell me, have you ever met Boris Becker?'

'Who?'

'This is Europe, isn't it?'

'No Bernice, this is England.'

'Ah.'

The Doctor hurried up the steps of Charing Cross tube station, and ran across the road into Trafalgar Square. Big Ben stood in the distance, chiming midnight in the lights of London. Lorries carrying British eggs and coal rumbled past, and the people walking by were dressed in afghans, in old flares, in big grey coats and tufty beards.

Funny how you knew an age by such trivia. There were some signs of something new in the occasional boy, his hair cut short, his trousers leather. Skinny tie and battered suit jacket. Half-way between rocker and punk, and feeling out of place. His hair was a passport to his own time, a time which was about to happen. The boy was soon going to find himself at home.

The Doctor envied him.

Benny slumped beside him at the base of Nelson's Column. 'How are you?'

'Wanted by the law. I'm guilty as well.'

'You fought the law and the law won?'

'Don't even think of writing that.'

'What's the charge?'

'Being an illegal alien.'

Benny sighed, realizing that she'd missed him in these last two weeks. 'Did Ace get here?'

'No.' A frown darkened the Doctor's features for a moment. Benny decided to drop the subject.

'I could murder a cup of tea.'

'So could I.' The Doctor pulled the TARDIS key from his pocket, opened up Nelson's Column, and let Benny in.

2

Wild Horses (Slight Return)

'Why did you give the order to fire?' Carpenter slammed his fist down on the table.

'No sir, I didn't give the order to fire,' Pike deadpanned. The two soldiers had retreated to the privacy of the safehouse kitchen.

'Then why didn't you give ... I mean to say, why did you begin the order to fire, but fail to ...' Carpenter stopped, gathering himself visibly. 'I shan't take this matter any further, Captain, but I regard it as a very grave error of judgement.'

'Yes sir, I accept that, sir.'

Carpenter nodded. The relaxed posture of Pike when at ease seemed to disturb him. 'We're still investigating how he got hold of the RSM's key card. Now, what have we done to recapture the alien?'

'Sir, I've ordered Number Two Platoon of B Company to maintain a ground-level watch for bug signals and noise across London. They're using tracking vans, so we'll be able to triangulate any source. Number Two Assault Platoon under Lieutenant Brown are searching the city in mufti, and a Broadsword unit is doing ... whatever weird stuff those guys do. Police and the intelligence services notified as normal, sir.'

'Yes. It's a pity we couldn't spare more men. This Black Star stuff is a matter for the regulars, really.'

'I gather the Brigadier finds it politic to serve the national interest at certain times, sir. Keeps the locals sweet.'

'Yes, that's probably true. Carry on, Captain. See you at training tonight.' Carpenter stalked out.

'Training . . .' Pike shook his head and sank into a lotus position on the floor. He closed his eyes. 'I got training of my own to do.'

The Doctor peered at Benny over his tea. They were sitting in wicker chairs in the console room. Benny had changed back into her chinos.

'Prison gives you time. Time to think. That alternative reality where the Silurians ruled . . . it wasn't a natural universe, it wasn't one that – '

'Oh, I know.' Benny cut in quietly, blowing on her mug. 'You can only care about people if they're real in some way. Very obscure, especially for them.'

The Doctor ignored her, taking a long gulp of tea. 'So if it wasn't a natural branching of the omniverse it must have been created artificially.'

Benny was interested, in spite of herself. 'That would take more power than something very powerful indeed. I mean, you can't just go creating universes can you? It laughs in the face of the laws of entropy and upsets causality's shopping trolley.'

'There are some powers in the omniverse that can do anything. The Guardians, for example. The only things that bind them are codes of conduct, civil laws designed to give sentient races some means of maintaining a stable existence. I sometimes wonder if that's the reason the Time Lords are so introverted . . . they've bargained with creatures who could pull the arms off spiral galaxies.'

'What about the Land of Fiction, though? I mean, you said that that place had been around for some time?'

'Yes, but it had been rebuilt. And instead of the Gods of Ragnarok, some new audience was using it, watching us. Somebody is doing this . . . letting old foes out of death's bag and causing new ones to be created, leading me a chase around other worlds. They've done it so they can set this game in motion, this invasion. I've been here two weeks, I've sniffed the air and sought help, and I still know nothing about it. Except the fact that a very old friend doesn't know me any more.' He looked up suddenly, blinking out of his reverie. 'At least you found Danny Pain. That's the only clue we've got. It's late, but do you fancy a walk?'

They wandered along the Embankment in the direction of St Paul's, watching the lights of the boats as they navigated the Thames.

'Well,' murmured Benny, seeing the Doctor was still lost in thought, 'while you were imprisoned, I was becoming important in the world of rock and roll. First hippies, and now punks. I'm really brushing up on my twentieth-century subcultures.'

'Good. What's Danny like?'

'Very sweet. It's like being in panto, being a punk. Except nobody spat when I was in Cinderella.'

'You were? Which part?'

'Principal Boy, of course. I can still slap my thigh with some style. I can't sing, so I sort of growl and it seems to please the audience, if their appreciation can be measured by how clear their throats are afterwards. The only thing is, why am I doing it?'

'It's part of a plan. My plan.'

'I did guess that, actually.'

'Have you read any newspapers? There are only two differences between this world and the one I'm used to. One is the Brigadier's reaction. That makes me worry about not existing, about having been killed before I met him . . .'

Benny raised a finger, then lowered it again. 'No. Go on.'

'The other difference is Black Star, who aren't historical.'

'Right, and everybody's talking about them. There's a sort of hysterical edge to the concerts, a real feeling of releasing pent-up fear. I've never seen so many curved shoulders and tense expressions.'

'In the real world, that was just a reaction, an ugly

29

glamour. This time, anarchy's real. There are powercuts and Wilson's resignation, a great upheaval of unease. But now there's real fear too. Real panic. And that's not how it's supposed to be.'

'It is actually frightening to hear you not knowing what's going to happen next. But what's all this stuff to do with Danny Pain?'

'The Master of the Land of Fiction told me that he features in the fiction of the invaded world. He's going to be a hero.'

'Now that does surprise me. He's very afraid.'

'Yes. But heroes are always afraid.'

They had reached a vantage point on the Houses of Parliament by now. The Doctor looked up to see the minute hand move to the top of the hour, one o'clock. Big Ben struck. Then struck again. And again. It kept on striking as Benny grinned.

'You can't depend on anything these days, can you?'

'Twelve . . .' the Doctor counted. 'Thir – '

The clockface erupted. Shards of glass sprayed out in a blast of heat that threw the Doctor and Benny flat. Light filled the sky in a nimbus around the tower, and waves swept across the water as smoking debris began to plummet into the river. The building had become a fast-burning candle.

Boats on the river began to sound their horns in alarm. As the echo of the explosion died away, distant sirens could be heard.

The river shone red with the fire. 'First strike,' whispered the Doctor.

Ace sat on the edge of a warehouse roof, looking out across the spread of disuse and neglect that was the Docklands. Better than last time she'd seen the city, anyway. Then it'd been half underwater and covered in jungle. Maybe that had been an improvement.

Alan's head blew sideways, the pistol jerked in her hand. Just a twitch away. Meaningless.

She didn't know why she'd come to Wapping on the

last tube. Stupid thing to do. Still, she was warm enough, and a fire-escape had given her access to this great vantage point. Down the river, some kind of fire was producing a cloud of smoke.

There was somebody sitting beside her.

She spun round, ready to fire a flechette into their neck. But they were gone. Or hadn't been there. Just the person who lives in the corner of your eye, the one who's just walked past the window but never knocks on the door. Or perhaps it was some old memory of sitting on steps with the Doctor, being explained to. We all like to be explained to sometimes. This time round, he'd left his instructions for Benny and run away. She hadn't asked what she was supposed to do, if anything. She didn't know the Doctor's game, which probably meant that it was going to hurt her.

Ace shivered, and glanced down into the street. A familiar figure was walking, kicking stones. Danny. Coincidence, or what? Yeah, probably what. She wandered along the edge of the roof, watching him. The way his shoulders moved. Then for a moment she just watched him as a target, saw a string of flechettes bursting open his spine. She raised her hand, wondering about giving the order to the armour. Blaster, smart-bombs, or flechettes. She'd repaired her wrist computer a week ago, and it still hadn't been tested. The suit seethed around her fist, currents jumping at her synapses, wanting to kill. They said the suits didn't want to kill, but they did.

She thought about something else, suddenly. Something about owls. She lowered her hand, and slid down the fire-escape, landing silently in the cobbled street.

She walked up to Danny's shoulder, and spoke into his ear. 'Hiya, what you doing here?'

Danny jumped about three feet, making Ace laugh. 'Yah! Why did you do that?!'

'Could have been worse.'

'Getting late, eh Stevens?' The Brigadier rubbed his brow,

leaning back in his chair. In front of him, flags were scattered across a map of London.

'Tell me about it, sir,' the corporal smiled ruefully. He had been standing at the door since Lethbridge-Stewart had arrived at the Ops Room in UNIT's London office. The Brigadier had dismissed the night watch, saying that he'd hit the bell if any news came in, but under a black alert, senior officers had to have a continual armed guard. Stevens, who'd been with the Brigadier since the Wenley Moor crisis, had volunteered. For the last hour, he'd ignored the fact that his superior seemed just to be staring at the map, not even moving a unit.

'Get yourself to bed. I don't think I'm taking too much of a risk in here, do you?'

'No sir, thank you sir.'

The Brigadier waited until Stevens had departed, then closed his eyes. He moved his lips at intervals, as if reciting something to himself.

Carpenter swept into the room, and the Brigadier stood up, turning to face him. 'Any news about Big Ben, Major?'

'Yes sir,' Carpenter saluted. 'One thousand pounds of plastic explosive, specially shaped, or so the Met think. Timer device of a fairly sophisticated nature, the remains of which we're in the process of obtaining from the Bomb Squad.'

'Tell them if they don't get their finger out I'll be on to the PM's office. How did they get in?'

'No idea as yet, sir. It'll take a few days to get any sort of forensic data.'

The Brigadier walked around the table, slapping his gloves into his palm. '*The Times* got a call ten minutes after the blast, codeword in the Athena series, so it's genuine. Black Star, if we hadn't already guessed.'

'Yes sir.'

'And this with Her Majesty's parade coming up. Are you sure they won't cancel?'

'No, sir, the Palace don't want to look like they're giving in to terrorist threats. We've got the route monitored every inch, we'll be searching the surrounding buildings the night before, and we're co-ordinating with the SAS, MI5 and Special Branch over security arrangements.'

'For once, I'm glad they're using us, Major.'

'Yes sir. Sir, the alien prisoner – '

The Brigadier looked out of the window, into the darkness. He paused for a moment. 'Yes, Carpenter?'

'I'm afraid he's escaped, sir.'

'He what?' Lethbridge-Stewart spun round, and for a moment the look on his face was almost amused. Then he exploded into anger. 'Carpenter, this is what you will do. You will concentrate on organizing the sensor sweep of possible Black Star arms dumps on the South Downs. You will cease to have any involvement with the matter of the prisoner – '

'Sir, Captain Pike – '

'Captain Pike,' bellowed the Brigadier, 'will be in charge of efforts to find the alien. And tell him from me, Major, that he is to shoot to kill! Is that clear?'

'Yes sir!' Carpenter clicked his heels.

'Dismissed!' The Brigadier turned back to the window as Carpenter exited. 'Damn him . . .' he whispered, a second later.

Danny had taken Ace to his squat, a trashed council house on an estate that seemed like part of a warzone. Ace liked it. The lounge had a vast black star on one wall, a shrine that was surrounded by comments and sprayed slogans. The furniture was scrappy and slashed, and the floor was piled with records, the remnants of roll-ups and literature.

'This is it,' Danny muttered, not looking at her. 'Coffee?'

'Yeah. Thanks. Where I come from, we'd call this a student house. How many you got living here?'

'Varies. Cob tries to keep a count, I'm not bothered. If somebody needs a place to stay, this is it.'

He went into the kitchen, and Ace picked up a pamphlet from the floor. It was a photocopied cut-and-paste job, a rip-off of Reader's Digest with the headline 'Holi-

33

days Under The Pavement'. 'Who are this Black Star lot, anyway?'

'Situationists,' Danny called. 'Artists who take what this crappy culture's got and change it into what they want. You want to do some of that tomorrow?'

'Violent, is it?'

'Nah! That's just the press mouthing off as usual. The state apparatus kicking into life now it's being threatened.'

Ace went into the kitchen, glancing around the piled washing-up and the general disorder. 'You're supposed to be signing a contract tomorrow.'

'Yeah, well, that is if I stay in the band. I'm not too sure about that contract, I'm strung out about that money business.'

Ace watched his thin arms as he poured two cups. 'What is it about you, anyway? You didn't want to talk to me tonight.'

Danny glanced up at her. 'Went too far. Sometimes you do, don't you? You're all right. We're just gonna drink this and sit in the lounge, then I'll go to bed and you can have the sofa, right?'

Ace paused before following him into the lounge. 'Damn . . .' she murmured, 'first Alan, now him. I must be getting old.'

Benny and the Doctor arrived back in Trafalgar Square at a run, to hear a great hooting of taxi horns. Above their heads wasn't the familiar shape of Nelson's Column, but the crowned figure of a miniature Statue of Liberty. Glancing along the Mall, between the burning facade of Big Ben and the incongruous sight in Trafalgar Square, a crowd of bemused and scared people were starting to gather. The first police cars had arrived, and there were strange individual screams, almost as if people didn't know what else to do. The city was giving out a roar, a kind of noise that Benny had never heard before. It was as if the buildings were starting to shout.

'Quick,' muttered the Doctor. 'Before they cordon it off.'

34

They dashed up to the statue. A police sergeant with a megaphone turned from advising the crowd to disperse and ran after them.

By the time he'd reached the base of the monument, the two strangers had vanished.

The Doctor leaned on the TARDIS console, stabbing at the chameleon circuit keyboard. 'I wonder if this is to do with our escape from the Land of Fiction . . .' He straightened again. 'There, we're back to being the Column.'

'Truth seems to be stranger than fiction.' Benny rubbed her brow, exhausted. 'Look, unless there's anything urgent going on, more urgent than the destruction and alteration of historic monuments, that is, I'm off to bed.'

'Fine.'

Benny paused at the door, and then turned back. 'How are you, anyway?'

'Fine.'

'She's probably in the YWCA or something. I'm sure she isn't in danger.'

'I'm not worried.'

Benny sighed, and slapped the wall as she left the console room. 'There are times,' she muttered, 'when I want to thump him.'

In the glare of Earthlight, just out of the shadow of the wall of Copernicus, three ships basked in the electronic storms that silently washed the lunar surface. Their surfaces were dull metallic, their light a subdued green.

Inside one of the ships there was a globe of what looked like green liquid. Oily fractals spun and broke on its surface. Static sometimes played between it and the metal bulkheads that surrounded it.

A scattering discharge of energy hit the globe, and suddenly it showed faces, places, maps. A news-reader shuffled his papers and thumped them on his desk, looking grimly up at an audience he'd never guessed at, the audience of the ever-growing emission sphere. Within hours, his image would have reached Mars, in four years it would have got to Alpha Centauri. And there would always be eyes to watch it, a sixty light-year globe of interest and examination.

The energy matrix halted the news-reader, and read new data into him. The image blurred and shifted, and in a moment flashed back the way it had come.

Alien eyes watched the process, and heard in their collective thoughts that it was good.

They'd put on some Bowie, about the only thing in the pile of records on the floor that Danny would admit to, and sat on separate chairs.

'Getting early, innit?' Danny smiled, after they'd talked about Eno. 'Time I went to bed.'

Ace was feeling washed out, a bit angry distantly, that all her close attention and special words hadn't even dented this boy's armour. 'You remind me of someone, you know. Somebody special.'

'Yeah? Well that was them, and this is me. Like Mike Yarwood says.'

'I like the way you tell the truth, that you mean what you say.'

'Me?' Danny picked up the cups. 'Nah, stop looking for somebody credible, love. You think that some people mean it and some people are just pretending? Let me tell you, everybody is pretending.'

He went out without another word. Then a second later he came back in, headed straight for her, and Ace thought, with that familiar shock of adrenalin, that he was going to kiss her.

He just touched the top of her head, with one finger. 'Don't knock friendship, friendship's hard. Takes more bravery than a quick shag does. Goodnight.'

Ace stared after him for a full minute. 'Bastard,' she shook her head, feeling mauled by his arrogance. She swung her feet up onto the sofa, sunk her head back into the cushion and kicked off her boots.

'Time,' she sighed, closing her eyes, 'used to be a friend of mine.'

As she fell asleep, the day started to arrive over London.

3

Transubstantiation Baby

They'd set fire to the cornfields, a blaze catching along the line of the downs. And a woman walked down through the fire, her hair catching light, her clothes starting to shine in the gleam of it. She wore shining black now, and her eyes were burning to the same rhythm as the fields.

The smoke obscured the sun, and she made grasping motions with her ever-mobile hands, the darkness spreading out behind her like shadowy wings.

Ace stood in the middle of the field, her feet planted in the ground in her boots. The woman and the fire were approaching her. She could feel the heat on her face, the gasping in her throat as the air started to thicken with blood.

Danny was beside her, his arms thrown up in a desperate appeal of sacrifice, his chest naked. 'I've offended her!' he choked. 'I've sinned against the goddess!'

'Let me run!' Ace's fingernails bit into her palms. 'Let this be a dream and let me run!'

The goddess stood before them now, and reached out a long-nailed hand to touch Danny's cheek. Stubble around her feet began to blacken and enflame as the fire grew behind her. 'Is this what you want?' she asked, in a voice that Ace thought was a terrifying song.

'Yes!' shouted Danny, his teeth and eyes clenched shut.

'It's not what he wants,' Ace was saying calmly. 'It's not what he wants.'

The goddess turned and looked at Ace, and she was

surprised, her face erupting in astonishment. 'It's you!' she said. 'You've – '

The flame washed over them and Danny screamed.

Danny was screaming.

Ace was awake. 'Come,' she said, and sat up.

Then, without thinking, she was running up the stairs, her arm suggesting a range of killing options.

She elbowed her way through the bedroom door, and snapped to find targets –

Danny, curled in a twist of grubby bedclothes, panting. She stepped up to him.

'Ah, yeah . . .' he muttered, blinking at her. 'Bad dream. Had them a lot lately.'

'Me too.'

He rubbed a hand back through his hair. 'Put the kettle on, eh?'

Benny strode into the console room in costume, a black leather and lace creation with black-and-white striped tights. She twirled proudly in front of the Doctor, who was concentrating on the TARDIS console.

'I sewed on every sequin.'

The Doctor looked up. 'There aren't any.'

'Just as well, I'm terrible at sequins.' Benny glanced in her mirror at her black lipstick. 'God, I look like a panda that's taken up prostitution. Punkerella, you shall go to the ball.'

'What does that make me?' The Doctor managed a smile.

'Baron Hardup.' Benny wandered over to the console and glanced at the chameleon circuit panel. 'So why the Statue of Liberty?'

'Something keeps urging the system to change. Something external. I've had to put up shields and set up a defence programme that'll reply in kind. That should disrupt the systems of whoever's doing it.'

'Perhaps the TARDIS is trying to tell us something. Could this, after all, be America outside?'

'Hmm. You've got your contract signing today, haven't you?'

'Yes, we'll hum and hah over the terms, just for show, and probably complain about the money, but we're going to sign.'

'You're probably being deceived. But staying close to Danny is more important than the band.' The Doctor went back to his instruments for a moment, and then looked up. 'Is that an awful thing to say?'

'No,' grinned Benny, charmed. 'You're doing okay. Open the doors and let me out. I'm not afraid to be seen in this outfit, and history awaits.'

'Indeed . . .' The Doctor activated the doors. 'That's what worries me.'

Kit's battered old Cortina drew up in front of Danny's squat, next door children and dogs glancing over at the garish vehicle.

Ace, Danny and Cob were sitting at the gate, sharing a bottle of Cabernet Sauvignon.

'Bit early for that, isn't it?' Kit called. He was wearing a suit that wavered dangerously between respectable and Teddy Boy. Danny had squeezed into a pair of tight leather trousers and a ripped up T-shirt. Cob was just Cob.

'The milkman left it,' Danny grinned. 'Drinka pinta day, that's what I say, my fine fellow! We driving there in that?'

'Just to the corner, then we walk. Don't want to cause a scene.'

'Of course not,' Danny jumped into the front seat, and climbed over the gears into the back.

The look on his face was one of sheer mischief, and Ace didn't know whether to frown or smile at it. She was still worried about her dream. It was as if the sunlit world might any minute dissolve into those burning fields. And this had started her on another train of thought, that she'd seen enough burning fields, and was quite enjoying living amongst normal people again.

And Bernice again, of course. Bernice this morning.

Ace got into the car, swigging from the bottle.

'Seen this?' Kit passed back a copy of the Daily Mail as he drove off. BIG BEN DESTROYED. CHAOS IN THE SUBURBS. The headline was supported by two photos, one of the blazing tower, one of crowds throwing stones and bottles at a police van. 'That was last night. Bloody Black Star. Good publicity for us now that we're punks though, eh?'

Danny sat up and grabbed the paper. 'My God...' he whispered. 'They actually went and did something meaningful.'

'Hooliganism, I call it,' Kit muttered. 'What's meaningful about blowing up a sweet old clock like that?'

'Sign of the times, mate,' replied Danny with a secret grin.

Robert Bertram walked up to the big window that overlooked the city, and put a hand up to the glass. He was half-smiling, like somebody trying to pretend that they were happy at a party. Outside the window, the morning was blazing summer already, the heat rippling the buildings and bridges.

He wandered back to his desk, putting the folder of papers back into his drawer. They were clippings concerning the riots from the previous night, riots that had erupted through Brixton and Camden Town like a flaming trail of petrol.

'It's not perfect,' he muttered to himself. 'But then, it was never going to be, was it?'

Benny sat in reception, reading Cosmo. As soon as Ace came in, she put it down. Then she picked it up again, wanting to look casual. Then she put it down again, aware of the messages she was giving out.

Ace sat down next to her on the plush sofa, Danny flopped down on the other side. Kit and Cob hovered, gazing at the gold discs on the wall.

'How, erm, did you get on last night?' Benny asked Ace.

'You mean where did I get to, why didn't I get home?'

'No, we were just – '

'Worried? Cheers, that's nice.' Ace quickly picked up the magazine and started flipping through it without looking.

'So,' Danny turned to Benny. 'Got home okay, then?'

'No, I was abducted by aliens and replaced by a clone.'

Ace looked up. 'D'you mean that?'

'No . . .' Benny sighed.

A smartly dressed PA walked into the lobby and smiled at the band. 'Plasticine? I'm such a fan. Mr Bertram will see you now.'

Robert Bertram was at the door to welcome them in, shaking their hands and gleefully directing them to chairs. It was as if, Benny thought, he didn't quite know how to be a businessman. His lack of front was quite charming.

'And I'm pleased to see you here, Ace.' He settled back into his chair, jumbling his fingers. 'I think a band should have friends, people to keep them together.'

'I'm just here for the ligging.' Ace had been staring out of the window, noting a worrying trail of smoke to the north. Looked like small-scale fighting going on. She turned to look at Bertram and found that he was smiling at her once more, looking her straight in the eye, right through the mirrorshades. Now, he must be comfortable with himself. She found that a grin had been torn from her again.

Bertram turned back to the band. 'I thought I'd demonstrate some of the technology that we're developing through various Priory subsidiaries to capture the new sound. All of this is British-made.' He picked up a remote control device and a section of wall swung out to reveal a CD player and a video-disc recorder.

Ace blinked, and glanced at Benny, who caught her look and shrugged.

'Compact Disc, we're calling it,' Bertram rubbed his hands together in pride, and held up a small silver disc. 'This is the one we recorded the other night at the concert, a test pressing. The system's already selling like hot cakes in Japan, and wait until they hear DCC! Video Disc is taking a little longer to get going, but it will, believe me it will! So, as you see, signing to Priory gives you access to the latest recording techniques, a real edge over competitors. Also, you'll receive prime-time rotation for any video on our satellite television franchise, which, if my negotiations with the Prime Minister are anything to go by, will soon be granted.' He stood up and spread his arms wide. 'I think I should go and fetch a contract, don't you?'

The band gave grinned affirmatives as Bertram left the office. Ace dived over to his desk, grabbed the CD and handed it to Benny. 'Give this to the Doctor, he might be interested.'

'Why?' Benny frowned and hid the disc in her bag.

'Just do it.'

Danny elbowed Ace aside and started to heave at a corner of the desk. Cob hopped up to help him. 'You're nicking that disc, then?'

'Look, he'd probably give it to us if we asked!' Kit shouted.

'Yeah, but it's not so much fun! Got to cover our tracks, mate!'

Kit glanced around. 'I'm, ah, off to the Gents.'

'Good decision,' murmured Benny as he left. Danny and Cob had picked up the desk between them. They were heading for the window. 'Danny, do I take it you have something of a hidden agenda?'

'Could be!' Danny laughed, and he and Cob swung the thing out at the city. It connected with the window, desk against skyline, and then the glass parted around it, smashed into fragments, burst out of the building.

The desk fell towards the street. A van had bumped up onto the pavement outside, and two men in balaclavas cheered as the desk thumped onto a mattress. They dragged it quickly to the vehicle, grabbing up every piece of paper that had scattered from the burst drawers.

'I dunno what that was about,' grinned Ace. 'But I liked it.'

43

That, of course, fitted in with what UNIT knew about Black Star. The leaders were probably remnants of the Angry Brigade, bohemians living in Chelsea or Ladbroke Grove. Personally, Claire had always liked the antiques and markets of those blossoming old terraces, and the way that people sat on the steps with their cats and typewriters. But associations of rainy afternoons with a battered Michael Moorcock paperback in Aldershot had given way to the sunny snarl of some alienated young kid, the kind of lunatic who makes fire-bombs in the corner of his flat and flops out all day reading Rousseau.

'Partial,' she heard the Brig saying. 'Don't be. You're a searcher of silences, you can't judge anyone. Don't even think the tea's good. Just concentrate on how you feel about it.'

They'd all held a mug of strong sweet tea to their lips that afternoon, holding it in both hands. She'd sipped it, and known some sort of momentary bliss.

'So, how's the tea?' the Brig asked.

'Very good, sir!' one of the trainees replied.

The Brigadier had shaken his head. 'Sometimes, McCardle, I wonder why I bother . . . what about you, Tennant?'

Claire had just smiled, and the Brigadier had smiled back, pleased. And now she found herself smiling again, at the little man who was wandering down the King's Road on this sunny afternoon, looking like Charlie Chaplin.

It was a pity that he was about to be arrested. But then, that was probably being partial, too.

Plasticine had left the Priory Building to go and find a pub.

Ace had carefully left her jacket in Bertram's office. She remembered it half-way down the stairs, and told Danny not to wait.

Robert Bertram was standing by the hole in his window, holding the jacket up to the light. He turned, expecting her.

'Perhaps I ought to offer you a contract too.'

46

'Can't sing, can't play.'

'Oh, that doesn't matter. Image is everything. And any-body who wears a jacket that anticipates the future of the American space program . . . you must have a prodigious imagination.'

'You too. You invented the CD player ten years too early.'

'Oh dear.' Bertram handed the jacket to her. 'I seem to have been found out. When are you from?'

'The eighties. Crap decade. What about you?'

'Oh, my child . . .' Bertram chuckled. 'I'm from another planet. Are you?'

'No.' Ace slipped on her jacket. 'But I know a man who is. Fancy a walk?'

The Doctor had bought an Evening Standard, and was examining the small ads carefully as he walked down the street, miraculously avoiding other passers-by. 'June the nineteenth. . .' he murmured, glancing up. 'Preparations for Live Peace, arms talks, Black Star. Nothing.'

Two men were walking towards him purposefully. They had leather jackets and new jeans. The Doctor glimpsed a similar pair behind him.

He dropped the paper and fled sideways. Down an alley.

The four men rushed after him, sprinting. They pulled hand-guns from their jackets.

The Doctor hit a wooden fence and rebounded down a back alley, knocking over dustbins. He dashed straight past two shop backs and hurtled at the white-painted wood of a third door.

It was open. He fell inside.

A large, powerfully built woman in a leather dress was arguing with a slender man in a Teddish waistcoat. He had a shock of red hair.

'I don't care what Bernie's doing,' the woman was shouting. 'You wouldn't get into this mess if Vivienne was here – '

'Excuse me,' the Doctor closed the door behind him. 'I hope I'm not interrupting, but I'm on the run.'

47

'Are you?' the man beamed. 'Don't fancy joining a band, do you?'

'I only play the spoons.'

The man frowned. 'Knives, yes. But not spoons. Come in and have a cuppa, anyway.'

Ace and Bertram wandered through Hyde Park, past tourists and office workers lounging in deck-chairs.

'So, d'you know the Doctor?'

'I must admit, I do. We met two or three times. He was in his first incarnation then, very hard to deal with.'

'Nah, I met him, he's sweet.'

'Well, yes, I suppose he could be. We were rivals of a sort. He tried to stop me meddling with time. I wanted to change things, make things better. He wouldn't listen to me. From what I hear now, though, he's started to agree with my methods.'

'Yeah, that's all he does now. Meddle.'

Bertram put his hands together, fretting. 'I had no idea he was here. Perhaps we should meet. I'm trying to save his beloved Earth now, after all. He wouldn't argue with that, would he?'

'Absolutely not. I think he's trying to do that himself, but I dunno any details. He doesn't trust me with that kind of stuff any more.'

'Why?'

Ace looked down at her boots, silent for a while. Then she decided. 'Because I went away, learnt about taking action. That makes him feel terrible, 'cos it's what he's like now, too. He'll blow up a planet or something, and he doesn't like the idea that there's someone watching who's played on the same pitch, who knows there might have been other ways to do it.'

'My dear, I'm so sorry.'

'Yeah.'

'The options are anarchy or fascism, one or the other. Every day, their control, control exercised through the most everyday means, gets greater. The only thing you

48

can hope to do is jumble the signals, create chaos. Because out of chaos comes sweetness. And, as I have said before, cash. You can play them at their own game, but don't stick around afterwards, because the military industrial complex is a jealous beast. It will have you for its own. Against that, we only have poetry and violence. This year, that will be enough.' The shop owner's careful, edgy voice underlined every syllable, and the Doctor had got the feeling that he was being lectured to. They were sitting in the back of the shop, drinking tea by a kitchen sink. 'Take these new CDs for instance – '

'CDs?'

'Yes, you must have seen them. Terrible little things. No soul. Their covers are so small that you can't communicate any extra information on them. Not much opportunity for messages. They're much more expensive to make in small quantities, so new bands can't cut just a hundred, and their retail price is much higher, so working-class kids cannot afford them. They are designed to take the music away from youth, and give it, wrapped in velvet, to age. Now, here's the interesting bit. The silence on them is pure silence. No atmospherics. No studio stuff that goes by subconsciously. It's all flattened out. The medium used to be a bit more than the message, but now the two are the same thing. Frightening isn't it?'

'Yes . . .' The Doctor nodded, serious.

'But you can, you must, subvert all that.'

'How?'

The man leaned closer. 'We're working on it.'

The Doctor's eyes narrowed. 'Do you know anything about Black Star?'

'Bunch of artists, aren't they?'

'Terrorists.'

'Same thing.'

Ace relaxed in a comfortable chair in Bertram's office. A new desk had already replaced the one that Danny had stolen. Bertram was pulling the cork from a bottle of wine.

49

Sweet tea-time noises and scents were filtering through the smashed window.

'Perhaps I should keep it that way.'

'Wait until winter. What are you doing running a record company, anyway?'

'Oh, I'm just killing time, and making some local currency so that I've got the means to alert people to these aliens when they arrive.'

'Who are they?'

'I don't know. I only know that future literature refers to them. They've done something horrid to the timeline, and I care about this planet too, I don't want to see it hurt,' He offered Ace a glass, but she took the bottle from the desk instead.

'Cheers. You're quite like the Doctor. Only nicer.'

'Oh, well, thank you . . .' Bertram jumbled his fingers and looked way. When he looked back, his face was serious. 'I've seen a lot of people under stress. How are you feeling?'

Ace took a deep breath. 'Oh, sometimes I think of putting a gun in my mouth. I mean, there was a time when I saw myself as a symbol against all that. I saw my life as an example, that if there was me, then there was justice, right? Didn't do drugs, held out for the sisters, put bacon sandwiches in the way of bulimia. Thing is, you get old, and you start to do the bad stuff yourself. Murder, sadism, all badness in the world lands at your door unless you're a saint. And the people around you can still con themselves enough to diss you, to think that they could never do that.'

'Ah, my child, we're all sinners though, aren't we?'

'I'm growing into that. But it's a defeat. We should all try to be perfect. We can all have wings instead of flechettes.' She passed the bottle back. 'Have some.'

To Ace's surprise, he did, swigging quickly, grinning and then gulping in a sudden comedy burp. 'I think I should, ah, confiscate that to preserve you from – '

'No, no, you do that and you're dead.'

50

'Did I say confiscate? I meant allow you to have as much as you want.'

'But you can have some. Why do you keep talking like a vicar?'

'Well, because I was one of the clergy once, a long time ago. I was very devout, yes, I kept up every article of my faith, was up in the monastery at all hours doing rituals.'

'You were a monk? What happened, did you get tempted?'

'No, almost exactly the opposite. I learnt of other worlds, worlds where everything I knew was meaningless.'

Ace was smiling a vulnerable sort of smile. 'I know about all that stuff. Is that what did you in? Seeing it all in perspective?'

Bertram nodded, relieved. 'Too much perspective. I took a while to realize how empty my revelation had left me. I became involved in politics, to try and create a purpose out of nothing. But that was full of betrayal. Finally, I retreated into pure hedonism, merely a desire for harmless fun. But I could not even be content with that. There is no justice, Ace.'

'Call me Dorothy. It's my name.'

'And you may call me . . . my real name is Mortimus.'

Ace reached out and touched his nose. 'You remind me of all sorts of things. Good things. What you've said is so like me. Except you've got old and it's all okay. Everything you went through . . .'

'Forgive me, but I doubt it. I was marooned on an ice planet – '

Ace bellowed a laugh. 'Me too!'

'And did you want to take revenge?'

'Yeah, after I'd worked it all out. But that's sort of part of a complicated ongoing thing. I s'pose I'm in the middle of that now.'

'Myself also.'

Ace took a gulp from the bottle, got up from her seat, and settled her head against the seat of Mortimus' wooden chair. 'Were you ever excommunicated or anything?'

'No, I simply left my order.'

51

'Will you do something for me, then?'

'Of course.'

'This is something secret.' Ace sat up and then knelt, putting her face close to the wooden grille at the back of Mortimus' chair. She closed her eyes and grabbed her hands together, the knuckles white with sudden decision.

'Forgive me Father, for I have sinned.'

4

The Valiant Trooper

'Take this with you.' The shop owner fastened a safety
pin through the Doctor's buttonhole. The shopfront was
plush black, racks of bondage gear and tacky leopard-
skin. The customers affected sneers as the Doctor stepped
past, but the owner shook his hand stickily on the doorstep. 'Remember,' he told the Doctor. 'Under the pavements, there's a beach!'

'I've said that myself.'

'Come and see our band. They're playing the 100 Club,
Tuesday after next.'

'If I'm not busy,' the Doctor demurred. 'You know how
it is. Time flies.' He glanced around the street, finding the
UNIT observer who was, fortunately, looking the other
way.

'Why are they after you?'

'I'm from outer space.'

'Yeah,' the shop owner saluted the Doctor with a little
flick of his tousled hair, 'aren't we all?'

Ace was sitting in a beanbag in front of the television.
The low sunlight had put a square of light onto the screen.
With one hand on the bottle, and another on an anachron-
istic remote control, she was channel-hopping while Mortimus had gone out on an errand.

She'd told him everything, every sin she could think of.
And some that she'd made up. He'd just taken it like a
jolly punchbag, sighing and reaching out to stroke her
hair every now and then.

She hadn't cried. Hadn't done that for years, forgotten how to do it.

Somebody from the Met was being interviewed on an afternoon documentary on BBC2. 'So, what do you think causes this violence?'

'I blame the parents. There's a lack of respect for law and order that permeates every level of – '

'Forfar five, East Fife four – '

'Tonight on BBC3, we ask the question – '

'And cue the Wurzels!'

'The music business doesn't help. I mean, I quite like some of Rod Stewart's tunes, but this – '

'This evening on BBC1, Professor X faces a sticky situation – '

'Oi've got a brand new combine harvester – '

Ace rubbed her forehead. She'd suddenly got a headache.

The Doctor had made his way back to central London, wandering along Tottenham Court Road. From what he'd learnt, the Valiant Trooper was in Fitzrovia, the fashionable quarter where the Woolfs had lived.

He'd have to visit them again, soon. Lots to talk about. Assuming he got out of this alive.

Down Windmill Street, past several other pubs, all with customers standing outside in the evening sunshine, office workers in their shirtsleeves and tourists in sunglasses.

The Valiant Trooper was packed, but a familiar face was sipping a pint of Guinness in the corner, his jacket dropped on the stool opposite. His stocky build would have deterred anybody taking it. He was reading the Exchange & Mart.

'Sergeant Benton!' The Doctor grinned over the top of the paper. 'I might have known it was you.'

Benton smiled back, but something about him was still guarded. His face was lined with cares that hadn't been there when last the Doctor had seen him. Well, last time in this world. In the real world. 'You got my name wrong, Doctor.'

'Did I? It must be the drink. I don't have one. Do they serve brandy?'

'Doctor . . .' Benton folded away the paper and tucked it into the pocket of his sports jacket. 'Tell me what you got wrong, or I'll have to turn you in. I've been regretting last night since I did it.'

The Doctor put a finger to his brow. 'RSM John Benton – '

'That'll do!' Benton grinned in relief. 'And the brandy's on me!'

Benny was leaning on Danny and he, to her surprise, was leaning back. They were in the Prospect Of Whitby, a Wapping pub with a dock that stretched out into the river. Plasticine were sitting along the wooden rail, watching the boats go by as the sun began its long journey down.

'I thought he'd go spare!' Kit was laughing.

'He expects to make more out of us than any desk could be worth,' Benny sighed. 'And that was not a good desk. But what I want to know is . . .' She frowned, staring at the pint of bitter in her hand. 'What do I want to know?'

'You want to know what I have done with the desk,' Danny told her. He was wearing his handkerchief knotted on his head. 'I have given it to a friend, who will be using it in one of her installations. You can meet her tonight, if you want.'

'Is she an anarchist, too?'

'Yeah, but she's sweet.'

'No buts about it. Jan was a sweet anarchist.'

'Who's Jan?'

'Nobody you know.'

Benton raised both hands in an exasperated gesture.

'It's just incredible! The Brig goes on sabbatical, to develop his Broadsword project – '

'Broadsword?' The Doctor asked.

'They're Special Ops, an elite unit. UNIT's version of the SAS. The Brig said that he needed somebody to do

55

what you used to do. Sort of . . . muck things around a bit.'

'That's a verv apt description. How long has he been acting strangely?'

'Depends on what you call strange. He's been on his Buddhist bit for a year or so, but he was still the same old Brigadier. But in the last couple of weeks he's just become distant and really officious. He's enforcing the whole rulebook, right down to dress standards, which we used not to worry about that much. And the organization itself . . . all these new men, and a lot of the old ones don't seem like themselves. We've got tons of new high-tech training methods, and I don't fancy a lot of them. What do you think, Doctor? Are we being got at?'

'It's possible. I'd like to have a closer look.'

'Well, if you really want to, I could get you into UNIT HQ tomorrow. There's a training session on, the Brigadier'll be there. Charlie on the gate's old-time UNIT, he'll just wave me through.'

'Yes. We'll do that. Tell me, why are you doing this, why do you trust me so much?'

'Well . . .' Benton shifted uncomfortably in his seat. 'Nobody else I could ask. Besides, you're the Doctor, aren't you?'

The Doctor grinned. 'Thank you,' he murmured. 'I'm glad somebody has faith in me.'

Ace threw her arms back and yawned. 'I gotta be going,' she told Mortimus. 'I'll see you, okay?'

'Indeed,' Mortimus nodded.

They had been watching telly all evening in Mortimus' penthouse atop the Priory building, chatting about their adventures. Ace had started to feel fuzzy, and she wanted to get back to her bunk in the TARDIS. Normally an evening in front of the box was the last thing Ace would think of as a night's entertainment, but Mortimus was good company and the programmes had taken her back to her childhood. Professor X, Saturday Night At The

Movies, The Generation Game, Basil Brush. It all added up to a safe feeling.

Ace wandered to the door, and Mortimus switched off the set. 'D'you want to meet the Doctor, then?'

'Why?'

'Because you're both fighting these aliens.'

'What aliens?' Mortimus stood quickly and put a hand to Ace's forehead. 'My child, are you feeling all right? Where do you think I'm from?'

Ace frowned. 'I . . . I dunno, where are you from?'

'Why, I'm your friend and your confessor. Everything that has passed between us is private, is it not?' His face hardened. 'It mustn't be told to anyone.'

'You're right there,' Ace nodded quickly. 'Can I come and see you again?'

'Of course!' Mortimus beamed. 'Perhaps we can find you something amusing to do.'

Benny gazed up at the desk on the gallery wall. It had been pinned there with spikes, and, like a butterfly, its papers were stapled up like great wings.

'I told Bertram that if he wanted it back, he could pay to come and see it, get Jackie some publicity. Maybe him or one of his goons'll buy it. The show opens next week.' Danny was sipping from a glass of wine, his tartan jacket incongruous in the white-walled gallery. 'All profits to you know who.'

'Who?'

'Black Star. Like that composite, Jack!' A short woman in red dungarees had appeared behind Danny. She looked very tired.

'Oh, that . . . That's something I found in the desk. He had a file on the riots, right? Lots of clippings. So I just stuck all the pictures together. There are compartments inside it that I couldn't get open. Are you coming to the meeting?'

Danny glanced at Benny. 'Yeah, sure. I dunno how secure my friend Bernice is, though.'

57

'Oh, I'm secure,' Benny nodded. 'I just know a lot of neurotic people.'

The Doctor was tapping on the TARDIS's navigation controls, trying to find the source of the stream of information that was attempting to reprogram the chameleon circuit.

Benton had dropped him off, making arrangements to meet him next day. The UNIT man had a touching belief that now the Doctor was around, everything would be all right.

A display appeared on the scanner screen, an orbiting satellite broadcasting data in a tight cone at the TARDIS, pin-pointed on the Earth's surface. The Doctor frowned and hit a few more buttons. A graphic of a shield appeared, and the beam bounced off it. 'That'll use less power, anyway ... but what's the point? It's like some sort of challenge. Challenges. Awful things. Competition things. But you have to answer them ...'

The doors opened and Ace wandered in. The Doctor looked up quickly, and then pretended to continue working. 'How are you?' he muttered.

'Fine. Just wandering about, not doing a lot. What's happening with you?'

'Oh, just tinkering with the circuits. Wondering. Wondering why I don't see you much.'

Ace sighed. 'I got stuff to do. Thought about starting a band. Gonna call them the Manic Street Preachers.'

'It'll never catch on.' The Doctor deactivated the control board and turned. 'Tea. Do you want some?'

'Yeah, okay. Could do with something to clear my head.'

They wandered into the kitchen area, and the Doctor gave the food machine a kick. It started to make tea. 'I met an old friend today. What did you do?'

'Talked to the record company people. Saw Benny again. I think she's getting really involved with that band.'

'Oh?'

'She might decide to stay here.'

'In 1976? Not Benny. The eighties aren't a good time

to turn forty.' The Doctor paused, and made a decision. 'I did wonder, would you like to go home, back to where you'd be if you'd stayed on Earth? We could make a short hop – '

'Piss off! You think I'd want to go back there now? Don't know me that well, do you?'

The Doctor handed her a cup. 'Perhaps not. I wondered why you came back. You seem . . . distant. Not really here.'

'Cos I'm not blubbering all the time and running to you for help? Yeah, right, I'm not here. You can just treat me like I'm not here, and I'll get off at the first place I like, okay? Don't trust me any more, do you?'

'I don't – '

'You've never even apologized for all you've done to me. You've never said sorry.'

The Doctor looked at her blankly. 'Sorry.'

'Yeah, right. I'm going to bed. Maybe I'll travel with somebody else, eh? Maybe I'll be somebody else's "companion"!'

And she left, holding the tea like it was a sacrament.

The Doctor's gaze was fixed on her departing. 'Somebody else?' he muttered. 'Who else is there?'

Benny and Danny sat with a group of black-clad people around a circular table. Whispers were being exchanged, and one place was still empty.

'It's like a seance,' muttered Benny.

'Exactly the opposite.' Danny was serious, nervously drumming his fingers. 'We're waiting for somebody who's come in from the South Downs. They're very important in the movement.'

There was a noise at the door, and Jackie led the new arrival in. 'This is our guest for tonight. He used to be a captain in UNIT. Call him Michael X.'

The man looked around, his angular face taking in the crowd at a glance. He relaxed, and smiled gently. 'No, just call me Mike.'

Ace wrapped the duvet around her and tumbled into

sleep. She didn't want to stay awake, the pressure inside her head was too much, crunched between sobs that wouldn't come and something hard and metallic that smelt of blood.

A big clock chimed midnight over the steps, and Ace turned to see a woman in a long red gown scampering away. She ran after her, but she was gone, leaving only a shoe that tumbled, toe over heel.

Ace picked it up and clasped it to her chest. It was an extravagant silver thing. She must find the owner.

She burst into a bar, looking over the customers quickly. A hooded figure turned its hidden face to her.

The shoe rattled off the bony toe, Death's skin as cold as glass. Ace shook her head, pleased that it didn't quite fit her.

The hooded woman pointed towards the door where a hooded man stood, his arms spread wide. In one hand he held the other shoe.

Death's hand closed on Ace's shoulder, breaking the rhythm of the dream. 'Death's Champion,' she murmured. 'All Eternals have one.'

Jan stumbled past the man, shrugging him aside as puffs of fungus burst from his chest, his arms, his head.

And his arms wrapped round her, fluffy mushroom lips finding hers. Like biting into a sea-slug. Ace munched on the stuff that was dripping down her lips, and it was white sticky poison, sweet and fatal.

She woke biting the pillow. The clock beside her bed said 11.59.

Ace waited for midnight.

In his office, Mortimus pressed a button on his watch, and jumped theatrically at the reading on the dial. He hit another button.

'Damn you!' he snarled. 'Will I never have you fully under control?' He started punching in a series of commands. 'Time to get you back under my wing, I think.'

'I worked for UNIT a few years ago, and it was during

60

that time that I developed my distrust of the state. Earth has been under threat many times in the past, and the public have never been trusted with that information. That's something we know from people like Hank Macbeth ... and, I suppose, from people like me.' Mike X had placed an automatic on the table, and was holding court. The audience, Benny thought, was a bit star-struck. They were listening intently, smiling the fond smiles of enthusiasts.

A balding old man in a black jumper nodded. 'That's why our magazines are so important. Information is power. We can deconstruct the messages that this society sends out, and reconstruct them in our own image.'

'Even the deconstruction's enough,' Danny chipped in. 'Anarchy is freedom from messages.'

'In the end, that is,' Mike reminded him. 'We have to take positive action first, and then diversify into the non-state. I know that's alienated a few of our pacifist comrades, but we're working for them, too. And we will not take civilian life.'

'So you have moral values!' A woman with a French accent laughed. 'I thought we had explored the narrow nature of all that years ago. You're taking on so much of their culture, you'll become decadent!'

The others shouted her down. 'No, no,' Mike insisted. 'The movement keeps its aim clearly in mind, and that aim is the dissolution of the state.'

'You say you won't take civilian life,' Benny raised a finger. 'What about the debris from Big Ben? What about the riots that followed?'

Mike frowned. 'There are different opinions held within the movement. Different approaches.'

'Yes ... I thought it'd be something like that.'

The meeting broke up in the early hours, Benny getting involved in conversations about the foundations of the Situationist movement and art terrorism. As the amount of red wine she drank increased, so did the vigour of her arguments. Finally she staggered upstairs.

61

Danny had passed out in a chair. Mike sighed and helped Jackie carry the glasses into the kitchen. 'Sometimes I wonder,' he smiled sadly. 'It's hard being a traitor, you know.'

'You're not a traitor,' Jackie wiped down the table, lifting Mike's gun with two fingers. 'You're actually fighting for what you believe in. How many soldiers can say that?'

'You're right there. I just wonder if – '

There was a crash from the gallery above them. Danny woke up with a start.

'I'll go!' Mike took his automatic from Jackie and ran upstairs.

'Think we should go too?' Danny asked.

Jackie shrugged. 'Yeah. If it's the police, you stall them.'

'Ta.' They followed Mike.

There was a blank space on the wall. The desk had disappeared. The papers and drawers that had been arranged around it had fallen to the ground.

'I think the butterfly's escaped,' Jackie muttered.

Danny bent to pick up a sheet of Priory Records stationery. 'Could be useful,' he grinned. He spent five minutes carefully folding it and slipped it into his pocket.

Mike watched the folding, and then clapped him on the shoulder. 'Go to bed, eh, Danny?'

Mortimus took a hesitant low-gravity step forward, and bowed before three metal chairs.

'You wanted proof of my techniques,' he grinned. 'Very wise, in the circumstances. Very wise indeed.'

'Get on with it!' snapped a voice from one of the chairs. 'Your frivolity is already tiring.'

'Certainly, your . . . your. . . . yes, indeed, immediately. Here we are.' He presented a metal tray, on which were laid out notes and letters, all in the same handwriting. 'The Doctor's warnings to himself. I'd know the hand anywhere.'

'Yes . . .' a gloved hand reached out to take a letter. 'So would we. You have removed them all?'

'I'm certain of it. There are none left.'

'So the Doctor is on his own!'

'Yes . . .' Mortimus nodded enthusiastically. Then he added under his breath: 'But not as much as he's going to be.'

5

God Save The Queen

Benny woke up and stretched, pleased at the warmth of the sunlight that was shining onto the bed. Her forehead hurt, and she couldn't remember much about the previous night. Well, that was okay. If anything too awful had happened, she would have remembered it.

Her elbow hit somebody's head. 'Ow!' said the somebody.

Benny opened her eyes and looked. Next to her lay Danny, looking awful.

'Oh my God!' She clamped the duvet down over herself, and thumped a solid furrow between them.

'Morning . . .' groaned Danny.

'Oh, yes, morning. And, erm, how are you?'

'Not good, Bernice. I was wondering, to tell you the truth, why we're in the same bed?'

'Well, obviously, because we both got back to . . . to wherever this is, and were so drunk that we thought nothing of stripping off like we were at home and going straight to sleep. That's how I intend to remember it, anyway.'

'Yeah, that seems – '

'I mean, you're the one who's allergic to the squelchy things in life. Didn't this situation present you with something of a challenge? Didn't you pause slightly before hopping into bed with somebody who could be your . . . older sister?'

'I hope so . . .'

'And you don't drink, either! My God, you really went for it last night, didn't you?'

64

'Guilty all the time. I try, it doesn't work. Why does my cheek hurt?'

'That would seem to indicate that I slapped you.'

'Aw no, I can't have given you any reason to . . . I didn't want to . . . oh no . . .' Danny dived under the pillows and hid.

After a moment, Bernice shoved her head under her own pillow. A narrow corridor of illuminated fabric connected her with Danny's tousled head. 'Do you have the taste of pizza in your mouth?'

'Yeah . . .' muffled Danny. 'Yeah, I do.'

'Well, only I had the pizza. So I suppose I kissed you. In a friendly sort of way.'

Danny made a little sound of agony.

Benny found herself getting annoyed. 'Listen, there are quite a few people I could mention who would enjoy the prospect of a snog with yours truly. What's up?'

'Can't talk about it.'

'Can you talk about why you can't talk about it? Hey!' Benny thumped the pillow in sudden realization. 'I know what happened.'

Danny raised his head. 'Yeah?'

'Yeah! We got back here, and I sat by you on the bed. Rather ill-advisedly, I elected to give you a friendly kiss. For reasons best known to you, you pulled away. I regret to say that I may have slapped you at that point.'

'Really?' Danny looked up, brightly.

'Really,' Benny nodded. 'So we both sulked and undressed under the covers.'

'Oh, well, that's really great. Cheers.'

'Don't mention it.' Benny popped out from under the pillow and lay back. 'Jan again. If I'd slapped him, he'd have fought with me.'

'Who is this Jan bloke?'

'He's somebody that Ace fell in love with.'

'Poor bastard.'

'I was quite fond of him in a –'

'In a friendly way?'

'Yes. When he died, she was really hurt. But so was I.

65

Only more slowly. I'm not really the sort of person who blubbers on people's shoulders though.' She leaned up on her elbow and pulled the pillow from Danny's head. 'You look really sweet in the mornings. All vulnerable, like a puppy.'

'I'm supposed to be the beast of rock and roll.'

'There are all sorts of beasts. Relax.' She leaned forward and kissed his nose. 'That's not so bad, is it?'

'I can live with that.'

'Hello you two!' Mike X popped his head around the door. 'What do you fancy for breakfast?'

Benny descended the stairs of Jackie's house, her hair wrapped in a towel. Thank God this was the seventies. Getting pissed and laid after the eighties was the closest thing to suicide she could imagine. Not that she had. No, there was Danny's absolute reluctance to thank for that. Either he had problems, or he thought she was really ugly. She stopped at a mirror on the stairwell. 'Problems, definitely,' she said, tapping her chin.

She sat down brightly at the breakfast table, and watched Mike X buttering toast. Jackie had gone back to bed, declaring that she was tired and everybody could help themselves. Danny was probably asleep in the bath.

'So you were with UNIT?'

'Right. Until I cracked up. Very liberating thing, a nervous breakdown. Getting out of it sorts out a lot that you never knew was wrong.'

'Marmalade, please. So why do you think you flipped?'

'Everything that being in UNIT does to you. You face things that you can't talk to anybody about, you get shot at by aliens. Even if you did tell somebody, there's this strange syndrome that comes into operation. The Dinosaur Effect, we call it. Loads of civilians saw those things in London, but the only people who still talk about it are the underground press. And they're still seeing them, of course. People just aren't prepared to live in a world where this sort of bother goes on. So they don't. If you get in deep, like Broadsword does, you have to worry about abduction, hot jobs – '

'Hot jobs? Is that something recreational?'

Mike sat down and handed her some toast. 'Spontaneous human combustion. Happens to UNIT operatives ten times more frequently than to civilians. Do you know UNIT loses about five troopers a year, always has? Loses as in misplaces. They either wander off the battlefield and just walk away, or they get stolen by the Greys.'

'Greys? Sorry, all these terms are new to me.'

'Greys are your bog-standard alien bogies, the sort who use flying saucers and are probably mythical. They're part of the UNIT man's nightmares because they're what you get most reports about, but we've never caught one.'

'Cybermen use flying saucers too.'

'Yes, they – how the hell did you know that?' Mike had straightened suddenly.

'I read it in a fanzine.'

'You can't have, that's – ' he stopped. 'Well, I suppose you could. That's one of the most important tasks of Black Star, to make people aware of the threats they face as a species.'

Benny tried to meet the man's gaze. After a moment, she succeeded. 'A minute ago, in connection with UNIT, you said "we".'

'Hard habit to break.'

Danny wandered downstairs, and took the piece of toast that Benny had been holding. 'Ugh,' he groaned. 'It's gone cold.'

The Doctor was taking an early-morning wander along Oxford Street. He'd gone as far as the door of Ace's room that morning, opened it a crack, and saw her sleeping peacefully, snoring.

On the floor beside her was a device. He'd tiptoed in and picked it up. It was his old temporal disruption monitor, something that he'd perfected after the Timewyrm business and hidden away in a storeroom somewhere. Ace must have found it. Strange that it was exactly the thing he needed. He hadn't realized it until then.

He'd pocketed the dial, and looked down at her. He'd once put presents in her stocking, like he was Father Christmas. And in the end, all she'd got was pain. Well, she gave plenty back. In sleep, she still looked so young.

He'd avoided the urge to kiss her forehead, and left the room.

And now it was hard to find urgency in the crowds and the sunshine. There was something desperate about the heat, certainly, something oppressive, but whatever was happening was slow. There were boys in leather trousers hanging out in front of a couple of shops, selling sunglasses and wristbands on this Sunday morning. They were playing dub music from bulky cassette players that hadn't quite evolved into ghetto blasters. And past the Doctor walked a girl with her personal stereo, blurting out Rod Stewart into the ears of the tourists.

The Doctor headed for the tube, fanning himself with a rolled-up copy of the *Sunday Times*. It was only when he got on the train that he realized what he'd missed. Personal stereo. That was too early too.

A thought seemed to strike the Time Lord as he gave up his seat for an old lady. Strap-hanging, he raised a hand to his face, and his fingers began to drum out a complex beat, his eyes looking beyond the world.

The look on his face was that of a hunter.

Benny and Danny had bought ice-creams, and were sitting on a rug at the edge of St James's Park. Barricades had been erected, and they were right next to them. Behind them, a crowd had been assembling for much of the morning. Mike X had left after breakfast, stating that he had to get back to HQ.

'So we're going to see a queen are we?' Benny asked. 'This would be Elizabeth the Second, wouldn't it?'

Danny stared at her. 'Yeah, unless summat's gone down at Buck House this morning. And while we're at it, we're on decimal currency, too.'

'I realized that,' Benny dug into the pockets of her chinos and found a few pound notes. 'When I paid for the cornets.'

'You're not a punk this morning,' Danny pouted. 'I'm upset.' He was in a T-shirt depicting two semi-naked cowboys, and was wearing a necklace of razor-blades.

'To punk or not to punk . . .' Benny licked her cone. 'I was just too tired. What's the parade in aid of, anyway?'

'Well, it's a rehearsal, innit, the parasite. She's gonna come and wave at us to show that our taxes are being well spent. Anne and bloody Mark, Jubilee next year. It's a circus. And there's that stupid concert Bertram's putting on at the end of the week, supposed to stop the kids acting up by having Cliff Richard get up on-stage singing "Devil Woman". Please.'

Danny turned as a heavy hand landed on his shoulder. 'Any trouble?'

'No officer, just exercising my right to free speech.' Danny stared up at the two constables who had made their way through the crowd.

'What right is that then, son? Do us a favour, pack away the shirt. There'll be the TV down here in a minute.'

'And what if I don't?' Danny squared his shoulders.

The policeman looked skywards. 'Then we could arrest you. Plenty of grannies back here might make a complaint. Queen herself wouldn't be too pleased. You punkers don't enjoy being in the back of the van, if I remember rightly.'

'Are you saying you'd beat me up?'

'I'm saying that you'd miss the parade and spoil your nice day. Go on, take it off.'

Danny looked between the policemen and Benny.

Benny stood up, and smiled. 'I say, officer. I'm sorry if we're causing offence, but this is an art item from my sister's studio in Knightsbridge. What's the name of your DCI?'

'I can't see how that's relevant, miss – ' The policeman had straightened up, his tone becoming more civil.

'Because Daddy knows quite a few of your people from his club, and I was just wondering – '

'I trust the young gentleman will find more suitable attire before the parade passes by.' The policeman tipped his helmet. 'Good morning to you, miss.'

As the policemen trudged off, Danny grinned up at Benny in amazement. 'That was incredible!'

'Sometimes . . .' Benny sat down and bit off the bottom of her cornet. 'I get my history just right.'

The Doctor had found himself jammed between two tourists as the underground train stopped between stations. The carriage had filled with people, and there was a crush of bodies along the aisle as well as in the spaces near the doors. They hadn't moved for five minutes now, and the heat was starting to get oppressive. And this was just the normal tourist trade. It would get worse tomorrow, with the start of Wimbledon.

'Anarchy . . . don't know what it means . . . Big Ben . . .'

'States as we know them . . . EEC . . . darling Harold . . .'

'The Standard was saying that . . .'

'Friend in government, says they don't know what they're doing. A woman just isn't . . .'

'Little runt over there, hasn't got the muscles on him to . . .'

'You and your bloody swastikas!'

The Doctor looked up from his shoes. A large man in a vest was prodding a boy in the chest, staring at his swastika earrings. 'First it's the bloody Pakis, then it's you and your punk whatnot. Fought the war for you lot – '

'I dunno what they were mate, they just looked – Christ!' The man had grabbed one ear-ring and pulled. Blood spurted from the boy's ear. He lashed out with a boot, catching the man across his groin. The man roared and landed a heavy punch square in the boy's mouth. Blood spat against the window. The crowd edged back. A random kick from the boy as he fell caught another man across his shins. He turned and kicked the boy in the ribs. A quick little kick, like he could do it and turn away again. He couldn't. Shouts were building in the carriage

70

now, and people were pushing against each other trying to get away. A man with a beach umbrella made a vast swinging turn and smashed it across the head of the kicking man, grazing him over the eye.

'Get off him, get off him, you're killing him!' The kicker turned and exploded into violence, smashing the umbrella man against the wall. He ploughed into him, yelling and screaming obscenities. The victim's girlfriend dived at the attacker. He punched her in the face, sending her flying into the crowd. The crowd shoved her back and she fell into the aisle, where feet were stamping around her as people tried to climb up onto the seats. Her glasses shattered under a shoe, and the glass was spread across the floor as she tried to climb up through the tangle of legs.

The Doctor reached out an arm, but found himself battered from right to left by elbows and pressing people. He pulled out the dial of the Temporal Disruption Monitor, hoping that this was somehow a time distortion, some kind of control . . . The dial showed no reading.

Passengers were trying to climb over each other now, as more and more were pulled, flailing, into the fight. There was a smash of glass, and a burst of foam blasted through the carriage. People began to slip and fall, crowding against each other in a pile along the length of the train. The Doctor grabbed a support pole and hung on.

'Stop!' he shouted, but he couldn't be heard over the screaming and yelling. In the aisle, people were lying three deep, covered in foam, making feeble movements to cover their faces and groins as feet and falling bodies slammed around them. Punches threw new victims spinning into this mass as the central fight, four men deep now, swung back and forth along the coach. In a corner, a Rastafarian was being held against a wall by the weight of bodies, his face a mass of blood. A Teddy Boy was slashing to his left and right with a razor, his expression half-way between terror and ecstacy. Splatters of blood flailed across the seats. People grabbed other people's hair and hauled themselves away, slipping into the muddle of bodies at the centre of the train. Collapsing so that their heads

71

slammed into the floor, under falling bodies and stamped-
ing feet.

The original punk was lost somewhere under a fighting
mob of men. Bloody debris filled the carriage, the atmosphere full of sweat and adrenalin. The Doctor noticed a
hand in front of his nose, reaching for the emergency
handle. He grabbed it and held it. 'No. They'll stop the
train before it reaches the station.' He didn't know if
the man heard him, but the hand grasped his and held
on.

The train started up again. Darkness hummed past the
windows as screams and laughter whooped at the little
lights that sped by outside. A minute later, a bundle of
thrashing, screaming, bloody humanity vomited out of the
carriage onto the platform. The Doctor was slammed
against the wall in the scramble to get out. He'd dragged
with him a boy, a fair-haired student, still clutching his
hand. The cries from the train were spreading through
the station now, tribal shouts spreading up the escalators.
The sobs and wails continued to slop out onto the platform, the doors thumping open and closed against hands
and feet sticking out at awful, broken, angles.

The Doctor looked down at the young man, and
realized that his eyes were closed. 'Are you all right?' he
shouted, shaking him lightly. There was no response. 'No
spinal injury . . .' the Doctor muttered. He put one hand
behind the boy's neck, and gently tilted his forehead backwards. Then, taking his hand from the neck, he pulled the
boy's chin up and forwards, leaving the mouth open. The
Doctor checked for breath again, and muttered an invo-
cation to Rassilon. He couldn't see any obvious obstruc-
tion in the boy's mouth. He pinched the victim's nose,
took a deep breath and sealed his mouth over the boy's,
blowing gently but firmly. He glanced sideways. The chest
hadn't risen. He tried again, making sure he was pinching
hard enough and that the seal was tight. Still no
movement.

'Recovery position,' the Doctor muttered. He turned
the boy's head sideways. Then he grabbed the arm furthest

72

from him, and crossed it over the boy's chest, tucking that hand, palm downwards, under his cheek as a cushion. Taking the arm nearest to him, he tucked it, palm upwards, under the boy's bottom. Then, quickly, he crossed the furthest ankle over the nearest. Then he grabbed the boy's belt with one hand, his shoulder with the other, and rolled his body towards him so that his trunk rested against his knees. He bent the upper arm and leg to prop up his hip, and the lower arm to stop him rolling backwards. He checked the chin again, and delivered four firm slaps between the boy's shoulder-blades. Then he rolled the student back and tried respiration again. Nothing was happening.

A firm hand closed on the Doctor's shoulder. 'Come on mate, we'll take over.' An ambulanceman took the boy's head from the Doctor, and kept up the respiration process. After a minute or so, he began compressing the boy's chest. After five minutes, he checked the pulse once more, stood up and shook his head.

The Doctor moved away. Ambulance crews were picking their way through the people on the platform. He was the last able person left. An ambulancewoman put an arm around his waist. He was surprised to find that he was shaking. 'It's all right,' he told her. 'It doesn't matter. None of this matters.'

'Hush. You're suffering from shock.'

'No. It's all right,' the Doctor whispered. 'I'm a Doctor.'

Mortimus danced in front of a panel of illuminated dials, watching a read-out as its needle jumped higher and higher. Behind him, anger radiated from the black depths of an opaque sphere, and he looked over his shoulder, amused, his hands clenching and unclenching. 'You object? You object to him being shown what these cattle of his are like? Oh no, I see . . . you object to the freedom that others are exercising. Well, I'm sorry you can't be free to torment them yourself!'

A light flickered on behind him. A warning beacon. Mortimus glanced up at it, irritated. 'Oh dear . . .' he muttered. He glanced at the panel. 'Ah well, I'd have to stop soon anyway.' He flicked a switch on the control panel, and the lights died.

Ace had spent the morning in Camden Market. She thought she preferred the place in her own time . . . whenever that was.

She'd been trying to shake the cobwebs out of her head since waking up. Something about last night . . . finding something, like in a dream, but expecting it to be there in the morning, only it wasn't. And now it felt, distantly, like someone was angry with her again. Well, that was nothing new. She'd made the decision to go and see Bertram again around lunchtime.

Priory was closed, of course, but the building security man had shown her straight up to Bertram's apartment. That was flattering. She found Bertram sitting behind his chair, watching the lunchtime news on television. Kenneth Kendal.

'Good morning to you!' Bertram beamed. 'How are you feeling?'

'Could be better. Feel like I've got a metal plate in my head.'

'How awful for you. I'm not quite feeling myself either. I was up late watching The Manchurian Candidate. Wonderful film. Did you, ah, see the Doctor?'

'Yeah. We had a row. He wanted to dump me back in the eighties.'

'And how do you feel about that?'

'Wouldn't fit in there, wouldn't fit in anywhere.'

'Oh, I don't know about that. I can think of quite a few places where you'd fit in perfectly. Shall I show you a video of some of them?'

'Yeah!' Ace sat down on the desk, intrigued. 'What sort of places?'

Mortimus activated a remote control, and the picture on the television changed to a swirling vortex. 'Places known to the CIA. Places of the mind.'

'The CIA?'

'There's no such thing as coincidence. They've been a front for us for years. If Kennedy had really got humanity into space travel, then – ' He spread his hands. 'But this is for the future. For now . . . look at the pictures and listen to the soundtrack. I think this will answer a great many questions for you.'

Ace pointed a wobbling finger at the screen. 'That darkness . . . that's not a place, is it?'

'That darkness, my dear, is the most suitable place for you. It's the place where all assassins live. This will give you the opportunity to see it, and then in a moment we'll go there properly.'

Benny had watched Grenadier Guards and marching bands and soldiers pass by, and was greatly interested. In her time, horses hadn't been used for anything so chivalrous. She'd read texts which insisted that the animals were still used for warfare in this century. Obviously corrupted sources. It was hard to tell between fiction and fact in a past century. Danny had taken off his T-shirt, revealing an agonizingly slim torso and rib-cage, and replaced it with one that bore a large black star on a red background. 'Yeah,' he commented. 'I ain't getting a tan.'

Behind them, the crowds were on their feet, cheering and applauding. There were, Benny thought, worse ways to spend a summer afternoon. The state landau was approaching, and a wave of cheering was resounding up through Horse Guards Parade. Above the street on the other side, people were leaning out of the windows of stern government offices, waving banners and flags. For once, they'd be glad that they worked on Sundays.

The wave of noise washed into their part of the crowd as the Queen came in sight, seated beside Prince Philip in the open-topped carriage. She was waving to the crowd. Beside the carriage walked a group of plain-suited bulky men, wandering in and out of the ceremonial guardsmen. They also walked along the edges of the parade, between the two rows of barricades. One glanced at Danny's shirt and frowned before moving on.

Benny was looking at the carriage, thinking how strange it must be to have a monarchy, when she saw that something strange was happening. A security man had jumped into the landau, but he flew back off it, his shoulder bursting into a red mist. The Queen looked up, and suddenly there was blood in the back of the carriage as she threw up her hand and fell, gunfire cracking out across the crowd.

The royals vanished into the carriage and it was spurred ahead, the parade clearing to let it through. Security men were running, guns out, along the road, squinting up at the buildings.

The crowd behind Danny and Bernice rose up, like one thing, and roared. The sound was terrible. They rushed, not away, but at the barriers. Danny hit the metal across his throat, and was barged with the crowd to the point where the metal bulged out into the road. His razor-blade necklace slid alarmingly across his skin.

Benny grabbed his arm, feeling the mass of bodies straining behind her. 'Come on!' she shouted, and put a foot on the shoulder of the man behind her. They were catapulted out of the crowd, rolled into the street in front of the barriers and bruised their elbows on the pavement. A security man spotted them, as they picked themselves up, saw the shirt, ran towards them aiming his gun.

Benny put her hands up. 'We're just getting out! We're just – '

The barriers behind them broke, and a screaming mob washed into the street like a tidal wave. A nauseous human screeching filled the air. The security man snapped up his arm, pointed the gun straight at Danny's head.

He was going to fire.

6

Another Girl, Another Planet

The security man spun as another shot rang out, blood splashing from his shoulder. The mob roared over them, sweeping him off in screams and buffeting elbows. Benny turned and gasped at the numbers that were rolling around them, pulling her and Danny down.

A pair of hands grasped theirs, and they found themselves walking quickly through miraculous gaps and spaces in the raging crowd.

'Come on,' the Doctor muttered. 'We're going.'

'Where?' gasped Danny, amazed at the strength of the little man's grip.

The Doctor looked at Benny, a cold determination in his features. 'Hunting,' he snarled.

'Back and to the left!' Pike's baton slapped the projection screen as the bullet sent the security man flying off the landau. 'That means, ladies and gentlemen, that the would-be assassin was somewhere within the government offices. Actually inside what we regarded as a secure zone.'

They were in an office in Whitehall: the Brigadier, Carpenter, and the Prime Minister seated, Pike standing by the projection screen.

'Thank you, Captain.' The Brigadier stood up. 'We've alerted the ports and airports, obviously.'

'Obviously.' Mrs Williams drummed her fingers on the table. 'We've been led a merry dance, Brigadier. Her Majesty actually suffered a deliberately inflicted injury today. That hasn't happened to a monarch since Charles the First

77

got his head cut off. I wouldn't grin if I were you, Captain Pike. It's a major publicity coup for Black Star.'

'How is Her Majesty?' the Brigadier frowned at Pike.

'She's shocked, of course.' Mrs Williams produced a cardboard file and flipped it open. 'I just wish that I could be certain that elements within our own security services aren't at least partially responsible.'

'For an assault on the monarch?' Carpenter almost laughed. He quickly regained his composure. 'That's an interesting theory, Prime Minister.'

'It's the civil disobedience this afternoon after the incident that worries me,' Mrs Williams continued. 'That is, I think, unique in the history of assassination. Normally people are quietened, shocked into inaction by such events.'

'Yes, well ma'am, that's part of a much wider pattern.' Pike deactivated the projector and sat down. 'We're looking at increasing waves of violence and looting. Summertime blues. Trouble, right here in River City.'

'You may be aware of an incident on an underground train – ' Carpenter cut in.

'I am indeed,' the Prime Minister closed her file. 'Which is why I've invited a guest along to this meeting. He's from the private sector, but I think we can learn something from him.' She gestured to the guard at the door. 'Show Mr Bertram in, please.'

'Bob Bertram?' Pike asked. 'Hey, wasn't he military adviser to Slade?'

'Captain Pike!' the Brigadier snapped. 'We already use a lot of equipment that Mr Bertram had a hand in developing.' But his expression wasn't pleased either.

Bertram wandered into the room and glanced at the gathering, rubbing his hands together in anticipation. 'Hello all,' he murmured. 'I must say, I'm slightly overawed at this honour, but I'll do what I can . . .'

'What honour?' The Brigadier glanced at the Prime Minister.

'I hadn't time to tell you.' Mrs Williams tapped a pencil

78

on her teeth. 'I consulted with your superiors in Geneva. Mr Bertram is to be UNIT UK's new scientific adviser.'

The Doctor led Benny and Danny to Trafalgar Square, still walking whatever path had taken him so quickly through the crowds.

Danny began to protest. 'Hey, Benny, who is this bloke? You said you'd lost your dad!'

The Doctor looked at him, as if only just realizing he was there. He stopped. 'I'm the Doctor. You must be Danny. Go home.'

'Doctor!' Benny tapped him on the head. 'Hello, anybody home? Stop being so rude, git features.'

The Doctor glared at her, still furious. Then suddenly he cracked into his seven-year-old grin. 'Guilty.' He turned and shook Danny warmly by both hands. 'Sorry. Pleased to meet you. You're very talented. Or will be. Eventually.' He flickered a pen out from behind Danny's ear. 'So can I have your autograph? It's not for me, it's for my granddaughter.'

'You're taking the piss!' Danny stepped back, angry.

'No,' Benny gave Danny a significant look. 'He's not.'

Danny fished in his pocket and found some paper. He took the pen from the Doctor, and, looking around as if to see there was nobody watching, scrawled his signature.

The Doctor took the paper and smiled, folding it into his pocket. 'Thank you. Now I need to talk to Benny. She'll see you tomorrow. Go home. Be safe.'

'Yeah, well, see you tomorrow, Benny. I'll be off home, better safe than sorry, eh?' And he wandered off in the direction of Charing Cross.

'Eight out of ten,' Benny opined. 'That was probably the best way to please him, but I wish you wouldn't send people away like that.'

'Best for him to be safe. And I wasn't trying to please him. I was scraping the bottom of the barrel, crossing the i's and dotting the t's.'

'And mixing your metaphors. What do you mean?'

'If his fame's an issue in all this, if he saves the world,

perhaps his signature's going to be useful. Perhaps . . .' He unfolded the paper and stared at it, pleased. 'Yes. He happened to sign a piece of Priory Records stationery. Perhaps I'll place it in his pocket, in the future. Perhaps that's all my future self needs to do . . .'

'I wouldn't rely on that, if I were you. I don't think your future self's involved this time.'

'No. But when you're looking for a needle in a haystack, it's easy to clutch at straws.'

'At least the metaphors are improving.' Benny put out a hand and played idly with the Doctor's lapel. 'I don't like seeing you so desperate. Has something awful happened?'

'Yes. To me. On the tube. People got hurt.'

Benny softened, seeing the tension in the Doctor's features. 'Including you?'

'Yes.' The Doctor followed Benny's gaze to Nelson's Column. Ace was sitting on the steps, idly tossing a knife to and fro.

'It isn't over yet,' Benny murmured. She would have hugged him, but she couldn't. Not in front of Ace.

The Doctor was checking the console to see if the TARDIS defences were still being challenged. Benny and Ace met in the wardrobe room.

'So how are you?' Benny selected a headscarf.

'Stop asking that. I'm fine.' Ace was searching through a baroque old chest. 'I'd be much finer if you pissed off.'

'What, so that you and the Doctor could get back to the old days?'

Benny regretted saying it as soon as it came out.

Ace didn't seem to react. 'No. The old days are gone. That's history. You can't change history. I just want you to piss off 'cos you're an irritating, selfish bitch who wants everybody to love her.'

'Oh, and that's really terrible isn't it!' Benny exploded, throwing down the scarf. 'You are so immature! At least I can still care about people! What do you feel about anybody any more?'

'I feel . . . something. I think it's hate. And I tell you

what . . .' Ace had found what she was looking for, a long-bladed knife with strange carvings on the handle. She flicked it up to the tip of Benny's chin. 'Don't shout at me again.'

Benny met Ace's expression. 'Why don't you just leave?' she whispered.

'I will,' Ace told her. 'But there's a couple of things I have to finish off first.'

The tube journey was absolutely silent. Benny sat on one side of the Doctor, Ace on the other. The Doctor had insisted that they wait for an empty carriage, which had taken a while. With him thinking and Ace plotting, Benny thought, there wasn't much left for a chatterer like her to do.

She hadn't meant any of it, obviously. It had all just come tumbling out, unreasonableness in the face of unreasonableness. Was it really selfish to want people to think well of you? Benny had called up enough people in the night, had even woken Jan up once to ask if they were friends. But that had been when she was much younger. Yes, fully a year younger in that last case. It was fine for her to talk about immaturity, a real case of the orange calling the non-orange thing orange. She had neuroses that were so big that other people felt them too. She'd watched Ace slip the dagger inside her jacket, watched her appreciating its potential to maim. Ace was a soldier, and Benny and the Doctor weren't. And that was the whole situation. If only Ace could see how much they both cared for her. The row would just give her more fuel for her bitterness. It was all going to end horribly. When it did, Benny would try to save the Doctor from it. And so she was silent.

The Doctor was angry. Angry like a caged animal that couldn't find anybody to attack. He knew that the enemy was here. But he didn't know exactly where. He'd become used to getting messages from himself. Complacent. Everything he loved was at risk. Again, Ace. Especially

81

Ace. He couldn't think for worrying about the fixed set of her eyes. And so he was silent.

Ace was comforted by the weight of the knife in her jacket. It could get her out of a corner, one she was going to be in soon, deliberately. There'd be a tiny chance to get out of it. Ace clenched her teeth against the blankness that had welled up inside her, and willed herself to go through with it. Traitors and assassins lived in a different place to soldiers, like Mortimus said. They lived in a place where everything they did had to have a calculated reason. Needed a lot of thought to stay in that place, lot of balls. She glanced at the Doctor. It was where he lived, these days. And now he was gonna feel it. Christ, she almost felt sorry for him. She stuck her hand inside her jacket and found the blade, and was silent.

Benton's Jaguar was waiting outside Amersham tube station. He'd left the door open, and was sitting inside in his sunglasses, studying a racing form book. When the Doctor and his companions appeared in the car-park, he clicked open the boot and went out to meet them.

'Afternoon, Doc. You must be Miss Summerfield and Ace. I'm John Benton.'

'Call me Bernice,' Benny managed a smile.

'Hi,' Ace flicked a hair off her forehead.

'In you get then, first-class compartment.' Benton pulled open the boot and motioned them inside. 'Special conversion job. I had it done years ago for an undercover operation.'

The Doctor peered in. The boot extended a long way back under the back seats. It was still going to be a tight squeeze. 'How far is it to UNIT HQ?'

'Only about half an hour,' Benton helped the Doctor get inside. 'You'll be okay.'

Benny glanced at Ace as she hopped in, and frowned.

As they rumbled along the road, something hard jammed into the small of Benny's back. It was a bottle of champagne. 'Hmm, nice of your friend to think of me, at least.'

The Doctor was curled up, thinking ferociously. 'I've often talked about how savage mankind can be . . . And then I talk myself out of it. How can the same race produce Michaelangelo's David and Belsen? Guernica and the air raid that inspired it?'

'St Etienne and Kellogg's Pop Tarts,' Ace added.

'But today . . . they just killed each other for no reason. Even Daleks are more civilized than that.'

'It sounds horrid,' Benny murmured, still glancing at Ace. 'But it is summer. There's a certain temperature that sets people off. And in the current political climate, I'm really not surprised.'

'It was more than that. It was influenced. Perverted. I will come here, I feel it. I will be Time's Champion here, and leave clues for myself. But I haven't found a single one. For the first time, somebody's playing the game against me. Somebody who knows exactly how I win.'

Benny opened the bottle, the cork flying around the boot, and took a swig. She handed it to Ace, gingerly, but the woman was content to take it and drink herself.

'You got that disc then?' she muttered, gulping the champagne.

'Oh yes!' Benny produced the CD from her pocket. 'This is for you. Ace nicked it from Robert Bertram's desk.'

The Doctor stared at the disc and pocketed it. 'Funny how things turn up, isn't it? That disc was how I first heard Plasticine . . .'

Despite themselves, Benny and Ace glanced at each other.

'What?' asked Benny.

'It was at a party in Finchley in the early twenty-first century. When I first met you, Benny, I realized that I'd heard your voice before. It took a week or two before I remembered that it had been on a live recording. You get some writing credits on the finished disc, as well. That's why I asked you to go and join Danny Pain's band. I knew you were going to.'

Ace started to chuckle. 'You see, Bernice? This is what

83

happens. This is just the start. Right now you're a person. Soon you'll just be one of his characters.'

'No!' The Doctor quickly responded, turning to face her. 'I don't have a plan, I don't know what's going to happen, you have to believe me – '

Benny would have liked to have said that she wasn't particularly bothered about all this. It hadn't, after all, hurt her. But she felt that she would be interrupting at just the wrong point. The car had slowed down, and she was worried about the noise. She put a hand between the two of them. 'It's okay, I don't mind. I like being in a band.'

'Yeah,' Ace muttered darkly, not looking at her. 'But will you like what comes next?'

Benton drove up to the gates of the old Buckinghamshire estate that was UNIT HQ and waved his pass at the sentry, who waved back and raised the barrier for him. He took the Jaguar round to the car-park, and left it there, walking up to a side entrance. So far, this was exactly what he'd have done on a normal afternoon.

What wasn't normal was that, a moment later, Ace led Benny and the Doctor, at a run, to the same entrance.

'This is where I leave you,' Benton muttered, glancing along what had been a servants' corridor. 'I'll be driving her out in about four hours' time, unless there's a flap on. I'm on leave, but we're all required to report in for this new training lark. Be in the boot.'

'There are other ways out,' Ace muttered.

'Yeah, but they all involve taking out UNIT troops,' Benton wagged a finger at her. 'And I don't want that, okay?'

'Fine,' Ace grinned.

The Doctor pulled the Temporal Disruption Monitor out of his pocket and tapped the dial. 'Ah. Yes. There's a powerful source of time displacement here. But it seems distant, like a secondary station . . .'

Benny noticed that Ace had stopped looking up and

down the corridor, and was staring at the dial, rubbing her forehead.

'Run that past me again, Doc?' Benton slung his kitbag over his shoulder, ready to move off.

'Evil, Sergeant Benton. Here in UNIT HQ.'

'Right ho then, Doc. I'll just pop off and do a bit of training; you sort it out, eh? See you later.' And he was off down the corridor.

'What a wonderful attitude . . .' Benny murmured.

'Oh it is,' the Doctor looked up. 'We split up. You two check out whatever these new UNIT training measures are.'

Ace nodded. 'What'll you do?'

'Improvise.'

The Brigadier walked down the line of UNIT troops, inspecting them. 'We're under the microscope at the moment. What with Black Star, the escaped alien and the assassination attempt on Her Majesty, we're expected to take the lead. Now, I can't pretend to you that we're gaining ground in any of these affairs. However, I can promise you that there will be some action quite shortly.' Lethbridge-Stewart stopped and turned, aware from his long experience that the troops were listening intently, despite their rock-like postures. 'I intend to engage the forces of Black Star, on the scale of a major skirmish, within the week. Our intelligence is up to it, I want to know that you lot are too. Are you up to it?'

'Yes sir!' the troopers barked.

'Good, I should have known better than to ask, eh, Mister Benton?' Benton, now in his fatigues, was standing at the end of the line. He smiled back at the Brigadier's amused glance. It was at moments like this that things seemed to still be like old times. 'Very well, I'll hand you over to Major Carpenter for Virtual Reality training. This room is Black Clearance only after you've fallen out. Dismissed.'

The troopers returned the Brigadier's salute and

marched out of the briefing room. Benton stepped forward.

'What is it, Benton? I'll be seeing to Broadsword in a moment, you know we have to keep their identities secret . . .'

'I understand sir, but it's . . . it's a personal matter. I've been worried lately, about all sorts of things to do with UNIT . . .'

The Brigadier looked up sharply. 'Well, we're all worried, man. that's what the job's about. Captain Pike!'

Pike had been loitering by the door. He marched quickly over.

'But sir,' Benton continued, 'quite a few of the lads are concerned too, it's just – '

Pike shrugged at the Brigadier and snatched his automatic out of his holster, jacking the safety catch and sticking it under Benton's chin in one smooth movement.

Benton jerked with a thought of tackling the man.

'Don't!' Pike advised him. 'Or I will kill you, bet on it.'

The Brigadier turned and called up to the room in general. 'Doctor? Is that really what you're calling yourself? Come on out, or we'll kill your accomplice!'

Benton opened his mouth in amazement. 'How did you – ?'

'We're not stupid, Benton, despite appearances to the contrary. Come on Doctor, you're running out of time!'

There was a rustle from the fireplace, and the Doctor hopped out from behind the redundant fire-guard, disturbing the dry pile of logs that lay there. 'You saw me come in?'

'We saw all three of you come in,' Pike corrected him.

'And of course, you knew I'd want to hear what you were telling your men, Brigadier. You know me too well.' The Doctor wandered forward, peering at Lethbridge-Stewart's face.

The Brigadier turned away. 'One of the most irritating things about you, Doctor, is your delusion that we are somehow old friends. I'm not likely to have my friends locked up, am I?'

Benton looked between them. 'But sir, it's the Doctor. I know he looks different, but don't you remember – ?'

'I don't know what you're talking about, Mister Benton.' The Brigadier picked up a telephone, and tapped the rest twice. 'Get me a security detail.' He looked up at the Doctor again. 'Good to see you again, anyway. When you're safely in custody, I'll have one less problem to worry about.'

Carpenter appeared at the doorway.

'Close your mouth, Major,' the Brigadier advised. 'Take these two down to the security wing, and try not to lose them this time.'

Ace and Benny were watching from a stairwell as UNIT troopers filed through a sliding doorway into what looked like an absolutely white room. The door slid closed after them.

'What's that for?' Ace asked.

'Could be some sort of virtual reality equipment,' Benny mused, surprised that Ace was communicating with her. They'd moved through the house at the younger woman's pace, hiding in what seemed to be impossible corners, passing just beyond the range of sentries and cameras. Benny had begun to admire Ace's skill and stealth.

'I didn't ask you, I was talking to myself.'

'It sounded like you were asking somebody.'

'Yeah,' Ace pinched herself. 'Weird. Let's get a closer look.'

They moved down the stairs. Ace put an ear to the door. Then, satisfied, she touched the pad that opened it.

Benny took a step backwards. Inside the room there was a jungle, a hissing, chirruping expanse of dense green foliage. Between the trees flew strange birds, and small creatures stumbled through the humus. A smell of chlorophyll and humidity wafted out into the corridor. 'That,' she whispered, 'is the most successful virtual reality I have ever seen. It's far beyond twentieth-century technology.'

'Yeah. Right.' Ace was staring into the jungle. It was as if she'd seen something. 'You stay here.'

'No,' Benny put a hand on her sleeve. 'Wait, I'll – '

'You follow – ' Ace knocked the hand away. 'And I'll hurt you.' And she sprinted off into the foliage.

Benny looked around the corridor. 'I am getting so tired of that attitude,' she sighed. She peered into the jungle. 'Oh well. Perhaps they've just got a large greenhouse.'

She stepped into the heat haze.

Ace had run after somebody that she thought she'd seen. A woman in a red velvet dress, standing against the greenery, grinning. Her nails and eyes were as red as her garment. She'd turned and walked away, with a toss of her long dark hair.

The woman that had been in her dreams for months. The woman who knew something about the locked door in the TARDIS that Ace couldn't open.

Ace scampered through the foliage, ducking under branches and hopping rocks, her arms extended before her. The combat armour had compensated for the heat. Suddenly a burst of gunfire cracked through the jungle, and a brilliant bird burst from cover in front of her.

She threw herself into the ground shrubs, and poked her eyeline up again in a moment. The shots had been a way off to the left. Not at her. The bird had fluttered into the branches of a tree, and she got a close look at it. It wasn't a parrot, but a long-tailed alien thing. Ace was so used to alien animals that it had taken a while for her to realize that it was out of place here. Bit specific for a computer animation too. The gunfire came again.

Ace crawled on her elbows towards the sound, and peeped through a gap in the tree cover. Three UNIT soldiers were firing at a floating silvery blur. It sent out a crackling sound and flickered tendrils of energy at them. Bullets were scudding straight through it, leaving vapour trails that hung in the air.

Suddenly it lashed out, and a trooper fell, frying in a blaze of silver. The other two turned to retreat, but the thing suddenly increased in size and lowered itself onto them, surrounding them in a halo of sizzling light.

Ace's eyes narrowed as the man who'd fallen got to his feet again. He wandered over to watch his comrades throwing themselves to and fro inside the blaze. His expression was disinterested. The two flailing men finally steadied, and stood upright. The silver cloud rose from them and sizzled off through the jungle, singeing branches as it went. The three men watched it go, equally content.

Ace crouched down into the foliage.

Benny was watching from behind a tree-trunk as Major Carpenter stood stiffly beside a group of three shimmering silver forms. The things seemed to fade in and out of humanoid form, flickering like television images.

Carpenter was talking to them. His lips weren't moving, but the attitude was obvious. Suddenly, he turned his head. Benny ducked, realizing that he'd just been told something that had made him look her way.

One of the silver clouds rushed at her.

She scrambled in the other direction, sprinting around the trees as it crackled through them. She glanced over her shoulder, and suddenly it was upon her.

The jungle faded into the distance. Benny found herself moving in slow motion, bouncing in low gravity. Static flashed around her. Blurred lines flickered across her vision. Suddenly there was a burst of activity. The lines fractured and assembled at a startling rate, and then –

She saw figures. A row of marching men. A military tune thumped away in the background. The men wore basic, functional garments, including large brown helmets. Their faces were stern. They were marching not with weapons, but with their hands clasped together in front of them. Around them a withering psychic haze fried the air. Banners of simple colours fluttered above.

And then they were fighting amongst themselves, naked. Two men grabbed each other, slapped arms three times in a ritual test of physique, then slammed their foreheads against each other, their faces contorted in con-

89

centration. The air throbbed, their eyes locked. There was a moment of realization, a spasm –

And one head exploded.

The other man delighted in it, throwing back his head in exultation, splashing the blood onto his cheeks as he slammed his head from side to side in ecstasy.

There was a baby, a poor baby with one eye, and hands left it on a hill to die. Benny reached out to touch it, but her hand swept straight through the mists.

A hard old man was concentrating in his simple robes. His muscular hands clasped harder and harder together, until a glow began to blaze from them. The glow spread out to engulf his entire body. And then he was the glow. The shimmering form lifted off the ground and rose to fly.

Similar ghosts drifted across a war-torn landscape, frying and burning as they passed through humanoid soldiers. More of them appeared out of nowhere, behind a group of the humanoids who had been hiding in a trench. The burning glow engulfed them, but one stumbled out, blazing. He walked towards the glowing phantoms, staring at his hands in amazement. The ghostly beings clustered around him, curious. He'd changed sides.

The picture flickered out, and Benny felt the pressure of the cloud around her increase. Something in her head folded painfully, and her teeth ground together as she fell to the floor, open-mouthed and unconscious.

Ace had made her way carefully past many isolated groups of soldiers. Some had been fighting with the glowing beings, some had been standing with them, as if communing.

Well, these looked like aliens to her. Question was, were they real or were they computer-created? The fried trooper had smelt fried. And where had that woman gone? Ace had some serious questions to ask her. Like how come she was in dreams and in reality too? It was like she had the answers to everything.

Ace came to a gateway. It was a huge gothic arch set

into the wall. Gargoyles leaned out over the peak of it, and under it was the entrance to a tunnel. The darkness of it made Ace feel nauseous, because it was some kind of inside darkness, a void that echoed in your head. How could you ever come back out of that?

In front of the gateway stood a figure.

It was Mortimus, clothed in a monk's robe, his head hidden by a hood. He was waiting for something. Waiting for her. His hands were clasped in front of him in concern.

Ace remembered raising her eye from along the barrel of the rifle. It was an elaborate job, shoulder rest and all. The air was hot around her, and the crowd was screaming down below in Horseguard's Parade.

Mortimus had put a hand on her shoulder. 'Why the third shot?'

They were standing in a little office full of filing cabinets. It smelt of wood polish and disinfectant. From lower floors of the building came the sound of orders and running boots.

'Tried to kill Bernice,' Ace whispered. 'Missed.'

'The more I know you, the more you remind me of myself,' the Monk smiled, leading her back to a particular filing cabinet.

'Really?' Ace had entered the cabinet before him. 'How nice for you.'

She might have turned away from him at the gateway, she really might. But then, deep inside the tunnel, a pair of gorgeous eyes flashed and there was a swirl of retreating scarlet.

Ace stepped out of the bushes. 'Nice world you got here,' she told Mortimus. 'You're not trying to stop these aliens, are you? You're working with them.'

Mortimus raised his head slightly, his eyes shining with excitement under his hood. 'Exactly,' he whispered. 'You've taken a sip from my cup, Ace. You've seen how complicated it all is, in the land of the assassin. Does it matter who we're working for?'

Ace paused. And then she grinned. 'No.'

'My dear . . .' Mortimus held out his hand. 'Come with me. I've got so much more to show you.'

So Ace took his hand and walked into the darkness.

7

Passengers

Benny woke in a blank white room, staring up at a circle of soldiers.

'There is yet another strange taste in my mouth,' she told them, lying there. 'It reminds me of that time I got my depilatory cream mixed up with my toothpaste.'

They dragged her to her feet. Their faces were set and stern, and Benny couldn't see an ounce of humanity in them. There was no sign of Ace anywhere.

Major Carpenter strode over to her. 'So we've got all of you!'

'You got Ace too?'

The Major frowned. 'No. Quickly then, where is she?'

'I have no idea . . .' Benny winced as her arms were jerked behind her back and handcuffed. 'I only hope she knows herself.'

She was marched through the building, back to the central hall. There, Benton and the Doctor were standing in front of the Brigadier. He'd had them similarly cuffed, and three burly UNIT men were standing by.

'Splendid!' the Brigadier nodded to Carpenter when he saw Bernice.

'There is one more insurgent still at large, sir.'

'We'll find her. Now, no mistakes this time. I believe, Major, that these three know a great deal about our current problems. I want to fly them out to Geneva as soon as possible. Let the interrogation boys have a go at them. Put a call through to RAF Lyneham, top priority. I'll be going with them.'

'Sir, is that – ?'

'Captain Pike will accompany me. Get me a chopper pilot and an air corridor to Lyneham by – ' he glanced at his watch, 'Seventeen hundred.'

Benny was watching the Brigadier's movements. She kept thinking about an actor playing a soldier. And he was rushing, as though this was a farce, and he had to get away before something awful happened.

Carpenter saluted and turned on his heel.

'Sir – ' Benton turned to the Brigadier. 'Can't you see this is all wrong? We haven't done anything, and – '

'Quiet, Benton!' The Brigadier bellowed. 'You are under military arrest, and will not address any member of UNIT unless answering a direct question! Is that clear?'

'Yes sir!' Benton snapped to attention and saluted.

'Interesting.' The Doctor managed to look relaxed in his bonds. Benny suspected that he'd perfected the technique with lots of practice. 'Captain Pike – '

'The same goes for you,' the Brigadier told the Time Lord.

'Really? But I'm not a soldier. How can I be under military arrest?'

'As a spy. Frankly, I could get away with having you shot, in the right circumstances. Bear that in mind.'

Pike shrugged at the Doctor sympathetically. He and the Brigadier retreated into a corner and began to look at a chart the senior officer produced from his pocket.

'Where's Ace?' the Doctor whispered.

'She's gone,' Benny told him. 'There's a virtual-reality generator here, one with incredible properties. It's almost like – '

'A parallel world,' the Doctor met Benny's gaze. 'Yes.'

'And there's something else. I saw – '

'Later.'

Carpenter marched back into the room, followed by a security detail. 'Chopper's ready, sir. You're on the 18.30 Hercules out of Lyneham.'

'Very good.' The Brigadier looked up from the map.

'Try not to lose this lot between here and the lawn, Carpenter.'

The helicopter was warming up on the sunlit lawn, a military Lynx in UNIT colours. Soldiers ran under the blades, leading Benny, the Doctor and Benton into the craft. Pike drew his automatic and hopped up behind them.

'Major Carpenter.' The Brigadier stood in the gust of the blades, holding on to his hat. 'You're in charge until I get back. I've posted standing orders about Broadsword ops, let them get on with it.'

'Sir!' Carpenter saluted. 'Good luck, sir.'

'We make our own luck, Major. Carry on.'

He sprinted under the blades, jumped into the passenger compartment and closed the door.

Carpenter watched as the craft receded into the afternoon sky. After a while Robert Bertram joined him, fumbling with his tie as he stepped out on to the lawn.

'I thought I'd stay out of sight. Is everything in order?' he asked.

Carpenter turned to him and smiled. 'Don't worry, Mortimus. Everything's under control.'

The Lynx sped across the green countryside of England, its camouflage reflecting the brilliant sunshine. Far below were rivers and railway lines, ancient hill-forts and modern towns.

Benny glanced out of the cabin window every now and then. It was hot in the cabin. They'd been airborne for forty-five minutes. The Doctor had his eyes closed, deep in thought. Pike was toying with his gun, catching her eye every now and then in what was either a reassuring or flirtatious glance. Benton was frowning, worrying to himself. The Brigadier was reading from a black file marked Above Top Secret. In the front of the helicopter, a pilot and navigator sat.

Benny was trying to get rid of a developing headache, massaging the bridge of her nose. She'd started to hear a persistent hum below the roar of the chopper, and little flashes of light were sparkling in her vision. Migraine? Hadn't had one since she was sixteen. Of all the times . . .

There was a flicker of something across her vision. A person, a corner of the eye person.

And suddenly, everything kaleidoscoped. She saw the Earth from above, the helicopter from below, the land from underneath. They flew upside-down. Three view-points clashed in her, and for a dizzying moment she was empty in the void, without a body, without history. The helicopter shot through a moment of blazing now. The rotors slowed, stopped, and the view swept round the aircraft. She could see herself, cowering, through the cabin window. The sky shattered. She saw the craft as a bird saw it, roaring by, as a mouse saw it, the shadow spreading across the grass, as the earth saw it, a part of itself held momentarily in the sky. Then she saw the sights. Cross-hairs. The helicopter was defined, finally, at the centre of them. Defined as a target.

'No!' Benny leapt forward and made a grab for the control column.

The pilot turned. Benny's hand slammed into the stick.

The Lynx banked sharply.

A bolt of fire screeched past, bursting across the tail in an explosion.

The Lynx went into a spin, fire blazing from its rudder. The cabin passengers sprawled onto the floor. The roar of the engines became a rising whine.

'We've been hit!' the Brigadier shouted. 'Crash positions!'

'Windmill to Lyneham B Tower, we have an emergency, we have an emergency – ' the navigator was shouting into his mouthpiece.

'Coming down hard!' called the pilot.

The Doctor reached out, his face set sternly, and took Benny's hand.

The helicopter swooped low over level grasslands, cutting across hummocks and ridges. Amongst the blazing tail, the rear propeller rotated and stopped in bursts, sending the aircraft into sudden spins.

It sped in an arc around a low grassy bank, and hit it a glancing blow. The tail erupted in a firework cascade of explosions, and the Lynx spun back around again. The rotor blades touched the hillside.

The cabin was slammed into the ground, veering sickeningly sideways. One rotor blade jack-knifed upwards, spinning off into the air.

'Get out of it!' The Brigadier grabbed Bernice and hauled her to the cabin door, kicking at the emergency release mechanism. Explosive bolts fired, and the doorway burst out onto the ground. The hiss of automatic fire extinguishers covered the crackle of hundreds of small fires. The tail was just a charred skeleton.

Pike and Benton grabbed the Doctor between them and vaulted out of the aircraft. Behind them, the navigator clambered out of his webbing and burst out of his cockpit door. In the pilot's position lay a mass of squashed blood and metal.

They sprinted across the grassy ground, panting in the heat and the fumes of the crash. Jumping behind a hummock, they took cover as the Lynx exploded, a ball of fire bursting skywards.

'Ground-to-air missile!' Pike shook his head in disgust. 'They're gonna be around here somewhere.'

'I'll put a call out.' The navigator pulled a handset from his leg pouch. 'We're in the middle of Salisbury Plain, there'll be somebody on a military frequency out here.'

'Very good, Molyneux.' The Brigadier stood unsteadily, walking behind the man. He reached for something at his belt.

Molyneux tugged out the aerial on the handset.

Benny looked up and gasped. 'No!' she yelled. 'Don't – '

The Brigadier turned, brought up his revolver and shot Molyneux through the back of the head.

The body fell lifeless to the ground.

'Poor chap was dead already.' The Brigadier helped Bernice up. 'Alien take-over and all that.' He turned to the Doctor and raised an eyebrow. 'Have a little faith in me, eh, Doctor?'

8

Complete Control

Benton's face lit up. Benny thought that he was about to hug Lethbridge-Stewart, but he finally just saluted, grinning. 'Good to have you back, sir.'

'Good to be back, Benton.' The Brigadier returned the salute. They were sheltering behind a low ridge, miniature explosions still flailing debris into the air from the helicopter. The landscape was flat and grassy, hummocks and windy stretches of pasture sweltering under the heat of the low sun. 'And it really is good to see you again, Doctor. We need your help.'

'So I see.' The Doctor was still concentrating furiously. 'You put on a good act. I nearly believed it. The last time I saw you was in an alternate world, and you weren't yourself there, either.'

'What, you mean like that chap with the eyepatch? I still remember that rather witty story you told me about him – '

'We haven't time. What's going on?'

'We're being invaded, as always. I had to get you out.'

'So you arranged this crash?' The Doctor dusted off his burnt safari suit.

'Unfortunately, no. I was planning to jump the crew at Lyneham. I can only describe that chap I shot as the living dead. I found his body myself, some weeks ago, in the grounds of UNIT HQ. Rather surprising to find him in the ranks next day. Now, we should be moving, that crash will attract attention. What's the lie of the land, Captain Pike?'

Pike was leaning on the bank, looking around with binoculars. 'Quiet, sir. I think it's good to go.'

'Very well. Doctor, miss – '

'Summerfield,' Benny shook the Brigadier's hand, still dizzy. 'Bernice. Professor. But if you're going to be formal I prefer Ms.'

'Muzz?' The Brigadier frowned. 'Ah well, then I shall have to try and call you Bernice.'

'Brigadier!' The Doctor was pacing impatiently. 'I need more information. Tell me more.'

'As we walk. I took up the ways of Buddhism by your example, Doctor. Don't tell me you've become hasty now?'

'There are some things more important than philosophy, Brigadier. One of them is winning. I do that. But not so much lately.'

'I can't say I'm surprised. Here – ' Lethbridge-Stewart slapped the file he'd been carrying into the Doctor's hands. 'We stole this from UNIT HQ. It's your file. Perhaps you ought to remind yourself of who you are.' And he strode off to consult with Benton and Pike.

Benny propped herself on the Doctor's shoulder as he flipped open the file. 'Goodness,' she mused. 'Did you really used to look like that?'

'I first became aware of alien incursion last year. Didn't have time to tell you about it during that Zygon business. At the time I thought it might even be them.'

The Brigadier and the Doctor walked at the centre of a patrol made up of Pike, Benton and Bernice. The latter two had been given automatics out of a sack that Pike carried across his back. They were trudging across Salisbury Plain, heading for a road, according to the Brigadier's military map. Lethbridge-Stewart had decided that they'd rent a car in Salisbury and head for London.

'I doubt that I'd have listened.' The Doctor fanned his face with his somewhat charred hat.

'No. Anyhow, it all started with the new training techniques that this entrepreneur fellow Robert Bertram

100

brought in. The virtual reality room. Lot of the men fell ill, started to hallucinate. And then, after a while, they'd stop complaining. First sign of trouble, your private soldier not complaining, eh Benton?'

'Yes sir!' Benton grinned.

'I thought that some sort of incursion might be going on,' the Doctor murmured. 'That's why I asked Captain Pike about his childhood.'

'So if I'd talked about spacedogs and spacebikes you'd have got me!' Pike called. 'Hey, I'm impressed.'

The Brigadier raised an eyebrow. 'I'm not quite as foolish as you paint me, Doctor. I realized that UNIT had been compromised when myself and Captain Pike here began to get headaches too. We're both Buddhists, visit the same meeting house. What the men saw as flashes of light and sound, we saw completely. Voices and images, familiar human beings giving us orders. A lot of things from the pictures I used to go and see when I was a boy. Quite disturbing to see Robert Donat getting all uppity. Sometimes they told us to conform and obey, sometimes they played on the more base emotions, tried to get us worked up.'

'I see. Subliminal control. That makes sense. I'm proud of you, Brigadier. You're learning.'

'Well, that's what meditation does for you. Anyhow, Captain Pike and I immediately pulled out of VR training, and I instructed Broadsword to do the same.'

'Broadsword?'

The Brigadier smiled proudly. 'Another chip off your block, Doctor. They're our intelligence division. If all's going to plan, they should have vanished from UNIT this afternoon. They're hand-picked to offer us lateral and non-military solutions, backed up by SAS training and sheer common sense.'

'Should I be flattered?' The Doctor half-smiled.

'Oh yes. Anyhow, the headaches and visions didn't stop. We were being affected by something apart from the training.'

'Had to go in for some severe self-examination to shake

it off.' Pike shook his head. 'Three days of fasting and stuff. I stared at my navel so much it got nervous.'

'An external source!' the Doctor muttered. 'Yes. I can see a pattern.'

'Jolly good,' Lethbridge-Stewart smiled. 'That's the best news I've heard in weeks. I'd have withdrawn all of our men from training and given Bertram a kick up the behind, except by that stage I didn't know who was under control and who wasn't. The invaders seem to be telepathic. At least, they were always one step ahead of us. On various occasions I realized that they knew information that only I could have told them. So I set up strict mental barriers. I didn't let myself recognize you, didn't let them know that I intended to get us all out of UNIT's influence as quickly as possible. And I arranged for our computers to download everything useful to a private data account that I've established in London.'

'You're the computer hacker that the Captain mentioned?'

'Indeed. I visited UNIT Central in Geneva, of course, and found them all just as dazed as the chaps at home. I realized that we were on our own: myself, Pike and, as it turns out, Benton here.'

'Benton . . .' The Doctor frowned. 'Why Benton?'

'Well, Doc, I was never too much into the new training stuff. Made excuses, did other duties when I could. But as for why else, I don't know.'

'Hmm . . .' The Doctor wiped his brow. 'I shall have to think. In the meantime, Brigadier, do you remember a UNIT lieutenant called Macbeth?'

'What, Hamlet Macbeth? Ah, yes. Left in sixty-eight. Managed to muck up the Paranormal Division. Compiled a rather stinging dossier on you – '

'Which was what you left UNIT Central with when you downloaded my file?'

'Ahem. Needed to know where to find you. Sorry and all that.'

'You're excused. What's he doing now?'

'No idea.' The two old colleagues began to talk about

102

the past, the Doctor complaining of his imprisonment in a UNIT safe-house on his last visit to Earth.

'History repeats itself,' the Brigadier began.

Benny frowned, squinting at the horizon along the barrel of her gun. All of this alien take-over stuff was sounding horribly familiar. She tried to concentrate on the buffeting sound of the wind, hummocking across the plain in the sunshine. She could feel the sweat on her back. The grains of dust that swam across her eyes seemed to be little people, icons and flying saucers, like in a computer game. Every now and then, words would buzz over her brain. In and out of earshot. News at ten, and from me. You shall have a fishy. Get yer trousers on, you're nicked.

'I'm worried about my other friend,' the Doctor was saying. 'About Ace. She vanished in your training room.'

'It happens,' Benton nodded. 'We've lost a few. Initially, it got put down to accidents. Soon nobody was mentioning it. Then they started to come back.'

The Brigadier sighed, straightening up as he walked. 'It must seem to you, Doctor, that we've taken far too little care of things.'

'Not at all. You did what you could, Alistair. You're up against some powerful enemies.'

'In the plural? What exactly are we fighting, Doctor?'

'I have some ideas. But you know me. I like to keep my aces hidden.'

'Yeah,' grinned Pike. 'I guess the enemy feels the same way!'

Benny blinked. There was something –

She snapped into a firing stance. Pike spun off to her right, yelling as something hit him. Benton jumped forwards to shield the Brigadier.

Something hissed through the air, and threw Benny's gun arm upwards. A sickening blackness thundered into her head, and she fell.

The black-clad commandos ran over the hill, yelling. Ten of them. Benton raised his rifle and carefully took aim at the leader.

The Brigadier pushed the gun aside. 'No, Benton,' he murmured. 'No point in killing just one of them.'

The Doctor raised his hands and smiled as the commandos surrounded them. 'Grace under pressure, Brigadier?'

'Best time for it, Doctor.'

'Don't know much about history . . .' the Monk sung tunelessly, bustling out onto the patio with a tray of drinks.

Ace was leaning back on the cool stone, sunbathing. It was a stately home, a vast lawn extending as far as a distant gatehouse. Lakes and forests shimmered in the heat haze. She took a glass of iced coffee gratefully.

'Beautiful, isn't it?' grinned Mortimus, sitting down beside her. He was still in his habit. His haircut made more sense like that, Ace thought. 'In this reality, we're the only people in the world. Doesn't make a blind bit of difference to the ecosystem. Oh no, my child, in lots of ways, this planet would be a lot better off without humanity.'

'Is that why you do what you do, then?'

'No, no! I quite enjoy the way humans bicker, you know, I do like a chat. And their conflicts! Goodness, nobody else fights quite the way they do, as various members of my race have observed. That's the trouble, you see. I like to meddle, to play around with possibilities. But I also like to be paid. My career with the Capitol managed to balance those two interests rather neatly. Now I'm a freelancer, and so my aesthetics have been somewhat compromised.'

Ace squinted at the sun through her mirrorshades. 'So. Like I said, you lied. You're actually helping these alien invaders, not fighting them.'

'Well, yes, in a way. At the moment. You could say that. I mean, one can hardly keep track!' The Monk glanced at Ace worriedly, fingering the sleeve of his robe. He probably kept a weapon there. 'You're sure that you don't, ah, object?'

'Maybe I would have, once. You want to tell me about it?'

'Oh, there isn't a lot to tell. I've got the power to create pocket universes, to fiddle about with things in whole new dimensions of my own. It's such a wonderful toy! Take this place, for example. The White Room uses this power to create its training simulations. As you've seen, it can connect to any other reality that my ... my new abilities ... have created. And I can also change the real universe, on a very limited scale. Grand, simple gestures are quite easy, but trivia is so difficult to organize. All this has led to a rather lucrative financial deal with my current employers, who want to, well, use Earth for a while.'

'Invade it, you mean?'

'Well, I suppose you could call it an invasion. I prefer to see it as active immigration. Besides, they'll be dislodged by the Dalek invasion of Earth in a few decades. They don't, ah, know that, though. They're a little slow about certain things.'

Ace flexed her arm in an aerobic exercise. 'Why shouldn't I just go and tell the Doctor about all this?'

'Because we have an understanding,' the Monk smiled. 'Besides, my dear, I really wouldn't try to do that. you'd find that you wouldn't be able to say the words.' His face clouded. 'Or make the gestures.'

Ace put a hand to her face. 'Sorry ...' she muttered. 'What were we talking about?'

'Everything and nothing!' Mortimus stood up, pulling her to her feet. 'You're very important to me, Ace. I've been alone for too long. All that time on that desolate ice planet. All that muttering away to myself. You could come and explore the universe with me, be my companion. We could put some things right, perhaps have some adventures. I wouldn't betray you, or abuse your confidence. We'd be equals.'

They walked around the big old house, Ace kicking stones. Her face was set in a grim unwillingness to show anything. 'I've done that. I've had that. Is that all you can offer me?'

'All? Dear me, no!' Mortimus clapped his hands together. 'Have you ever thought, my child, how easy it would be for me to create a world where . . . let us choose a random example . . . where one Jan Rydd was still alive?'

Ace stopped and put a hand to her chest. For a moment she turned away. When she turned back again, she had an outrageous grin on her face, baring her teeth up to the gums. 'Nah . . .' she whispered. 'Nah. Be just a dream, wouldn't it? Like the Land Of Fiction. You don't get me like that.'

'Well then – ' Mortimus took her by the shoulders. 'Consider how easy it would be to change the course of history in your universe. I could have Jan plucked from the deck of that shuttle . . .'

'How do you know about that? Did you see it?'

'Are you sure that you remember him transforming into a Hoothi creature? Are you sure that you didn't turn away at the last moment? Say you're uncertain. I can bring him back to you. In the real world, here and now. Or wherever you wish. Ace . . . Ace! One life, one big important life like his, it's no trouble either way. If you want him back, I can give him to you.'

Ace took a great swallow of air. 'What do I have to do?'

The meddling monk grinned. 'I have a list.'

'Brigadier Lethbridge-Stewart, serial number – '

'Not now!' The guard in the back of the jeep tapped the Brigadier's shoulder with the butt of his sub-machine-gun.

'Up to you, old chap, it's all you're getting.'

The Doctor had been watching their journey across the plain, his hands bound behind his back. The jeep had followed military tracks and tank trails, hopped off onto older cart paths on occasion and sometimes had just driven across the grassy stretches. Judging from the changing position of the sun, they seemed to be following a very confusing route. The unconscious bodies of Benny and Pike lay in the back of the vehicle. Another jeep, which had a handheld missile-launcher stowed aboard, had sped off in another direction once all the balaclava-clad terrorists had hopped in. They'd taken Benton with them. As the jeep carrying the Doctor had made its way across the plain, the Time Lord hadn't seen another person, much less the military presence that he'd expected.

'I really think you should blindfold this man.' The Brigadier looked up at his captors. 'He's a civilian.'

The guard simply shook his head.

'I'd prefer to see . . .' the Doctor murmured.

'I don't think so, Doctor,' the old soldier whispered. 'If they let you see everything, it means they're going to kill you.'

'Ah, well, that's been tried before. How are Benny and Pike?'

'They used some sort of anaesthetic darts.' The Brigadier glanced over his shoulder. 'We've used similar things on occasion. I dare say they'll be all right.'

'Why did you stop Benton firing?'

'Oh, I suppose that's the old Right Occupation rule for you. One's way of life must not be harmful to others.'

'Is that reasonable for a soldier?'

'Of course, Doctor. The samurai were Zen warriors. A warrior knows it's a mistake to take life needlessly.'

'Yes . . .' The Doctor seemed surprised. 'That's good. And it's good to see you so well.'

'Ah,' harumphed the Brigadier. 'Well, as I said, it was you who first got me interested in the Eightfold Path. Although, I must say, I'd have thought that with all your good karma you'd have given up on the reincarnations and achieved nirvana by now.'

'Well you know how it is. I've turned down enlightenment before now. I never have the time.'

'That's because you're a Bodhisattva, Doctor. You're postponing your own peace in order to save as many others as possible. You take them into you and make them part of you.'

'Do you really believe that?' The Doctor looked out across the plain, his hair ruffling in the summer breeze.

'Yes, in a very English sort of way. You remember Harry Sullivan? He went off to do good works with the UN. I visited him in Eritrea, got things moving with the food convoys down there. He's picked up a certain quality from you, an unwillingness to give in. And as for Miss Smith – '

'Oh, she was like that when I met her. They often are. Like Ace. Only she's learnt all the wrong things from me. She's a soldier now, you see.'

'Then I think,' the Brigadier raised an eyebrow, 'that you'll find she bears up. Whatever you may think of it, Doctor, the military lifestyle does give one certain qualities.'

They were approaching a farmhouse. The Doctor smiled gently. 'I never doubted that.'

Ace was walking along a sunlit forest path, brooding. The way back to the White Room, to the real world, had started off as a dark tunnel. But gradually it had gathered trees and foliage and the smell of gentle oak on an English summer's day. The path had become soft dust, and Ace scuffed it as she marched, breathing in great gulps of balmy air. The sun was spilling through the gaps in the trees, sparkling off her shades and lighting up the path with reflections that danced and jumped like fairies.

Still she marched, not listening to the distant cooing of doves, and ignoring the clatter of a fox somewhere breaking through a thicket. She only wanted to get back to UNIT HQ, and then to do what she had to do.

She came to a branch off the main path. The branch was lined with small stones, and gave the impression of being brushed and cared for. In a tree beside it sat two owls, looking down on her.

Ace stopped. Something about the birds struck her as comical. 'You two shouldn't be out in daytime,' she told them. 'Well nocturnal, you are, so flap off home.'

With a clatter of wings, the owls took off and flapped

off down the side path. They turned a corner and vanished amongst the trees.

Ace frowned. 'Wait a minute,' she told nobody in particular. 'I'll be back.' And she dashed off down the path.

When Benny woke, she noticed several things. One: she was tied to the Doctor. Two: they were both secured to the legs of a rather wonderful old table in a farmhouse kitchen. Three: a group of black-clothed arms bearers were standing around them. Four: the Brigadier, Pike and Benton were tied to other points around the table legs. Apart from Pike, everybody else was awake.

While she was shuffling these facts into an order of importance, she noticed something else too. The visions were still going on. They'd been temporarily banjaxed by the effects of the drug – there was a puncture wound in her arm, she noted – but they were still going on. The room was fizzing with static, weird pictures swimming in and out of her vision.

The Doctor was gently trying his bonds. They were tied expertly. It would take at least three hours to even start to fray them against the table leg. And that was only possible if their captors left them alone. He exchanged a meaningful glance with Benny.

The door opened, and in walked Michael X. Benny gulped down her nausea and called to him, trying to sound friendly and confused. 'Hey, Michael! Let us go. We're supposed to be on the same side, aren't we?'

But the Doctor's reaction was very different.

'Mike Yates!' he smiled. 'What are you doing here?'

Yates peered at the Time Lord, blinking. Then he smiled back. 'Doctor? I see, you've got another new body going. As you can see, civilian life didn't really suit me. Good to see you too, John, Brigadier.'

'You're a bloody traitor, Mike!' Benton looked away. 'I'm not saying a word to you.'

'You're not even going to tell me how it's going with Violet?' Yates moved to the window and hitched up the curtain a fraction to glance outside.

Benton shook his head. Benny caught the ghost of a smile from him.

'So Mike,' the Doctor began. 'How's the holistic centre going?'

'Doctor!' the Brigadier exploded. 'I don't want to know about Yates' grubby little civilian life! The man's a traitor! Once was bad enough Yates, you were being controlled, but this! How could you, man?'

Yates shrugged, ignoring his old commanding officer.

'Really, Brigadier!' called the Doctor. 'You're acting as though these people are the enemy.'

'We are your enemy.' Two new arrivals strode in, sten guns swinging from their shoulders. The speaker was a young woman in a black beret and leather jacket, her eyes concealed by sunglasses. 'If you're not sure, I am.' The accent had a hint of American to it.

Behind her, an older man in a flak jacket wandered in. 'D'you want me to check up on the stuff in the attic?' And he was from Ulster, Benny registered in between flashes of static.

'Sure,' muttered the woman, pulling a knife from her belt. 'Everything's going to plan. We'll be here for five minutes.'

The Irishman nodded and left. Yates remained beside the window, watching.

'So who are you?' asked the Doctor, as mildly as if they'd just met at a party.

'Julie Q, Black Star chair. One of several.'

'Not Julie Quinlan?' Benny frowned. She sat up against the table leg. 'Yes, we're in the right time period, aren't we? I recognize you from a book jacket. You've started writing novels by now, haven't you?'

Quinlan stared at Benny, taken aback. 'Yeah. Just to make money. Shopping and screwing books. Ripping off the bourgeoisie.'

'Don't do yourself down. I really enjoyed the one about the tennis players.'

'Look, don't think this'll save your life –'

'Absolutely not. I just like meeting my favourite authors

110

in odd circumstances. I read it on the beach. That lead character of yours, Marcus . . . what a charming rogue he was.'

'I don't do sympathy these days, kid. Marcus was unbelievable.'

'I'll say.'

'I'd prefer to be remembered for my serious work, like my music journalism.'

'I've read a collection of that, too.'

'I don't believe this. Mike, can you – ?'

Benny ignored the fuzzing in her head and made herself continue to smile at Quinlan. 'It was quite brave, to isolate yourself from the rest of the staff on your magazine. Barbed wire around the desk, all that. I liked that piece you did on the . . . what were they called? The thin ones from New York?'

'I suppose you mean the Ramones. What are you trying to do?'

'Just expressing appreciation,' Benny tensed as a new wave of giddiness washed over her. 'I'm quite a fan of yours.'

'Right,' Quinlan stooped down and stuck her knife under Benny's chin. 'So I get to slice up a fan, I've always wanted to do that. That would, let me tell you, give me a real kick. Here's how it goes. If your pals don't give us the complete details of UNIT's surveillance flights over the South Downs, I'll torture you. Right here.'

'What's the alternative?' Benny asked. 'Being tortured in the lounge?'

The knife moved to Benny's mouth. 'Brigadier Lethbridge-Stewart, if you don't give me what I want, I'll take her face apart. You'll hear the screams.'

'Believe me, Miss Quinlan,' the Brigadier called, his tone even. 'I always hear the screams.'

Benny looked up at Quinlan, trying to make eye contact. 'You don't want to do this, do you? You're forcing yourself.'

'Yeah. Right. You think that'll stop me? You gonna tell me what I want to hear, Brigadier?'

The soldier shook his head. 'There's no point in asking, you'll get no reply.'

Quinlan pressed the knife across the corner of Benny's mouth. A drop of blood appeared. She tried to keep eye contact with Quinlan, but the room was being obliterated by a growing howl of electronic fuzz. The cut had somehow accelerated what was happening in her head. Her mouth tasted full of blood and iron, and felt about a mile wide. Soon everything would be white. 'I'm going to die,' she whispered. Nobody heard her. Quinlan had stood up, glaring at the Brigadier. The Ulsterman had returned, and gave her a quick nod.

'Stop it!' the Doctor was shouting. 'We're not your enemies!'

Yates spoke up. 'You've got to admit it, Doc, UNIT have done some things that are below the belt. Like taking a shot at the Queen.'

'What are you talking about, Yates?' the Brigadier asked.

Quinlan laughed. 'That so-called assassination attempt. Beautiful PR. Nothing to do with us. Typical of your manipulation of the media, trying to whip up public feeling against the movement.'

'Do you seriously expect me to believe that somebody in UNIT is . . .?' The Brigadier's voice trailed off. 'Sorry. Force of habit.'

'Correct, Brigadier.' The Doctor was struggling against his bonds, frantically trying to sit upright. 'An agent provocateur. And I'll bet that there are internal ructions within Black Star, aren't there? I'll bet that some of you are objecting to the degree of violence, the public atrocities. Am I right?' He stared at Quinlan wildly. 'Am I right?!'

'Why should I tell you anything?' Quinlan spun the blade in the air and caught it again. 'You're the problem. We're the solution. So you're not gonna talk, huh?'

'I'm not going to tell you anything about meaningless things like the UNIT patrols. They won't find anything.

They're not trying to. There's a world to save. Let me out of these bonds!' The last was a sudden bellow.

'Ah, don't get so excited.' The Ulsterman took a quick glance behind the prisoners' backs, adjusting the binding. 'Ropes are fine.'

'Two minutes left,' Quinlan glanced down at Bernice's slumped form. 'She's no fun any more. Somebody talks, or I shoot one of you before we leave. You, for instance.' She kicked Benton.

'Madam!' shouted the Brigadier. 'You will either respect the Geneva Convention, or you will respect my rank and kindly shoot me instead!'

Ace had come to a clearing in the woods. In it was a handsome cottage, its white brickwork shining in the filtered light of the afternoon sun. The door was standing open.

She approached it cautiously, noticing that the owls had taken up residence on the chimney pot. There was a smell of roses and afternoon cookery wafting from the door. A long time ago, the smell would have taken Ace back to the Sunday mornings when she cooked with her mother. The Yorkshire pud and the gravy. Now it just made her smile, not knowing the reason.

Inside the cottage, it took Ace a moment to get accustomed to the darkness. The interior was cool, and the gentle creaks of old wood sounded every now and then. The kitchen was empty.

There was a sound upstairs.

Ace crept up the stairs, feeling very young. Good, somehow. Hadn't felt it in years. Like it was summertime inside her again.

She pushed back the bedroom door.

On a four-poster bed lay the woman from Ace's visions. Dark-haired, in a long red velvet dress. Golden chains hung from her ankles and wrists, connected to the bed's woodwork. She was asleep, her hair spread out on silken pillows.

113

Ace somehow knew what she was supposed to do. She bent forward and kissed the woman gently.

The woman's eyes opened. 'You're here!' she whispered weakly. 'Break the chains!'

Ace's weapons systems informed her that they registered no chains, no house and no woman. She tugged at the golden shackles hopelessly. 'I can't,' she muttered. 'What can I use to break them?'

'You must find a way before we meet again.' The woman's gaze settled on Ace, and her blazing eyes peered straight through her. 'Whatever the Monk may tell you, whatever else he has promised you, if you free me I shall grant you whatever you most wish. Now you must go back to your own world. Leave me. I am tired . . .' Her head settled back down onto the pillow, and her eyes closed once more in sleep.

Ace made her way out of the cottage. The sunlight seemed lower now, as if evening was approaching in this strange world. The owls called after her plaintively. After a while, she found the path again, and marched at double time towards the whiteness which was shining through as the trees thinned out ahead.

A few minutes ago, her choices had all seemed so simple.

'Stop this macho idiocy!' The Doctor snarled at his captors. 'You're Black Star. Anarchists. You stand for the freedom of the individual spirit. But you're doing what tyrants do everywhere. Back to the ropes, the knives and the hot irons! Back to human against human, thrashing around in the blood!'

'This is what you drove us to,' shrugged Quinlan. 'This is a game you invented.'

'Be quiet!' the Doctor snapped. 'I haven't time for your excuses.'

Quinlan pulled out an automatic from her belt and took vague aim in the Doctor's direction. 'Just as well,' she smiled.

The walkie-talkie Yates was carrying buzzed. He switched it on, gave a call sign and listened briefly. 'Sky-watch,' he told Quinlan. 'Just as we thought. We've got UNIT jeeps, six of them, coming in fast.'

'Are the charges set?'

The Ulsterman nodded. 'Soon as they break in, the whole place goes up. Over two hundred pounds of explosives in the attic. But listen, shouldn't we take this one here –' he gestured to the Brigadier, 'back for interrogation?'

'No,' Quinlan shook her head. 'Let them find his body. Okay, let's move out.' Yates and the Ulsterman made for the door.

'That's right, Yates, leave your friends to die!' shouted the Brigadier. Yates turned and scowled as he left.

Quinlan stopped at the door and flicked the aim of her automatic around the room. 'Nah,' she finally laughed. 'You can wait.' And she left. A moment later there came the roar of jeeps from outside.

Benny let out a long breath of relief and fear. 'Doctor,' she said as carefully as possible. 'What the Brigadier was saying earlier about headaches ... Listen, there were aliens in UNIT's training room. Big cloud-like things. They were ambushing and controlling the soldiers.'

'Did you go near one?'

Benny paused, biting her lip. 'Yes. I can't see, the room's gone white, there are a lot of people in my head and I feel like I'm going to die.'

The Doctor frowned. 'That's because you are. Unless I do something about it. Brigadier, get us out of here before we're all killed.' And with that he slammed his forehead to the back of Benny's head and concentrated. They both froze, in some sort of coma.

'Oh, that's flipping fantastic!' Benton shouted. 'Soon as somebody opens the door, the whole place goes up. Even if the troopers defuse the bomb, they'll be out to kill us! And now those two have joined the Captain here in cloud-cuckoo-land!'

From outside the farmhouse came the distant sound of approaching jeeps.

'Give me a moment, Benton,' murmured the Brigadier. 'I'm thinking.'

9

Intertextuality

'Now pay attention men . . .' The bulky little military man was inspecting his ragged band of troops. 'We've been instructed to fight the invader on his own terms. Now, what do you think that might mean?'

'Permission to speak sir!' shouted an old soldier. 'These aliens from foreign parts, they don't like the cold metal, sir. They don't like it up 'em!'

'Well, yes, but apart from that – '

A young boy spoke up. 'My Mum says that alien creatures have masses of legs and a huge pulsating brain and big pincers that sort of reach down and – ' He made a pincing motion.

In the corner of the hall stood Benny and the Doctor. The creases in Benny's brow smoothed themselves out.

'How do you feel?' asked the Doctor.

'Absolutely fine. Which is odd.'

'Not very. We're inside the cause of your headache. If we succeed here, then you'll be fine outside. If we don't, it'll kill you.'

'And I was getting so worried. Tell me, is this an alien mind-control sort of situation?'

'Yes.'

'Glad it's something that I'm used to, at least. I'll really miss being controlled by aliens when I leave your company.'

'When's that?' He was looking at her urgently.

'Not for a long time. Don't worry.'

'I wasn't – '

'Yes, you were. And you're worried about Ace.'

'Yes. About her. And humanity. And me.'

'Two out of three are doing okay.'

'Which two?'

'That's another question. But don't worry. I decided to stick around a little while ago. Unless that is, I start doing things like sticking my hands out in a strangling motion and muttering "kill the Doctor". Then you can just get Captain Pike to shoot me.'

'All right.'

'Joke.'

The Doctor had opened the back door of the hall to leave. He turned back for a second. 'I know.'

Tim was busy dusting his silver-foil collage of the alien leader when Graeme burst into the room, carrying a mysterious parcel under his arm.

'Isn't he wonderful?' Tim breathed.

'Wonderful?' Graeme quickly hid his package behind a chair. 'You don't know what he looks like! Under that lot he could be a . . . well, a roast chicken!'

'I don't care! The aliens are bringing values that we need to this planet. Values like discipline, leadership . . .'

'Terrible fashion sense. No, no, Timbo, we've been living under the alien yoke too long. That's why I've developed . . . this!'

'A cardboard box?'

'No, it's what's inside the box. Meet Eric!' Graeme reached into the box and plopped a small brown creature down onto the table. 'A devastating new breed of hedgehog I've developed.'

'What does it do, run over lorries?'

'Watch!'

Tim gasped as a stream of spines embedded themselves in the dartboard. 'That's incredible!'

'No it isn't,' Graeme mused, inspecting the board. 'He didn't end on a double.' Another spine thudded home. 'That's better. No, I've been demonstrating Eric in front of the whole cabinet. I set him loose on a flock of sheep!'

'But they're simple, woolly-minded creatures with no will of their own!'

'True, but I think they were impressed with what he did to the sheep.'

The door crashed open and Bill entered, dressed in combat fatigues. 'Where are they? Lemme at 'em!'

'Bill, you seem troubled,' mused Tim.

'Troubled? I'll give those alien monsters trouble! I'll give them – '

'Have you gone and done something silly?' asked Graeme.

'I have not!' Bill threw himself into a chair and put his feet up on the television. 'I've joined Black Star. Best decision of my life, mate. Oh, you may well mock – '

'We're mocking, we're mocking,' the others chorused.

'But I've been training at a secret camp on Salisbury Plain. Now, I could do with a comfy night in, let's see what's on the box.' He picked up a remote control and looked at it. Suddenly he threw it down. 'That's the trouble with these new inventions! They're designed to give us, the proles, something fun to play with while the aliens take over!'

'Now, just a minute – ' Tim wagged his finger.

'And CDs? CDs are just what we've already heard, sold back to us in a more expensive way! It's like these privatizations that Maggie's on about, selling back to us everything we've already got! God help us if she gets in power! No mate, this whole country's just going into a spiral of buy buy buy – '

Graeme and Tim looked at each other. 'Bye bye,' they told Bill and left. Bill settled down and cracked open a can of beer.

'Blinking companies,' he muttered. 'Nobody cares about anybody any more unless they can sell them something, and the police are ready to back that up with a truncheon or two. And now these punks come along, just kids trying to have a bit of fun. That'll be illegal soon. No mate, I want to be anarchy. I want to be me. Let 'em stop me.'

119

There was a knock at the door. Bill wandered over and opened it.

There was a policeman with a gun.

'That's just typical, that is!' he shouted. 'That's just – '

The policeman blew him across the room. The bullets blasted his body into fragments, splattering the walls with blood.

In Surbiton, Margo used her handset quickly, and switched off the television with a wince. 'Why do they have to do that? I mean, Jerry, shot by a policeman! Honestly, that used to be such a jolly programme. They're all like that nowadays.'

'Yers . . .' Jerry nodded, glancing up from his *Telegraph*. 'Tell you what, I'll make us a nice cup of tea. And then we'll have a listen to that new Mantovani CD. That'll make you feel better.'

'Oh yes.' Margo hopped up from the sofa and followed Jerry into the kitchen.

The Doctor and Benny peered up from behind the sofa, where they'd been hiding and watching the programme.

'So, where are we exactly?' asked Benny.

'The Mediasphere.' The Doctor looked about him cautiously. 'Time Lord intelligence thinks that it's a development of the technology used in manipulating the Land Of Fiction.'

'You once told me that "military intelligence" was a contradiction in terms, like "internal market" or "sports personality of the year".'

'Yes. But the Capitol often gets it right. They've got their fingers in more pies than Mr Kipling. They still employ agents, covertly, to interfere.'

'Of which you're one?'

'Occasionally. Unwillingly. Unwittingly.'

'So explain.' Benny wiped a finger of dust off of the top of the television. 'This is a place of fiction, right?'

'Right. A sort of easy-access Land Of Fiction. Wherever there are intelligent beings, a community of fiction evolves in their collective unconsciousness. Usually it's completely

120

inaccessible except by shamen, mystics and other careful adventurers. But one species has evolved to take advantage of these gatherings of myth and story. They developed the Mediasphere.'

'As in created it?'

'As in moved in and built houses. They live here, at least part of the time.'

'Hey!' Benny smiled. 'I just realized, and this gives me a rather nostalgic feeling. You know who we're fighting!'

'Oh yes. I've worked it out. An old enemy.'

'Going to tell me?'

'Not yet.'

'More nostalgia.'

'We're psychically present in the collapsing and reforming energy wave that the invaders are using to manipulate the media of planet Earth. This is what they use to take people over.'

'There was somebody who wrote a lot about this kind of stuff in the late-twentieth century. She said that watching television was really bad for you. She must have been one of these anarchists. What was her name? Mary – '

'Exactly the opposite. Interesting how alien invasions muddle local politics though, isn't it?'

'I'll write a thesis. Go on then, how come I've got myself plugged into all this?'

'You made contact with one of the aliens. It started to process you. A few doses of that, and all that you think is censored by them.'

'So this is in my head?'

'Not entirely. We're inside the collective unconscious of Britain, circa nineteen seventy-six. It's a particular image of what the world is like. And it's being abused.'

'I've always wanted to be a zeitgeist. Wait a minute, do missile sights count as media?'

'Possibly. You saw the helicopter targeted?'

'Right. Bizarre point of view, too. All diffuse.'

'Yes. That makes sense. When you're plugged into the Mediasphere, you start to access the viewpoints of other users, such as the alien who shot us down.'

121

Benny paused, waiting for a fuller explanation. When none was forthcoming she sighed. 'So, where do we go from here?'

'We take soundings. We see what it's like. We see if we can detach you from the Mediasphere discreetly.'

'What, no horrific encounters?'

'It's possible. This is the seventies. "Love Thy Neighbour" is in here somewhere.'

They walked through a door into a darkly lit control room. A group of serious young people in flares were gathered around a pulsating globe. One of them was gesturing violently at the others.

'No, John, no! You don't understand! It's rock and roll, man, smash the system, smash everything!'

'I don't think that would be a very good idea, Mike,' replied John, the most serious of them all.

'Indeed,' boomed a voice from the globe. 'There are forces out there, Mike, that could destroy us if they tried. Military forces. We have chosen to remain on this planet, and so we must live by the rules of their civilization.'

'And what if we don't like the rules? What if we want to make our own rules? I've had it with you lot! I just want to play with my band, and make a million pounds!'

The others sighed as he stormed out.

'Let's follow him,' the Doctor suggested. 'He might be going to make a million pounds.'

'Not in those trousers.'

Mike slouched down the street, his thumbs stuck into the pockets of his jeans, his hair lapping at his collar. He swung into a barbers, and came out a second later with a spiky crop of gelled anger and the whiff of Hi Karate. He swung into a boutique, and came out a second later with a ripped vest, a leather jacket and tight trousers. He scooped a bottle of milk from a doorstep and swung it aloft in the rising sunshine, laughing as he swigged from it.

'Now . . .' he muttered. 'I gotta find some mates.'

'Are we going to watch all of this?' Benny frowned.

'This isn't the eighties. He means friends.'

'Oh.'

Mike skipped round a corner and gathered a gang of similarly clad kids about him. They poured off the doorsteps, swinging in to join him, one on each arm, forming a chain across the street. In the chain swung Rastas and rockabillies, lesbians and looters. Some of them had stars on their brows and cheeks, some of them had the furrowed, angled faces of the new wave. Their knees knocked in their thin pants and the sun dappled off their belt buckles. They marched with a jaunty crunch of boots.

But at the other end of the road, a larger group was forming. Alf Garnett and his men were pulling lead piping from the pockets of their long cardigans. A single black man was nodding wisely, wagging a finger sadly at the approaching rebels. He had white sideburns and no weapon.

'Get 'em!' Alf shouted, and the men sprinted forward.

The gang stopped in amazement.

'Coo, it was never like this with Roxy Music!' Mike exclaimed. A saxophone blared a long squeal, a catchy tune sprang up, and the kids turned and ran from side to side across the street, their feet staying together in funny little speedy steps. They dodged between housewives in headscarves. One of them was knocked off her feet, and retaliated with a swat of her handbag. 'You are awful,' she shouted after the running punks. 'But I like you!'

'Is this getting us anywhere?' Benny asked.

The Doctor was turning slowly, his finger hovering like he was trying to home in on something. 'I'm trying to find the centre of all this. The radiant point. Ah.' He set off like a bloodhound. 'This way.'

They walked for a while down the suburban streets, past uniformed coppers who strode past with a jaunty whistle, husbands in knotted handkerchief hats who were washing their cars, and kids who cycled up and down on their Raleigh Choppers. They wore bright T-shirts, flared denims and collar-length hair.

'I'm worried about the Brigadier . . .' The Doctor began.

'Well yes, he is about to be blown up by two hundred pounds of explosives.'

'Oh, he'll get out of that. No, I'm worried that I've met him at all. You see, when I next see him, he'll act like he's never met me in this body before. And he certainly hadn't met Ace.'

Benny moved her finger and lips, working it out. 'When you next see him . . . I see. I also see why you don't think he's going to get killed.'

'No, time doesn't work like that. She's ferociously neat, she – '

'She?'

'Time.'

'Are you two going out, or what?'

The Doctor frowned. 'Once. But now she's seeing somebody else. As I was saying, she's ferociously neat. If the Brigadier gets killed by that bomb, I'll just have all my further adventures with somebody else standing in for him. Things will change as little as possible. I just know he'll get out because he's good at that sort of thing.'

'I'm so relieved.'

'But nevertheless, between now and our next meeting, something awful is going to happen to him, something that triggers his breakdown.'

'Perhaps he gets shielded from the bomb blast by my poor body.'

'No.' The Doctor folded his hands behind his back. 'The bomb's in the roof.'

Benny stopped for a moment. 'It's all right for you,' she called. 'You can regenerate!'

A little further on they came to a street corner, where a funny little man in a gaudy costume was sitting on top of a pillar-box.

He was gesturing to an invisible audience. 'The prologue . . .' he began.

'Excuse me – ' the Doctor tapped him on the shoulder.

124

'You're excused. Don't bother me while I'm narrating. Go on, hop it.'

'I was wondering if you could tell us the way to the centre?'

'The centre? Well, what sort of centre do you require? The civic centre, the garden centre – ' he glanced at Bernice. 'The bedroom centre?'

'Just the centre,' Benny told him. 'The centre of everything.'

'Ooh, well, it's been a long time since I've been there. And it's an arduous journey, yes, very arduous, all uphill. Why, just the other day, an old man came up to me, very old, carrying a great burden on his back, he was. He asked me about the centre, and about how he could get it up.' He turned back to his audience. 'Don't.'

'Could you show us the way there?' asked the Doctor.

'Oh, all right!' The man hopped down from the pillar-box and opened it. 'Get in.'

'Into the pillar-box?' the Doctor asked.

'You're surprised?' muttered Benny.

'Yes, into the pillar-box,' the man explained patiently. 'I'm Professor X, and this is my TASID.'

'TASID?' The Doctor hopped inside.

'Yes, I bought it off of a bloke called Sid.' Professor X waited until Benny had stepped inside the post-box, and then followed. He turned back to his audience before he closed the door. 'Amateurs.'

The interior of the TASID was a brightly lit control room, full of computer banks and big levers.

Benny giggled. 'It's like a pantomime version of the TARDIS!'

'Titter ye not!' The Professor pulled down a central lever. The sound of an ignition trying to start came from the central console. Finally, the TASID groaned into life. 'Yes, I've never been quite comfortable with my position as a fictional character . . .' the Professor opined.

'You know?' The Doctor grinned. 'How interesting!'

'Know? Well, of course I know. What kind of fool do

you think I am? No, don't answer that. I was never happy with my slot, you see. Caught between Basil Brush and Bruce Forsyth.'

'It could be worse,' the Doctor told him.

'Ah, here we are! Brace yourselves!' With a crash and puff of smoke, the craft stopped. 'The centre's just over there.' He pulled another lever to open the doors. 'And don't tell them I helped you. Ooh, they're touchy.'

'Thank you.' The Doctor doffed his hat and Benny blew the Professor a kiss as they left his vehicle.

'Weren't they nice?' The grinning man addressed his audience. 'Such nice people. Now, where was I? Ah yes. The prologue . . .'

Benny and the Doctor stepped from the post-box on to another stretch of suburban street. But the view here was quite different. In front of them, three terraces of houses curled and twisted upwards into a skyward vortex. At the centre was a white point. Benny blinked at it. The sound of birdsong and the distant tranny tones of the Rubettes continued as normal in their part of the street. With a clank and a grind, the TASID faded from sight.

'That's what we're looking for.' The Doctor pointed up at the centre of the vortex.

'You surprise me.'

They wandered along the street as it curled upwards. Benny gazed down at the landscape that was unfolding beneath them. Union Jacks fluttered on tiny church spires, and the distant songs of choirs rang out across miles of rolling countryside. Black horses gambled across the fields. There were grimy mill areas, and round them swept clock-like shadows of moving darkness, lights going out under the sweep of them. Suburbs clustered underneath the span of the streets they were now walking, men with bowlers and briefcases marching along, past little tie-dye enclaves of hippie self-sufficiency enthusiasts and their rabbits.

'Jerusalem, as Blake would have it,' Benny sighed. 'Pretty, isn't it?'

'Pretty Vacant, as Johnny would have it . . .' murmured

126

the Doctor as a milk-float buzzed by beside them. It looped the loop over their heads a second later, heading for the blazing white light at the centre of the vortex.

'What happens when it hits the light?'

'Watch.' The electric vehicle entered the light and vanished. 'It's only an image. There has to be a milk-float in the Mediasphere, so that one's reappeared in another location. This is all just a dream. The aliens who live here aren't corporeal.'

'Isn't this their natural environment, then?'

'No. They do have a homeworld. But when they're there, they resume their humanoid form. They're scared, terrified, as most military races are. They won't risk combat while they're in their physical form.'

'I think I saw some of that homeworld when I had my close encounter.'

'Yes. That makes sense.'

The Time Lord and his companion stepped into the light that blazed at the end of the street. Everything blanked out around them as the light got brighter. Their shadows vanished, and the void shone empty white.

'Very like the Land Of Fiction,' Benny opined. 'White with a hint of white.'

'The aliens may have dealt with higher powers to gain this technology. The Eternals meddle. Time and Death especially. Or perhaps this is down to the Gods Of Ragnarok.'

Ahead of them appeared three silvery blazes of light. Benny flinched. 'Here we go again. Do we try and avoid them?'

'No, I like to meet who I'm fighting.' The Doctor stepped forward, doffing his hat. 'Hello. I'm the Doctor, and this is my friend Bernice.'

The three creatures hissed forward menacingly. 'Oh yes, Doctor . . .' crackled their leader in a voice like electricity. 'We know who you are!'

'Then you must remember. Remember what happened to you last time.'

'We remember,' blazed the shape. 'We remember how

127

your people time-looped our homeworld, shut us in a chronic hysteresis! This, Doctor, is the time of our revenge! For do not the greater powers of the universe tremble in fear and cry out in terror at the very name of the Vardans?!'

10

Cliffhanger Deconstruction Season – Ah!

The Brigadier struggled against his bonds. 'Can't get out of the house,' he muttered. 'They'll have wired every entrance.'

Pike had woken up and was struggling too. 'We'll have a few seconds after they open the door. They'll want the troopers to come inside.' Suddenly he was free. 'Hey, that was easy, wasn't it? Let's try for second base.' He flicked out his knife and cut away Lethbridge-Stewart's bonds.

'Free the others,' the Brigadier told him. 'I'll try the attic.'

He sprinted out of the lounge, thinking about UNIT procedure for surrounding a target. They'd take a few minutes to position men at every exit. Then three troopers would run to the front entrance. Then they'd all die.

He quickly found an overhead trapdoor, out in the hallway. A step-ladder was propped against the wall. Convenient. He clattered it upright and climbed up to roof height, placing a palm against the trapdoor. Opened upwards. Better. He pushed up very slightly and flicked his penlight beam into the crack. Plastic thread. Penlight in mouth, he pulled out his Swiss Army Knife and cranked the sharpened blade. It must be a pressure trap. They couldn't rely on the upper edge of the trapdoor snapping the thread, so it was pulling it that would kill you.

At least, that was the sixty-forty option.

He gently placed the blade against the thread. It snapped. No explosion. He threw back the trapdoor, and clambered up into the attic.

The bomb sat like a spider in the middle of the wooden

joists. It was a cone-shaped slab of white plastic explosive, pointing downwards. Electrical detonators implanted in the plastique were connected to wires that ran off in all directions. Individual circuits. There wasn't even a central box. Where did these people get their ordnance from?

In a moment of nausea, the Brigadier realized that it was impossible. Each detonator would take about a minute to safely remove. And knowing this lot, there was probably a motion detector somewhere amongst them.

'What would you do, Doctor?' the old soldier asked the ceiling. 'Yes, I know. Something damn stupid.' He glanced at the circuitry, and reached out a gloved hand.

Captain Healing stood on a low hill, overlooking the farmhouse. Below him, UNIT troopers had taken up position in cover at various strategic points. He plucked a walkietalkie from the jeep beside him. 'Trap Two to all traps. Move in, repeat, move in.'

The Brigadier ran back into the lounge, narrowly avoiding Pike and Benton struggling with the rigid bodies of Benny and the Doctor. 'There's a cellar door along the corridor,' he called. 'Get them down there.'

Benton and Pike dragged the bodies after them. The Brigadier plucked Pike's automatic from his belt as he went by, and flicked off the safety catch, pulling out his own revolver for his right hand. He ran to the front door and checked that it was bolted, before returning to where the two soldiers had kicked open the cellar door and were hauling the bodies down a flight of steps.

There came a shout from outside. 'Here they come,' whispered the Brigadier, taking position on the corner. Pike and Benton had vanished into the depths. He was afraid. After all these years. Every time. He checked his watch.

The door burst open. 'One hippopotamus!' shouted the Brigadier, opening up with the automatic. Two UNIT troopers flew back, blood splattering the hallway. The third fell into a firing position and raked the end of the

130

corridor with a burst from his FN, splinters of stone spattering up around the Brigadier. 'Two hippopotamus!' The Brigadier turned to find, as expected, a soldier taking aim through a lounge window. He squeezed off two shots from the revolver and the man fell. 'Three hippopotamus!' He turned back to the hall and emptied the automatic into the prone trooper and another who'd burst in, yelling.

He spun back around the corner and sprinted, hoping they hadn't got another man to that window yet. He'd just swung onto the cellar steps when there was a clash of glass and shells whipped up the wallpaper behind him. He slammed the cellar door behind him and dropped the wooden brace into place across it.

Pike and Benton were huddled in a corner under a mass of old sacking, sheltering the bodies of the Doctor and Benny under their own. 'Four hippopotamus!' the Brigadier yelled, diving in to join them.

The wooden cellar door erupted in a hail of machine-gun splinters. The noise was deafening. The Brigadier grabbed Pike and Benton by the shoulders.

'Five hippopotamus! Six hippopotamus! Seven hippopotamus!' they shouted at each other.

The door gave way. The Brigadier closed his eyes and put his fingers in his ears.

And then the world went white.

The explosion blew out the walls of the farmhouse, sending the bodies of UNIT troopers flying like dolls. Heat and shrapnel flashed across the jeeps. Captain Healing grabbed his shoulder as something white hot cut to the bone.

He ground his teeth, concentrated, and evaporated into a blur of electricity.

'The Vardans?' Benny frowned. 'I think you'll find that your enemies tremble with mirth and cry out things like "Oh good, it's only the Vardans, thank goodness it wasn't somebody serious like the Daleks". You are, after all, the only race in history to be outwitted by the intellectual

131

might of the Sontarans.' She glanced back to the Doctor, who had a look of amazement on his face. 'Well,' she shrugged. 'It's true.'

The Vardan leader bellowed with electrical rage. 'I will strike you down, Doctor! That an undisciplined traitor such as you once defeated us!'

'Keen on discipline, aren't you?' the Doctor mused. 'Very serious. Very kinky. Who are you working with this time? Who rescued you from the time loop? Don't tell me you're managing on your own?'

'You expect us to answer your questions? Do not doubt our new power, Time Lord! Why have you found no clue to our plans? Why have you found no quick escapes or easy answers? It matters not that you know of our presence on Earth. We are nearly ready, ready to triumph! And then nobody shall dare mock the might of Vardan military supremacy!'

'Dare?!' the Doctor roared, stepping up to the blazing cloud. 'Do you think I need help from my future self? Do you think the Ka Faraq Gatri needs help from anybody to destroy parasites like you?'

The Vardan commander paused, buzzing with internal information. 'Yes,' it concluded. 'Do not bluff us, Doctor. This time, we know how helpless you are.'

'It's past tea-time.' The Prime Minister looked up from her desk at her two visitors. 'And I'm tired. There was an all-night sitting last night. The miners again. Please tell me this is urgent.'

Robert Bertram stepped forward, nervously fiddling with his tie. 'It's quite a delicate matter, Prime Minister. You see, it's about UNIT. We've reason to believe that the organization's been . . . compromised.'

'In what way?'

Carpenter turned his gaze on her. 'I don't feel comfortable with this, Prime Minister, but I feel it's my duty to speak up. A core group of UNIT officers has been plotting with foreign forces.'

'What do you mean by foreign?' The Prime Minister

got up from her desk and closed the door to her Private Secretary's office.

'Foreign as in Foreign Hazard.'

'Evidence?' The Prime Minister settled herself back in her seat, prepared for the worst.

'This afternoon, we lost a helicopter over Salisbury Plain. On board were Brigadier Lethbridge-Stewart, a UNIT captain and two prisoners, one of whom was, ah . . . foreign.'

'You had an extraterrestrial in custody and you didn't inform my office? Major Carpenter – '

'I did not inform you because my commanding officer instructed me not to do so. Brigadier Lethbridge-Stewart has always been more concerned with the international scene than with what he called . . . local politics.' Carpenter adopted a supercilious smile. 'I protested, of course. But that apart, in the helicopter crash we lost two men. One of them was shot by the Brigadier's own revolver.'

'He could have lost his weapon to the enemy.'

'There was no sign of enemy activity in the area of the crash. The helicopter was brought down by a surface-to-air missile of the kind used by Black Star on previous occasions, but we have no reason to believe that they intervened at the crash site.'

The Prime Minister shook her head. 'No. I don't believe it.'

'Ma'am, I realize that the Brigadier was a great friend of your predecessor, however – '

'Excuse me.' Bertram was pulling something from his briefcase. 'I think this will settle the matter. As UNIT's new Scientific Advisor, I gained security clearance Above Top Secret, and thus access to a great many restricted files.' He placed a tiny television and video set on the Prime Minister's desk, and slotted in a miniature disc. 'We have references to an extraterrestrial involved with the Brigadier from as far back as the sixties. It's possible that UNIT Geneva know of it, but the British government were never informed.'

The Prime Minister used the controls to review microfiche copies of files. 'This is incredible. Do you think this has anything to do with Black Star?'

Carpenter inclined his head. 'It's possible. We don't know where the terrorists are getting their ordnance. An off-planet source can't be ruled out.'

'I don't – '

Bertram leaned closer. 'Insurrection and terror are recognized opening tactics for alien invasions. The Autons, for example, or the Yeti. And, Prime Minister, I think you'll find that this is the most damning evidence we have for you . . .' He flicked another button.

The Prime Minister blinked. 'RSM John Benton. Security clearance card necessary to free the extraterrestrial prisoner and to enter government offices along Horse Guards Parade. Expert shot. On leave on the afternoon of Sunday the twentieth.'

'He was the other prisoner that the Brigadier seems to have . . . rescued.'

The Prime Minister sighed. 'I think you have a case, Mr Bertram.'

'Are you declaring a Foreign Hazard Emergency?' asked Carpenter.

'Yes.' She opened a drawer in her desk and pulled out a document. 'Damn it.'

'Good.' Bertram rubbed his hands together. 'If I may, I think I have a few suggestions.'

The Doctor raised a finger to the Vardans as they moved in for the kill. 'Benny's having trouble with the conditioning.' He took a step backwards, thinking ferociously. 'Why?'

'Because I'm not from this era,' Bernice muttered quickly. 'I know all the characters, but my brain's not really part of these fictions.'

A great ozone tension was building up around them now. The hairs on the back of Benny's neck started to prickle. There was a Vardan cloudform on every side, and the crackling was rising in pitch.

The Doctor smiled and took her hand. 'Ah well. Looks like it's all over. And so we face the final curtain. Askescharr, Olympus Mons, Harcalkas. Close your eyes and think of Mars.'

Benny did so. The background blurred, the white void becoming vaguely red.

'Any last words, Doctor?' crackled the Vardan leader triumphantly.

'Yes.' The Doctor looked up at the blazing alien, his eyes narrowing. 'Upload Benny. Download Ace.'

Everything vanished.

Captain Pike blinked, and then forced himself to open his eyes. He was lying in a cellar, with a woman's body underneath him. The roof had collapsed and all around was murky debris. A beam had fallen, missing his head by about a foot. Benton and the Brigadier were struggling to shift the mass of wreckage they were lying under.

Pike lifted Benny up gently and wiped her face with his handkerchief. 'Hey, did the earth move for you too?'

Benny's eyes opened. 'Hoi, leave off! Who are you?'

'Captain Pike. UNIT, ma'am. Don't you remember?'

'UNIT? Hey, is the Brigadier about? Wicked!' She sat up and put a hand to her face. Then her hair. Then her chest. 'Aw no . . . what's going on? Professor?'

The Doctor groaned and sat up. He grinned. 'Upload Ace. Download Benny.'

Benny blinked. 'Oh no . . . for a minute there . . . I was . . . I didn't . . . Doctor, where was I?'

'In the TARDIS telepathic circuits. Ace used her own memories to reconstruct the ship. The ship kept a copy. I just ordered it to switch that with your memory for a moment. That, and the instability caused by your knowledge of Martian literature, cut off the link to the Mediasphere completely.'

'Thanks, I think.'

The Doctor stood up, helping Pike and Benny to their feet. 'Well done, Brigadier! Creative, at least. Where are we?'

135

'In the cellar.' The Brigadier and Benton had succeeded in freeing themselves. 'I managed to alter the timer on every detonator on the bomb. Just a matter of turning each a couple of notches. Thank you for your help.'

'Oh, I was doing something far more important.' The Doctor peered around the gloom in interest. The remains of the doorframe lay under a collapsed wall.

'Question is, sir,' Benton muttered, 'how do we get out?'

'Oh, that's easy.' The Doctor walked over to the remains of the door, and lifted the heavy wooden beam that had blockaded it. 'Ask yourself, Brigadier, why would you want to lock a cellar from the inside?'

'Because there's another way out?' suggested Benny.

'A secret passage,' Pike grinned. 'At least, that's how it always goes in Scooby Doo.'

'And they'd have gotten away with it too.' The Doctor paced slowly across the floor, tapping it with his foot at intervals. 'If it weren't for us meddling kids. Ah.' The noise from the floor was suddenly different. 'There it is.'

'I don't understand, Doctor,' the Brigadier knelt on the flagstones, brushing off his uniform. 'Why should there be a secret passage?'

'Because it's something that Black Star were trying to hide.' The Doctor felt around the edges of a particular flagstone. 'The size of that bomb. It wasn't just designed to kill us and the UNIT soldiers. It was designed to bring the house down. Here we are.' With Benton's help, he lifted the flagstone. A ladder led downwards into a dark passage. 'After you, Brigadier.'

They trudged along the stone corridor, bending low. The Brigadier led the way, shining his penlight ahead while the others walked behind, weapons drawn. Water dripped from the ceiling. The stone was cooler than the dusty heat of the cellar, at least. Benny was just glad that her headaches had gone. Alien possession, she decided, was something she would try to actively avoid in the future. They'd been going for about five miles, she judged. The corridor wasn't old, it must have been specially built. Quite an engineering achievement.

'The Vardans,' the Doctor said suddenly.

'Who are they?' asked the Brigadier.

'The aliens who are taking over your men.'

'Oh, glad we've got that sorted out. How do they do it?'

'In one of two ways. Either they interfere with their brains, take over their senses and control their perceptions, or if they're too strong-willed, they kill them with an electrical charge and take their place. Vardans exist in two forms, a sort of electronic cloud or a humanoid one. They can tailor the appearance of the humanoid form to suit their needs.'

'So we've no way of telling who's human and who's not?'

'No.'

'Damn,' the Brigadier took a long breath. 'I had thought they were all duplicates.'

'I'm sorry – '

'Never mind that. How exactly do they take over people?'

'One way is through direct contact, but your soldiers would have reacted badly to that. Some of them would have escaped the Vardans in the training area and told tales. No, it must have started off more subtly than that. The Vardans can travel down any wave-form, even thought. They inhabit the electronic media.'

'What, you mean television?'

'Exactly. The Vardans start by influencing humans through broadcasting. They're weakened by continual exposure, and thus easy prey when direct contact happens.'

'That's why I didn't get nobbled!' Benton grinned. 'Haven't got time for the box, Doc. There's never anything good on.'

'There certainly isn't now. You were lucky. You must have been next on the list to be eliminated. The Brigadier and Captain Pike used their meditation techniques to stop

137

the Vardans from infesting their thoughts. Few of the men will have been so lucky.'

'So how did they get all this stuff together?' Pike asked.

'They were a militaristic race. Very spartan. They lived by the principles of martial meditation, survival of the very fittest. Eventually they transcended their physical bodies, possibly with aid from one of the greater powers of the universe. They tried to invade my homeworld, Gallifrey, once. They'd done a deal with the Sontarans. That alliance didn't last long. The Vardans tend to make deals with other races . . .'

'Possibly because they're still regarded as a bit of a joke,' Benny added.

'Yes, but Earth doesn't have Gallifrey's electronic defences. Your average Gallifreyan could have easily prevented a Vardan from taking her over. Humans aren't so hardy. And the Vardans are showing such subtlety! They knew that I'd be prepared to stop them, so they interfered with the timestream, played me at my own game. Or rather their latest ally did . . .'

'Doctor.' The Brigadier had realized that the Time Lord had started musing to himself. He pointed to a light up ahead. 'I think we've arrived.'

Captain Pike cautiously raised the trapdoor and peered out. He'd lifted up a rug in front of a fireplace. The surroundings were those of a small cottage. Facing him was a man in an armchair, sitting with an automatic pointed at him and a glass of Guinness at his elbow. It was the Ulsterman.

'Now . . .' he smiled, 'I suppose you're wondering why I called you here today?'

'Yeah.' Pike climbed out of the trapdoor. 'Got any real beer?'

'Red Barrel?'

Pike shrugged. 'Hell, that'll do. I'm not about to go out for a six-pack.' Behind him, the Brigadier emerged from the trapdoor, levelling his pistol at the Irishman.

'Don't fret, Brigadier,' the man told him. 'I wouldn't

have freed you if I was going to kill you, now would I?' He put down his automatic. 'I just didn't want you lot to leap in and shoot me.'

The Doctor hopped up into the room. 'We haven't been introduced,' he said. 'I'm the Doctor. These are my friends.'

'The Doctor!' The man laughed and stood up, extending his hand. 'The name's Kevin Doyle. If everything I've heard about you is true, you certainly deserve a pint!'

'Well,' said the Doctor brightly, his hands clasped in front of him. 'Why don't we all compare notes?' They were sitting in a circle of comfy chairs. The UNIT men were sitting straight and tense, watching Doyle. He, however, had done nothing more sinister than brew a pot of coffee.

'Perhaps it's down to me to begin.' The Black Star man rubbed a hand through his slick black hair. 'I am an anarchist, like they say, but I'm worried. I can't expect you lot to make a lot of the differences between Black Star philosophy as practised and the origins of our movement. But differences there are. I think we've got imposters and double-agents up our arse. Now, I had thought it was you lot, until very recently. I got into a little altercation with a mate who didn't seem to know what was what any more. Ended up blowing his brains out across a hayrick. I've seen human bits often enough, lads, and that's not what they look like.'

'So that's why you loosened our bonds?' the Brigadier asked.

'You're right. Old Julie used to be a fine tactician, a real inspiration, but she's getting more and more desperate now. I think she knows we've been had, only she won't admit it to herself. When you said – ' he gestured to the Doctor, 'that we weren't enemies, I found myself in agreement. I could hardly tell Julie that; she'd have shot my goolies off.'

'And why should we believe this change of heart?' The Brigadier raised an eyebrow. 'I know what the informer situation is like where you come from, Doyle, and – '

'Oh, please! My family's Unionist, and I couldn't give a toss. I was an artist before all this mess started.'

'That,' murmured the Doctor, 'is the important bit. When did Black Star stop being artists and start being terrorists?'

'It was last winter. The winter of '75, I mean. Me and Julie were living in the same squat. I was painting, she had a regular column in a music paper, tons of review copies. We made a kind of living off of the record and tape exchange. She was over in New York all the time, going down CBGB's, talking to Richard Hell and all that. And often I went along too, took the other free ticket that her ex used to get. Quite a buzz, getting on a plane without a penny in your pocket and cadging drinks off of Patti Smith.'

'Were you two together?' asked Benny.

'None of your business,' frowned Doyle. 'I was just having a good time in London, hanging out south of the river, checking out the galleries. I hung around with Jamie Reid and that lot. One weekend, after me and Julie had just got back from two weeks in the States, Jamie introduced me to this kid actor who was in some children's TV show. Gary, his name was. Now he was young and beautiful, he wore a leather jacket. He was sixteen playing fourteen. He wanted to show me his programme, of course. So one afternoon I popped a few and went over to his place when his mum was out. Christ, she'd have been worried by the company he was keeping. He switched on the television, and I watched. I'd been away, I was loaded, and I saw it. Behind the children's TV show, there were messages, control things. There were creatures in there, telling me to perform acts of violence. I switched it off. Gary was upset, he hadn't seen anything strange about it at all. For a long time I thought it was just nerves, you know, getting strung out. Then people began writing about this stuff in the underground press. There was talk of mind control all over the place. I talked to other people who had seen it, and their experience was the same as mine.'

'And you thought that this was, like, a trick of the establishment?' Pike asked.

'Sure. We figured that they'd finally found a way to control people directly. A few of us dropped out, wrote a manifesto, created Black Star. There was an awful lot of ordnance left over from the Angry Brigade, whole dumps. And you know, once you've taken up a position like that, there are always people willing to train and arm you.'

'I dare say,' mumbled the Brigadier. 'But it's still not enough, is it? Your people have intelligence systems and supplies that would put a standing army to shame. What's this Skywatch, for instance?'

'Satellite surveillance system. It's how we avoid military activity on the Plain.'

'My God . . . How did you manage that?'

'I don't know. Julie always knew more than I did.'

'Interesting.' The Doctor was playing cat's-cradle games with his fingers. 'These double-agents, as you call them . . .'

'I'd prefer to call them frigging aliens, if it's all the same to you.'

'Vardans,' added the Brigadier knowledgeably. 'They can look like human beings, you know.'

'Thank you, Brigadier. Do you think they've been active in making Black Star attacks more violent?'

'Indeed,' Doyle took a sip of his Guinness. 'All these riots, with our lot in there whipping it up. That doesn't make sense. It's supposed to be public targets, not private housing. All property's theft, but that's not the way to win public support, is it?'

'Indeed not,' the Brigadier cut in. 'Granted, civil rights aren't what they could be, but isn't it better to work inside the system, to write to one's MP?'

Doyle smiled sadly. 'There is no way to protest peacefully. I still believe that. You can't upset the status quo from within. Money guarantees that. But we thought we were going to be making grand gestures, rewriting hoardings, blowing things up. And even that . . . the charge of explosives in Big Ben was much larger than it should have been, civilians could have been injured in the blast. I

141

never saw myself becoming part of what is now, I'd say, a disciplined and ruthless army. An inhuman one.'

'You seem to take all this talk of aliens in your stride,' the Doctor murmured.

'Well, that's partly down to you, Doctor,' Doyle grinned. 'You're quite a hero to our lot.'

'What?' The Brigadier frowned. 'How?'

'Through the underground press. Fanzines, whole books. We like to keep alive the stories of alien invasions that you lot try to hush up. And your man here's always on the side of the rebels. He's the purest sort of anarchist.'

'Indeed?' The Brigadier looked at the Doctor with a sort of proprietorial fondness. 'Well, Mr Doyle, it's my opinion that the Doctor symbolizes the best values of British life. Eccentricity, the creative amateur, and civilization. Now, I may have had my horizons broadened recently, but I still believe in civilization. I'm quite looking forward to my little acre when I retire.'

'You'll retire at the expense of everybody your society treads on, from Africa to the beggars in your own cities,' snapped Doyle. 'You're – '

'Hush.' The Doctor stood up, and every eye turned to him. 'Here's the plan. One, nobody watches television or listens to the radio.'

'I never do,' Doyle frowned.

'I guessed. Two, we have to get to the members of Black Star that haven't been controlled or replaced. Convince them. Work with them.'

'Ah, well, that's what I thought,' Doyle grinned. 'That's why I stayed here. We're five miles or so from the farmhouse. We wanted to destroy it 'cos otherwise you lot'd find the tunnel. Now, nobody's going to be expecting us to be assembling as close to our last base as that. Besides, I've had a message that they'll have moved on from the wreckage by midnight.'

'How – ?!' The Brigadier was exasperated. 'How do your people know so much about what we're doing?'

'Search me. We're fortunate enough to have access to

a lot of buildings down here. Most of them seem to be just standing empty.'

'Very fortunate . . .' the Doctor murmured darkly.

'There's a major operation going down at dawn tomorrow. I got permission to put together a special ops team for it. I chose all the good lads. And of course Julie'll be with them. They'll be here for you to convince at four a.m.'

'Four o'clock in the morning?' groaned Bernice, looking out of the window at the setting sun. A distant plume of smoke and the moving lights of helicopters marked the remains of the farmhouse. 'Please tell me that this place has got a bath.'

11

Finally Facing My Waterloo

Ace found Danny down on the sands by the river, watching the lighted boats go by. The night was warm and the air tasted sweet.

He was wearing his sunglasses, hugging a timber. He looked up when Ace hopped down the ladder from the jetty above. 'Hey. How'd you find me?'

'One of the barmen at the Prospect told me you came down here. I can see why. I like it.'

'Yeah,' Danny turned back to look at the black water. 'So what're you doing?'

'Not much. Saving the world.'

'Seen Benny?'

Ace ignored the offhand plaintiveness in his voice. 'From a distance.'

'I got told to go home by that weird old bloke. So I did.'

'After he got your autograph?'

'You saw that? He asked for it. All I had was some Priory Records paper. He was so eager that I thought he'd ask me to sign his forehead.'

'That's just the Doctor. You don't have to do what he says.' Ace sat down on some old bricks beside Danny.

'You know, this is where they used to execute pirates. They'd bury them in the sand up to their necks and wait for high tide. It was a really great spectator sport. Brutal, eh?'

'I've seen worse.' Ace made the decision. 'I haven't got long, Danny, and I wanted to see you.'

'What, you dying or something?'

'Maybe. Just soldier stuff. Dunno who I can trust, except you.'

'How can you trust somebody who only knows three chords?'

'Maybe 'cos of that. And 'cos we had the same dream.'

'What, the woman in the cornfield? I don't think we did, I don't think any of that psychic stuff is true, that's all Mike Oldfield.'

'You said that you'd offended the Goddess. That sounds really down to earth, right?'

'Well,' Danny shrugged his bitterly thin shoulders. 'I can't help what I say in dreams. Dreams are where we're free, they would have us believe.'

'You remind me of somebody.'

'You and Benny both. Must have been a kid, that one.'

'We were lovers.'

'Yeah? Well, that's nostalgia for you, innit?'

'What did you do to offend this Goddess of yours, anyway?'

'Well . . .' Danny took a deep breath. 'If you're gonna go away anyway, you might as well go thinking badly of me.'

'I won't think badly of you.'

'You will. There was this girl, mate of a mate. Met her at a club. This is when I was still looking for something to be, in my rocker gear. I was really young.'

'When?'

'Last year. We got pissed, 'cos I drank then, and she told me that she'd been raped. Long time back. Didn't know the guy. Before that, I'd kind of been thinking that maybe, well, yeah, but that stopped me from thinking that. We went back to her place, and spent a few hours talking about stuff and listening to Lou Reed. I was well out of it, but I knew what was going on, I wasn't totally gone. For some reason, I took her hand, and kissed it, and tried what I thought was gonna be the ideal bloody seduction number on somebody who'd been raped. I told her that she had every choice, that everything was up to her. And she just froze. She went out, told me she wanted to go to the loo, fetched a couple of her flatmates, who came in and sat with us. I felt like a worm. I left, and thought about it a bit, and then went back and knocked on her door again, wanting to explain, wanting to get back to that great evening of talking and stuff. There was also this element of realizing what I'd done, what it'd sound like to other people. I wanted to establish my own version of the truth. She called the coppers. Don't blame her. I got taken to the nick, and would have been up on something, 'cept she didn't want to press charges. The bloke who'd introduced us saw her a few days later, and she said that she'd just felt unable to tell me to piss off, that she'd felt that rabbit in the middle of the road feeling that you get, I suppose, when you've been through that. I wrote her a letter, trying to say that I really liked her, and that I didn't go back to her place thinking about sex. Shouldn't even have written the letter. Well, after that, I couldn't go to the same clubs, couldn't hang out with the same mates.'

'Couldn't?'

'She didn't want to see me. I didn't want to limit what she could do. Everything changed. So that's what I've done. My expertise lies in the field of human betrayal.'

Ace put her hand on his shoulder. 'I – '

He shrugged it off. 'I didn't ask. Feel sorry for her. You feel sorry for me, it means you don't understand how bad she felt. I'm the villain, okay? Me.'

'If you want to be the villain, that's all right.'

'Good.'

'But we all want to be the hero, right? You know we all want to be the one who saves the day?'

'Yeah. I know just where I am.'

'Do you often dream about it?'

'Yeah. Often.'

'And is that woman in the dreams?'

'The one with the hair and the eyes? No. I dunno what Freud would have said, do you? Dirty old man. You and me, we had the same dream . . . I still can't believe that.'

'I met her. She's trapped. Just like you are.'

146

'Yeah? That's probably my fault too. I probably tied her down.' Danny sighed, throwing a chunk of brick into the river. 'So where are you going, then?'

'Where the traitors live,' Ace told him. 'Where it's dark.'

'Give them my love. I had this other really weird dream the other night, and it seemed really real, like I'd woken up.'

'What was that?'

'Well, I woke up beside Benny, and – '

'What?'

'We were sleeping in the same bed, that's all. No squishy noises. No panting.'

'Doesn't bother me.'

'I'd had a few for the first time in years, 'cos I felt safe, right? There was no – '

'Tell me about the dream.'

'Yeah. Right. I woke up in the middle of the night, and my jacket was hanging on the back of the door, except it was really bulging. Something was inside it. I walked over, had a good long look. In my breast pocket, there was this object. It kept changing, in my hands. It was a little wooden door, and then a bike exhaust, then a stone from some kind of wall.'

'Yeah? What did you have in your pocket in real life?'

'Just a folded up piece of paper, must have been the one that I signed for the Doctor later on. From that desk . . . hey, Ace, I must have been really out of it. I remember a desk disappearing.'

Ace folded her hands into a spire. 'The changing thing . . . was a piece of paper from a desk that disappeared?'

'Yeah, Bertram's desk.'

'Bertram's desk. And the Doctor's got it now?'

'Yeah. What would Freud have said?'

Ace laughed. 'He'd have said . . . "wicked".'

The Doctor stepped silently through the darkened cottage kitchen, staring at the fractals breaking on the surface of his cocoa. The Brigadier and Benny had taken the two upstairs rooms. The Doctor had told Benny that he'd come up eventually. Probably not true.

Pike was sleeping beside the fridge, the door open. A crack of orange light shone across his face. The Doctor reached out and gently closed the fridge door.

Pike sprang up, cranking his automatic out from under his pillow. He stared at the Doctor for a second, and then waved his hand in apology. 'Hey, I need my night-light.'

'Sorry. I thought it was a mistake.'

Pike lay down, and opened the fridge again. 'No. It's a habit. I like being near electrical devices, okay?'

The Doctor heard Benton snoring in the lounge, where Doyle also slept. 'It must have taken those two a while to get to sleep.'

'Yeah, they don't trust each other at all.'

'Do you trust Doyle?'

'Yes, I do. He's putting his ass on the line for us. Mind you, if things go wrong tomorrow. I'm gonna put him between me and them.'

The Doctor nodded and wished Pike goodnight. He went to the door of the cottage, and plucked his safari jacket from its hook. Then he went out into the night.

Ace and Danny had been throwing stones into the water for an hour. The boats went by on the river, and there was music and singing from some of them. Ace was trying to find something good to tell Danny, but couldn't think of anything. He'd done something wrong, he was paying for it. The military bit of her, the Ace that had seen men flogged for looting, said that the only question was how many lashes. Still, something had been changed by this meeting. She now had a vague line. Something to hang on to.

She looked up, warned of something. It took her a second to realize what. On the far bank, in a muddle of building works and warehouses, a fire had bloomed. Suddenly a shattering explosion broke the night's silence. Red fire blasted into the air.

'Petrol drums,' she told Danny.

148

The boy clambered to his feet, putting a hand to his brow to peer across the water. 'Something's going on on that boat, as well.'

In the middle of the river, a pleasure cruiser was slowly turning round, the music blaring from its dance floor mixing with the sound of screams. The propeller was kicking up spray as the rudder swung the boat randomly. Then it stopped turning and headed straight for Ace and Danny's quay.

'Let's go,' muttered Danny.

'No, we can do something,' Ace told him. 'They're gonna need help.'

Within a minute, the cruiser impacted against the jetty. The crash set off alarms in the empty cabin of the boat. It jammed itself between the jetty's wooden supports, propellers still spinning.

Ace climbed up onto the woodwork, and hopped onto the roof of the pleasure cruiser. From below there were screams and shouts.

In front of her, a man in a tuxedo burst out of a hatch. He carried a heavy meat knife. Ace flinched towards her flechette reflex, but stopped herself. 'Now wait a minute,' she told the man. 'Think about this.'

Danny was standing on the dock, his sunglasses reflecting explosions that were detonating all along the far bank. The traffic along the river had started to spin in the same giddy way as the cruiser, tugs and launches randomly going haywire.

And then he felt it himself.

With a yell, he leapt over the railing and landed beside Ace. He launched himself at the man with the cleaver. The man swung at him, but Danny somehow dodged and grabbed his arm. With a heave, he had the weapon, and the man had fallen flat to the roof.

'Hey!' Ace grinned. 'I was doing okay – '

Danny raised the cleaver over the man's head, and glared down at his victim's ecstatic grin.

'Danny! No!' Ace caught his shoulder.

A roar escaped the boy's teeth, and he swung the weight

of the cleaver, round and round in a giddy dance, like it
was a hammer he was about to throw. Ace staggered
aside. With a squeal of pain, he swung it down. The blade
sliced into the toe of his boot.

Danny shouted and fell. Ace ran to him, and helped
the shivering and sweating boy to stand.

'Couldn't do it!' Danny spat. From streets away came
the sound of ambulances.

'Good . . . that's good.'

'Thank God for guilt, eh?' Danny laughed. 'Guilt and
steel-toed Doc Martens!'

Ace hugged him in relief. Behind them, the man who'd
held the weapon was getting to his feet, staring in horror
at his blood-stained sleeves.

Danny turned to gaze at the scene of devastation on
the south bank. He didn't hear, over the hooting of boats
and the cry of sirens, a strange and ancient sound of
grinding power. 'What's going on, Ace? What's happening
here?'

When he turned back to her, she was gone.

Across the plain, the sky was bright with the sweep of the
Milky Way. The Doctor stared up as he wandered away
from the lights of the cottage. It was Keats, wasn't it,
who'd been caught in a storm wandering across these
flatlands? One of those young lads with big shirts, anyway.
Too long a sacrifice can make a stone of the heart, he'd
said. He'd repeated it over and over so that the Doctor
could compliment him on his greatness. Still, he must have
known that it was true.

The Doctor smiled grimly up at all the stars he knew.
There was the distant sun of Iceworld, and there was
Skaro's home star, still twinkling now in the seventies,
back before he snuffed it out. He'd killed a star. The
Doctor shook his head. How far had he come to even
contemplate that? The young man in the Underground
had died holding his hand. Out of an eruption of hate,
the sort of hate that humans did so well.

The Doctor had once played at Find The Lady with the

150

young David Bowie, his white-trousered legs crossed in the back of a punt that Romana was stoically poling. They'd been discussing transcendence, and Bowie had flipped card after card down apparently without thought.

'You need three players for this game,' Bowie had grinned. 'I know what you've got, you know what I've got.'

'Oh yes . . .' the Doctor had boomed offhandedly. 'But it's fun finding out, isn't it?'

'Not for me.' The fringed young man had flickered a final card into the bottom of the boat, its vinyl reflecting the sunshine. 'I had the Queen of Spades.'

The Doctor closed his eyes at the thought of the man with the razor, cutting face flesh in the carriage. The Death Card, the Ace or Queen? And wasn't he the Hanged Man, dangling by his umbrella from some precipice?

'I've been such a fool,' he whispered. 'To lose her.'

The light from the cottage increased for a moment. The Brigadier was standing on the step, his hands tucked into the pockets of a dressing gown. 'Bit late isn't it, Doctor?'

'Perhaps too late.'

The lights arrived outside the cottage at four on the dot. Benny, Doyle, Benton and Pike had woken to their various alarms half an hour earlier. The Doctor and the Brigadier didn't appear to have gone to bed.

Benny pulled the curtain aside. Three jeeps were speeding up the track, their lights low. Behind them, the first blue of dawn was gleaming under the stars.

She stifled a yawn and tucked an automatic into the waist of her jeans. 'What's the plan?'

Doyle glanced around, uneasily. 'I'll meet them in the kitchen. Try and talk to Julie. You lot stay in here. If you hear shots, you'll know what to do.'

'Panic,' Benny muttered. She joined Pike behind a pair of armchairs. 'How are you this morning?'

'Sleepy. Didn't get my third cup of coffee.'

'Poor baby.'

Benton propped himself up against the sofa, FN at the

151

ready. 'Don't you think you ought to get under cover, sir?'

'No, Benton.' The Brigadier glanced up at the Doctor, who was engrossed in an examination of the china on the mantelpiece. 'I think we'll be safe enough here.'

There was a knock on the kitchen door. Doyle left, nodding over his shoulder to the UNIT men. He closed the lounge door after him.

The Brigadier instantly took up a position by that door, pulling his revolver from its holster. He listened closely. The Doctor looked up and turned to face the door, standing in the centre of the room.

There was a minute of whispered conversation from the kitchen. Then a shout.

The door burst open. Quinlan dived in, brandishing a sub-machine-gun. Behind her came twenty troopers, Mike Yates amongst them. One grabbed for the Brigadier, smashing his gun hand against the wall. Pike leapt into a firing stance, but Quinlan shoved her gun into the Doctor's stomach. 'Move and he's dead.'

Yates snapped up his automatic and shoved it into her neck. 'Ditto.'

Quinlan turned and smacked Yates across the face, sending him flying. 'Yeah, like I didn't expect that? You think I'd trust you with live ammunition?' She turned her gun on him.

'Lilac Time!' shouted the Brigadier.

Half the troopers spun, covering Quinlan and the others with a clank of safety-catches.

Silence. The Doctor turned slowly, examining the situation. Everybody waited. 'Well,' he said finally. 'Who's tea and who's coffee?'

Doyle neatly stacked a pile of sugar-lumps on a tray. Benny was rummaging around the cottage's store cupboards for cups.

In the lounge, terrorists, UNIT troopers and UNIT troopers pretending to be terrorists sat in a circle around a pile of weapons.

Benny brought the first tea-tray in. 'I see you're being disarming,' she murmured as she handed the Doctor a mug. 'Oops.' She glanced down at her waist, handed the tray carefully to Pike and threw her own gun into the pile.

'Violet is a code-word for an agent working undercover,' the Brigadier explained, glancing at the remaining members of Black Star uneasily. 'Lilac is an instruction to break that cover. Since Captain Yates here had already done so, I thought the time was right for the remainder of Broadsword to do the same.'

Claire Tennant had pulled the balaclava from her head. 'We've spent months establishing ourselves within Black Star. When the balloon went up, it was just a question of going undercover again. Sorry, and all that . . .' The last was with an unsorry grin.

'I can't believe it!' Quinlan erupted bitterly. 'So you're the bastards who've been undermining us for the last few – '

'No!' Doyle squatted beside her. 'They're not. That's just the point. Listen to them!'

Quinlan turned her head away. 'You're a traitor.'

Yates had been sitting in intense concentration, staring at his hands in a manner that struck Benny as almost guilt-ridden. 'I think you should all listen to me,' he muttered. He looked up at Quinlan. 'Julie. I didn't mean to frighten you just now . . .'

'And you're the worst. You spoke so well about the cause. Will you just stop pretending?'

'I have,' Yates cast an agonized glance at the Brigadier. 'I've stopped pretending that I could kill somebody in cold blood. I've stopped pretending that I'm a double-agent. I obeyed the order the Brigadier gave me, to leave them at the farmhouse. Even though it went against everything I wanted to do. I don't want to be put in situations like that any more. When this is all over, sir, I don't wish to return to UNIT or renew my status. I believe in what these people are trying to achieve. When I was recruited there was a lot of talk about pacifism, about destroying

153

preconceptions rather than lives. Maybe we can get back to that.'

'Pacifist terrorism?' the Brigadier snorted. 'Really Yates, I said deep cover, but I didn't expect you to go native.'

Yates sat upright in his chair and sighed. 'Well, sir, I suppose that's why you chose me for this job, wasn't it? I already had a credible background as a UNIT deserter. I feel like I've become somebody who deserts. I feel like I've got a lot to desert from. Perhaps Black Star is where I've been going all my life.'

Quinlan shook her head violently. 'I can't listen to this, Michael. If you're so into what we're doing, why did you betray us?'

'Because you're being used. Just like UNIT are being used. The aliens are exploiting both of you, just like the powers that be exploit class and race differences. Divide and conquer. Julie, do you remember what happened to Puckey and Douglas? The patrol went out with them, they came back without them. They've been slowly knocking off everybody you trusted, right in front of you. When you started this, you wanted an end to sides, nations . . . causes. But you were just as vulnerable to all that stuff as anybody else. The cause took control, and it became the limit of your imagination. We're talking about one species attacking another, all our dreams of anarchy hijacked. When are you going to see it?'

Quinlan closed her eyes, and put a hand to her brow. She stood awkwardly. 'You've got details of all this? Facts?'

'Lots,' Yates told her. 'You can see the files.'

The Brigadier realized that the Doctor was looking at him expectantly. He stood up also. 'I don't agree with what you do, Miss Quinlan. Not in the slightest. But let me tell you this. We're both in need of help. And I don't intend to put my politics before my planet.' He offered his hand.

Quinlan shook it. 'Okay. An alliance. For now. And you can thank God for traitors.'

Benton cast a thankful glance skywards. 'Halle – bleed-in' – lujah!'

The six jeeps sped across the plain out of the approaching light of dawn, their radiators rippling the cool morning air. In the back of them sat some sort of army, a ragged gang of Broadsword and Black Star troopers, comparing notes and telling stories.

The Doctor had been brooding, his gaze drifting across the grasslands in the darkness, thinking about all the animals and plants that the Vardans would exterminate in making this world theirs. And the humans. The humans would be possessed or burnt. And they'd respond with that meaningless violence of their own, that childish thrashing of each other. There'd be treachery and pain enough then.

As the darkness grew warmer and the sky got lighter, the Doctor realized that some of the soldiers in the jeeps were singing.

'La la la la, la le la lah! La la la la, la le la lah! Le lah lah!

'Iggy Pop?' asked Benny, sitting beside him.

Julie Quinlan nodded. 'A song about how everything belongs to us. A fantasy, right now.'

The Brigadier turned from the front seat where he sat beside Benton, who was driving, and handed Quinlan a map. 'Do you want to go over the mission again?'

'Right. This is June the twenty-first, okay? The morning of the summer solstice. Black Star are planning to attack the yearly gathering of Druids at Stonehenge.'

'What?' Benny frowned. 'That's not really your job, is it, persecuting religious minorities?'

'This is before the resurgence of interest in paganism in the eighties,' the Doctor told her. 'The Druids here are a sort of elite society of the rich and famous, people who can afford to indulge in a folly at this time in the morning. Some of them are serious and sincere, but it's a media circus. Usually it's a few people in sheets and a couple of tired photographers.' He turned to Quinlan. 'Was this one of your ideas, or one of the Black Star committee's?'

'Mine. We were going to disrupt the ceremony, maybe snatch one of the VIPs for ransom. It's Doyle's people, plus two more assault groups. I can't say what they're gonna do now.'

'So it's up to us to meet them at the rendezvous, see if they've also been compromised, and if so, engage the enemy!' The Brigadier smiled confidently. 'Do these Vardans good to sustain a few losses, if they're as nervy as you say, Doctor. Oh, excuse me.' The Brigadier's walkie-talkie had buzzed. He picked it up. 'Greyhound . . . sorry, Bloodhound Leader.' He listened for a moment. 'That's very interesting, Captain.' He turned to Quinlan. 'It seems we have more in common now, Miss Quinlan. Pike's been listening in to the local radio traffic. My little gang-show here have officially become *persona non grata*. They've declared a Foreign Hazard Emergency.'

'What does that mean?'

'It means that we've ceased, as far as the Geneva Convention goes, to be people. We're the aliens, now. They can do what they like to us.'

'Yes . . .' the Doctor nodded. 'I'm starting to recognize the enemy's style. He likes turning my own conceits back on me.'

'They searched the farmhouse ruins. There are UNIT patrols out on the plain looking for us.'

Quinlan nodded. 'Skywatch'll keep us informed. If my committee haven't decided to finish me off, that is.'

'Skywatch.' The Doctor nodded. 'Yes. A satellite in geostationary orbit, relaying information to your ground forces. He's become cleverer since last I met.'

'Who is this you're talking about?' Benny asked.

'Not yet,' the Doctor told her. He turned to Quinlan. 'You've got a patron, haven't you? Somebody who's part of the establishment that you're fighting?'

Quinlan paused. 'We've got several – '

'He owns the satellite and gives you the Skywatch data. He wants you to prosper, at least for now.'

'I can't – '

'I'm right, aren't I? Your whole organization is being used. And I know who's using you.'

'He's not using us, we're using him. Sometimes it's necessary to make compromises with society in order to undermine it.'

The Doctor settled back in his seat, satisfied. 'I know him. I have to find him. Before this game gets out of control. Don't bet on anything, Brigadier. This isn't the time for taking risks.'

'Perish the thought.' The lights of a highway were shining against the darkness ahead. The Brigadier began to carefully load his revolver. 'I haven't lived this long, Doctor, by being foolish.'

'No . . .' The Doctor stared at the approaching lights, his hands jittering again. 'I hope that after all this, I can say the same.'

The Monk stepped out of the darkness, his hands clasped behind him.

Ace was running her finger down one of the stone columns of his TARDIS, wondering at the frost that had caused condensation to form there. The Monk had landed his craft on the boat, an extra funnel appearing out of nowhere. Ace had jumped down it, not wanting to have to say goodbye to Danny. This was the final clause of the deal that Mortimus had put to her, the final act. She didn't want to start asking Danny about the rights and wrongs of it.

The Monk's TARDIS was more spaciously designed than the Doctor's, with dark, high-ceilinged cloisters. It echoed with the cold. The elegant carvings and gargoyles were poised, waiting for something. The only sound was the distant drip and echo of water, melting and refreezing.

'Why do you keep this place so cold?'

'Oh, just to help me remember.' Mortimus glanced around at the architecture, a sad smile playing on his features. 'Revenge doesn't burn, Ace, like the poets say. You can lose it, if you stay somewhere comfortable and kind. This way, I still live with the cold. The cold remains part of what I am.'

Ace half-smiled, like that was a joke. 'Yeah, I remember how that feels.'

'Thank you.' The Monk reached out and touched Ace's hair, hesitantly. 'Thank you for helping me, child, in my hour of need.'

'No problem. Don't worry about it.' Ace concentrated on the pillar.

'We're nearly there, after all. Just a few more moves and this game will be over. Then we can leave, and find out who we really are, you and I. You and I and Jan. We'll all be free of our responsibilities.'

'Yeah, I could do with that,' Ace smiled. She'd heard a bitter laugh somewhere in the darkness of the catacombs, maybe the red woman again. 'So, what do I do?'

The Monk produced a length of rope from behind his back. 'As a former companion of the Doctor's, I think you'll be familiar with your part.'

12

Calling Occupants of Interplanetary Craft

The jeeps of the Brigadier's bizarre army were speeding across country. The singing had stopped now, and the combined forces of UNIT and Black Star were just grimly smiling, clapping palms or shoulders, and immersing themselves in the ritual of weapons checks.

Benny could feel the fear in the pit of her stomach again as she mechanically loaded and unloaded the automatic. She hated combat, really loathed it. And she wasn't particularly keen on the company of soldiers. She felt like she was being dragged into a slaughter, a grand loss of heads and limbs. It was like being the pacemaker at the front of the charge of the Light Brigade. She could see the soldiers coping with it, could feel the exhilaration of this plunge into violence. But she didn't understand volunteering for it.

The Doctor worried her, too. He was just sitting there, a curious blankness in his eyes, like he was just letting it all happen. He did not, Benny realized, have anything approaching a cunning plan.

'Where's the rendezvous again?' the Brigadier called, wrestling with a map as Benton made the jeep scud faster across the hummocks of the plain.

'About two miles away, here – ' Quinlan reached over and tapped the paper. 'On the rise beyond those barrows. We'll be hidden from Stonehenge itself there. Skywatch says we're clear, there's just minimal security.' She held up a portable computer, about the size of a pocket calculator. A display showed a graphic representation of the area, small boxes standing for police units.

The Doctor took the computer and checked the logo on the back. 'A Priory company.'

'New from Taiwan, they call it a Warboy. Receiver's in the unit itself. We pay for a direct uplink to the satellite.'

'Privatized satellite surveillance?' smiled the Brigadier. 'What will they think of next?'

Up ahead, three more jeeps were parked by a hummocky ridge. An ancient row of round barrows ran across the skyline. The Doctor frowned, dropping the Warboy into the back seat of the jeep.

'They're ours,' nodded Quinlan. 'Let me talk to them first, okay?'

'By all means,' the UNIT man removed his cap.

They drew up alongside the Black Star jeeps. A man turned from viewing the plain below and waved cheerily to Quinlan.

'That's Birney,' Quinlan smiled. 'He's okay, he still talks about the old times.' Beside them, Pike's jeep pulled up, driven by a Black Star commando. Doyle hopped from it and helped Quinlan out of her jeep.

'Come on then,' he told her. 'You go and tell them what's what.'

She smiled at him, and ran over to the man in the black fatigues.

The Doctor was shaking his head. 'That noise – ' he whispered. Then he shouted. 'No! Come back!'

Two Lynx helicopter gunships roared over the ridge, the barrels of Vulcan cannons spinning on mounts at their sides. Their spotlights swept over the gathering. They bore UNIT insignia.

Quinlan stepped back from the man she called Birney, her hand still extended. She gazed upwards. Then she grabbed for her gun.

Birney fired first, emptying a magazine into her chest. She spun away in an explosion of blood. The body fell to the ground, lifeless.

From behind the jeeps appeared troopers, snapping their sub-machine-guns into firing position.

'Julie!' Doyle yelled.

'She's dead!' The Doctor grabbed him and hauled him into the jeep as it screeched off in a muddy arc.

Gritting her teeth, Benny flung herself down onto the back seats and fired two bursts of two at the troopers. A man flew backwards, clutching his chest. To her right, Pike's jeep was speeding away. Their group's vehicles were separating into a great fan shape. Overhead, the helicopters swung, selecting their targets.

The Brigadier grabbed his walkie-talkie. 'Bloodhound Leader to all units. Head for that hillside to the north. Abandon your vehicles when you can!' He threw down the radio and pulled a sub-machine-gun out from under his seat. 'Anybody ever taken a gunship out with a sten gun, Benton?'

'Haven't heard of it, sir.' Benton swung the jeep into a tight series of random swerves as bursts of cannon fire ripped up the ground beside them. The gunship was roaring after them, its rotors whipping the grasslands into waves.

'First time for everything, then.' He turned and aimed. 'Ready? And brake!'

The jeep slid to a halt. The helicopter thundered overhead, and the Brigadier fired upwards as it passed, emptying a full clip into the tail rotor. A small explosion puffed up, and the chopper swung giddily round again, hanging in the air above them. Fire was blazing from its tail.

But the cannon was pointing straight at them.

Benny jumped up from the back seat and aimed along the barrel of her automatic, one hand steadying the other. She could see the pilot through the canopy, see his hand closing on the gunnery trigger on his joystick.

She shot out his canopy.

Helmet.

Head.

The helicopter lurched wildly to one side. Benton wrenched the gears and the jeep shot off backwards, sending Benny tumbling into the back seats. The gunship swung into the ground and exploded, the concussion throwing up a blossom of earth and debris.

161

'Good work!' shouted the Brigadier. 'We make a good team!'

'We are not a team!' Bernice yelled at him, gulping in huge breaths of air.

There was an explosion somewhere behind them. One of the jeeps was a flaming mess, the other helicopter rushing through a cloud of smoke that poured from the wreck.

'Stonehenge, head for Stonehenge!' Doyle called.

'Yes,' the Doctor nodded desperately. 'If we can get ourselves mixed up with the Vardan forces, the gunships won't know who to shoot at.'

Benton swung the jeep and the Brigadier picked up his walkie-talkie again. 'This is Bloodhound Leader, all units head for Stonehenge. Engage the enemy at will, over.'

Multiple call signs answered, including, Benny noted thankfully, the voice of Mike Yates. She ran a hand through her hair as the jeep bounced across the country-side. 'I'm not a soldier,' she whispered. 'I am not a soldier.'

In the distance, Stonehenge stood against the blue, throwing long shadows in the increasing light. The jeeps roared across the grasslands towards it, a great plume of smoke rising behind them.

There were figures milling around at the stones, a TV van and a couple of police cars. The Doctor pulled out the Warboy and switched it on. No indication of the heli-copters, of course. They'd been very precisely betrayed.

Doyle put his hand on the Doctor's shoulder and handed him a pair of binoculars. 'My God, Doctor, take a look at that.'

The Doctor peered through the binoculars at what lay ahead. A group of men in white robes and all-concealing hoods were standing around the central stone of the monument. And on that stone, tied down and struggling, lay a young woman.

'Ace,' the Doctor growled. A moment later, he added: 'But there's something wrong with the stones. Where did that central one come from?'

Ahead, two UNIT armoured personnel carriers were

162

rumbling towards them, trying to block their path towards the stones.

There was a sudden woosh and one of them exploded into a flaming ball of wreckage. 'Ah,' murmured the Brigadier. 'Somebody found the bazooka.' Benton swung the wheel in that direction, and they raced past the moving APC, gunfire from its side ports skittering across the jeep's rear bumper. A moment later, they were obscured by the wreck.

The remaining helicopter gunship roared high into the sky overhead, turning to gain a better view of the battle below.

The TV crew were running for the safety of their van, and uniformed policemen were dashing back towards their cars. The men in the white robes seemed not at all disturbed. One of them pulled a shining silver blade from his belt and stepped purposefully towards the central stone.

The first light of dawn sliced through the crack in the heelstone, and illuminated a line down Ace's abdomen.

The man with the knife turned his head upwards. 'Artemis!' he bellowed. 'Come!'

He raised the knife.

The Brigadier's jeep skidded through the rope that cordoned off the stones, and hit one of the megaliths sideways. The Doctor jumped out, sprinted three steps and grabbed the hand that held the dagger, forcing it back until the man dropped the weapon. 'You!' he shouted at the cowled figure. 'What insane scheme are you planning this time?!'

'You mean you don't know?' The figure laughed, taking a step backwards. 'Why, Doctor, my plans are already complete. Look!'

Climbing from the jeep, the Brigadier and company gazed up at the image that was forming above the stones. A concussion of vast black wings was fluttering against the risen sun, crossing and recrossing in impossible patterns. From it, a huge, very female mouth appeared. Suddenly the stones were swept in shadow and a frost condensed across them.

The hooded figure clapped his hands together. 'Artemis arises!'

'You fool . . .' the Doctor whispered. 'What have you done?' He dashed over to Ace, leapt up onto the altar stone and freed her from her bonds.

'Doctor . . .' she whispered, grabbing him. 'There's something I have to tell you, before it's too late . . .'

The Doctor glanced up at the multi-dimensional creature unfolding above them. 'I don't know if I can get us out of this, Ace, any of us. I don't know if I can win this time.'

'I know.' Ace pulled his head close and whispered to him.

Benny's mouth opened in shock. She snatched for her gun.

Ace thrust a dagger deep into the Doctor's chest.

He screamed. Ace laughed. The centre of the altar stone opened like a trapdoor and they both fell through it.

'All the world's a stage!' The Monk leapt up onto the stone and spread his arms wide. 'And I've got a backstage pass!'

A bullet from the Brigadier's revolver ricocheted off a forcefield around the hooded figure, as he dropped into the stone also. It flashed through a series of different shapes: phone booth, van, motorcycle. Then it vanished with a grinding roar.

The men in white robes sizzled into a circle of floating Vardans. The gunship took up position overhead once more, in the midst of the monstrous apparition that was starting to roar and scream above the stones. The little circle of jeeps that had screeched to a halt by the monument was swiftly being surrounded by the running forms of hundreds of humanoid Vardans.

The Brigadier raised an eyebrow. 'Suggestions, anybody?'

13

Vicious Circle

The Doctor landed in a heap on the frosty stone floor of
the Monk's TARDIS. He was clutching his chest, his face
contorted in agony. His hand was covered in blood. 'The
old wound,' he gasped through clenched teeth. 'Have
you . . . killed me?!'

Ace dropped down into a crouch beside him. 'Yeah,'
she nodded. 'Eventually. I chose the entry point carefully.
It'll take a while.'

'Let me regenerate now . . .' the Doctor hissed at the
gothic arches above him. 'Let me be rid of this life.'

'Not yet, Doctor.' The shadow of the Monk passed
between him and the light source high overhead. He had
pulled the cowl from his features.

Drips of condensation were falling into the Doctor's
face, and he had begun to shiver. 'I knew it was you . . .'

'It's nice to see you again. Sorry about the cold.'

'Mortimus. The time meddler. You and the Vardans.
What are you planning?'

'No, Doctor. No explanations. And no regeneration,
either. It will be a long time before you will be allowed
that mercy.'

Between them, Ace and the Monk hauled the Doctor
to his feet, causing him to shout in pain. Blood had
started to stain the front of his safari suit. They carried
him through dark corridors, their breath billowing in the
air. The Doctor got the impression of a vast cathedral
with spires, stairways and echoing chambers. He seemed
to falter between unconsciousness and waking as they
carried him.

Finally they lay him on an angled slab of marble. In front of it stood a screen. The Monk connected a few plugs and slotted a cassette into a machine.

'Torture?' asked the Doctor.

'Of a sort.' The Monk grinned. On the screen appeared a grainy image of the Doctor as he once was, a white-haired dandy. He was battling a minotaur creature, leaping away from it with graceful bounds.

'How did you – ?'

'Oh, I've been watching you for a long time, Doctor. Ever since we last met. I've taken care to piece together your career. I have visual records of all of your adventures . . . well, nearly all. There are some that I have yet to recover. I wanted to study your methods. And I discovered, to my surprise, that those methods had undergone a change. You used to rely on your survival abilities, your expertise at getting out of situations.'

'Used patterns. They'll always arrest you. Tell you the plot. Then you escape.'

'So I note. However, recently something strange has started to happen.' The picture switched to the Yorkshire coast, to the Doctor moving a single piece on a chessboard. 'You have started to break the First Law of Time. You leave notes for yourself, place advertisements that you'll know you'll see. On some occasions, you seem, and this is just a suspicion mind you, to have prior knowledge of events. You have meddled far more than I ever did, far more. And have the Time Lords imprisoned you for it? Have they tried to have you executed? No!'

'Got tired of putting me on trial.'

'Or would they only try one of their own? Some of the things you do, Doctor . . . aren't they a tiny bit beyond what a rogue Time Lord could achieve?'

'No.' The Doctor turned his anguished head towards Ace, and saw himself reflected in her mirrorshades. Her mouth was set in a hard line. 'How did you meet the Vardans?'

'In my explorations of the universe, I discovered a planet that had been time-looped. Varda, as it turned out.

They were living out a few seconds of one particular day, over and over again. I used my new resources to free them, and they were grateful. They were looking for revenge on the Time Lords, on the Sontarans, on all sorts of people. I suggested that a good first step might be to take Earth, positioned as it is at a tactical site of Sonataran interest. This idea worried them. They were aware of your, somewhat narrow I must say, interest in the planet. "Oh no," I said. "I can handle him, I can stop him in his tracks." They commissioned me to conduct a feasibility study into how best to achieve their aims. I swiftly came to the conclusion that this meant getting rid of you.' The Monk wandered across the Doctor's field of vision, running a finger along the frosted stone wall. 'At first I succumbed to the delights of my new-found power – '

'Power?' the Doctor croaked. 'Power to change the universe. Create new ones. What power? The thing over the stones? Have you set it free?'

'I shan't tell you anything of that, Doctor. I used it to kill you, in an earlier incarnation of yours. Quite crude. I should have known that doing that would only create an unstable mini-universe. But what you did to that universe . . . you have changed, haven't you?'

'Perhaps. I had to do it.'

'The end justifies the – '

'No.'

'You're starting to become what you fight. You've stared too long into the void, Doctor. Has the healer really become the warrior?'

'Some things . . . must be beaten. You . . . must be beaten.'

'Hah! This hypocrisy of yours. Anyhow, after the Silurian fiasco, I decided to delay you while I set about putting my plans in motion. I'd read about the Garvond in the Red Book of Gallifrey. I was gaining more subtle control of what I'd got my hands on, so I started playing with tiny things in your past, getting you lost in all the little dislocations of your life. That Aztec creature, for instance. Huitzilin. Beautiful thing, I thought. I felt a great sympathy with its plight; an identification, if you will. I wanted you to start seeing the universe as it is to the rest of us, a place where cruel and offhand things happen. A place of bad surprises. I've always had the urge to control it, to make it better. And I've always been punished for it. I wanted you to understand.'

'I've always –'

'Finally,' the Monk continued, 'I needed you out of the way for a bit while I removed all your future notes and escape clauses. Hence the Land of Fiction. The Master of that place views me as some kindly benefactor, someone who will occasionally watch his adolescent fantasies. Most of them involve something the humans call –' he glanced at Ace for confirmation, 'Def Leppard?'

Ace nodded grimly.

'I did, after all, remove him from this timestream and give him infinite power. He ought to be grateful. The Land is such an interesting place, I couldn't leave it to fizzle out once you'd destroyed the central structure. Now it lives again, even if the Gods of Ragnarok have no time for it any more.'

'You thought I'd be caught by any of these things?'

'Oh, I knew you'd get out from all of these traps. But in the process I've learnt so much about you. And about Ace. The Vardans, incidentally, have promised to pay me a small fortune in gold.'

'Not the money. Revenge. You're full of revenge.'

'Perhaps. I don't like to admit it, though. No, I shall allow you that hit. Your final point, Doctor. I am consumed by revenge. I am only just seeing the light at the end of the tunnel, thanks to your young protégée here.'

'What about her?' The Doctor's voice became a little more firm.

'Why, she makes me feel young. She gives me ... another perspective. Once this messy business is over, the two of us will roam the universe, interfering. Putting right the things that have gone wrong. Talking of which, we'll have Jan with us too.'

'That's impossible.'

'Because it breaks the First Law, the one you break all the time?' The Monk cast a glance at Ace. She was impassive, her hands clasped behind her back. 'No, the three of us will go out into the universe, doing good and battling evil. We'll return to that rather jolly business of mine that I pursued before you decided to . . . meddle.'

'There's a difference. Between what you and I do.'

'Really? You think so? And what might that be?'

The Doctor smiled deliriously. 'Skill.'

The Monk frowned. 'Vanity, as I think you'll find, Doctor, is a mortal sin. If I might indulge myself with a little self-analysis, I dare say that's why I chose this particular method of helping the Vardans. I've taken everything you are: your companion, your position with UNIT, your beloved human beings, and I've shown you the truth behind those romantic ideals. Ace is a person with feelings of her own, not somebody who'll blindly love you. UNIT is an organization hobbled by the feudal politics of Earth. And human beings are merely naked chimpanzees, fighting over whatever bone you throw them. Rather than skill, Doctor, I'd say that the difference between us is one of scale. You enjoy being a big fish in a very small pond. I enjoy being a citizen of the whole universe.'

'But not a gentleman. Human beings . . . are good. Underneath.'

'Oh, when they can be so easily – ' The Monk stopped. 'By Rassilon. You're still doing it, aren't you? Still hoping that I'll give away my plans? I've seen so many others do that, and I still nearly fell for it. No, I'm not telling you anything, Doctor. You may die in ignorance, as well as in total defeat.' He looked up at Ace. 'I think I've finished. Let's get this over with.'

They hauled the Doctor's body upright again, causing him to cry out. In the corner of the room stood a vertical black cylinder, about the size of a person. A pressure lock was open at the top. Two ladders led up to it. Ace picked up the Doctor's frail form and carried him to the cylinder.

The Monk watched, an agonized frown on his face, as Ace lowered the Doctor into the cylinder. A blue liquid came up to the Doctor's neck, and then up to his nose. Curls of blood tainted the liquid. He began to struggle.

'Don't worry,' the Monk said, almost gently. 'It's an oxygenated solution, constantly replenished through a microscopic dimensional link. It's perfectly breathable.' He glanced up at Ace. 'Put him under.'

Ace took a hold of the Doctor's hair, and pulled him up slightly. He stared at her, blinking and choking. 'Ace. Don't.'

She pushed his head down into the liquid and slammed shut the lid, spinning the wheels to lock it, her mouth clenched tight. There came a noise of thrashing movement within the cylinder. After a few moments it subsided.

The Monk walked up to the cylinder's frosted surface, and put his palm to it. 'I know you can hear me, Doctor. This is what I'm going to do. I'm going to take you to a planet I know, and leave you there. You'll regenerate, eventually. And then you'll try to get out of the cylinder. You'll find that you can't. You may live out all your remaining regenerations like that, starving to death time after time. Or you may find some way to kill yourself. Or, perhaps, if you're very lucky, somebody will come along and rescue you. But I'd say that's unlikely.'

There was no response from inside the cylinder.

Ace and the Monk walked to the console room along a corridor flanked with gargoyles.

'How are you feeling, my child?'

'Empty. A bit scared.'

'That's the future. It's scaring both of us. Don't you feel guilty?'

'No. Stopped feeling that a long time ago. I'm just doing to him what he did to me.'

'As I believe I said, we have much in common.' The Monk entered the control room of his TARDIS, an ornate gothic dome, and began adjusting settings on the console itself, a marble rose design that reminded Ace of some ornate tombstone. 'We're still having control problems. I really shouldn't have sent out that message to alter the

170

Doctor's chameleon circuit. I wanted to interfere in everything he did. That seems so childish suddenly. The thing is, he's reflected the beam somehow, caused minor technical faults to start breaking out.'

'Is it serious?'

'No. The defences are holding up. It'll probably clear itself once we're away from Earth.' He hit a final control, and the central stone column of the console began to rise and fall in flight.

They heaved the metal cylinder out onto the barren surface of the ice plains, billowing blasts of snow getting into their eyes and mouths. They left it in the vague shelter of a hillside.

The Monk turned back as he trudged to his TARDIS, now looking every inch a rocky outcrop. He took a last look at the prison of his old enemy. 'I didn't want it to fall over,' he muttered. 'That might somehow allow him to escape.'

Ace glanced up at him. 'Will he be cold?'

'No. No, not at all.' The Monk paused on the threshold of his TARDIS. 'Let's get some heating on in here,' he murmured. 'I've been cold for such a long time.'

They went inside. The outcrop faded away, with a screech that was lost under the noise of the gale.

The black cylinder stood on the empty ice, gaining a covering of snow.

14

Wish You Were Here

Benny ran through the monoliths. Gunfire splintered the rock beside her as she threw herself to the ground. The Brigadier hauled her up, pushed her flat against a stone, and then spun round it to fire two careful shots.

'He's dead!' she gasped. 'The bitch killed him!'

'No time for that now.' Lethbridge-Stewart glanced quickly over his shoulder. Between the stones hovered a cluster of Vardans, taking their time in a slow advance. They could afford to. From the roadside, from all over the plain, a circle of humanoid aliens were closing in on the three remaining UNIT jeeps. The vehicles had formed a defensive circle by the stones, in slight cover from the hovering helicopter gunship. That was standing off at least, waiting to pick them off if they broke away.

Benny and the Brigadier were trying to make it into the jeep circle. Benton had already dashed across the gap between it and the stones, flinging himself over the seats under covering fire from Doyle.

And above them still floated the terrifying form of a four-dimensional mouth, polished teeth slowly opening and closing. Benny stared up at it, and then blinked. It had vanished.

'One less thing to worry about at least.' The Brigadier raised an eyebrow. 'Shall we, Miss Summerfield?'

'Why not?' Benny slotted the last magazine into her automatic and glanced at the distance. Thirty metres, maybe. Junior sports day. Bye, Daddy.

Yelling, the two of them broke from cover, Benny firing wildly behind her as they sprinted across the grass.

Bullets whipped up the mud at her feet.

Benton sprang up from behind the jeeps, firing a full burst from his FN.

The automatic stopped firing.

The shout sustained.

The side of the jeep hit her thighs.

Doyle grabbed her arms and pulled.

Bullets sliced where her feet had been.

She tumbled over the back, into cover, and yelled into the ground.

The Brigadier bounced off the back of a jeep into a crouch.

'Close thing . . .' he smiled. 'What's our situation, Yates?'

'Bad, sir.' Yates gestured at the ten or so commandos around them. 'We've sustained heavy losses.'

'I'll say,' muttered Doyle.

Benny made herself sit up and pay attention, firmly pushing away Doyle's arm as it held her. 'The Doctor . . .' And then, seeing the way the Brigadier had fixed his calm smile on her, she changed what she was going to say. 'What would he do?'

'Win,' Yates muttered. 'Question is, how?'

Corporal Tennant crawled on her elbows from the other side of the jeep circle. 'We're completely surrounded, sir. There's none of these Black Star hats with us now. I think a couple of them might have got away. Do you want us to make a go of it?'

The Brigadier considered. Doyle and Benton were leaping up at random intervals, firing quickly over the blockade. 'Professor Summerfield here's a civilian . . .'

'You will not surrender on my account!' Benny shouted at him. 'Sir!'

'Bullets seem to slow the fuzzy sods down.' Doyle dropped back into their position, reloading. 'Didn't expect that.'

The Brigadier made his decision. 'Doyle, you will remain here with Miss Summerfield and be taken prisoner.'

173

'All right, Brigadier,' Doyle nodded. His face had lost some of its animation now Julie Quinlan was dead. 'Good luck to you.'

Benny looked around in growing horror. 'Please, don't do this, there has to be a way – '

The Brigadier turned away. 'Benton, start up the jeep that's pointing to the road. Broadsword: two in the back, the rest on foot, we scratch the jeep as soon as we're on the road itself, take the first car that comes. They may not want to sustain this action in public sight – '

'You won't last more than a minute!' Benny grabbed his shoulder.

Lethbridge-Stewart swung round, and his expression silenced her.

Yates raised a hand. 'Wait, sir! Something strange is happening!'

A modulated warble was growing in volume, starting to eclipse the sound of gunfire. The Brigadier peered up quickly over the jeeps. The advancing energy forms had stopped in their tracks, their blazing growing more intense with what seemed to be a massive effort to move forward. The humanoid Vardans were having trouble too, twitching and jerking. One of them exploded into a sudden sphere of energy, which froze just as quickly.

Above them, the helicopter shot off suddenly towards the south, spinning away into the distance. It hit a hillside and exploded.

Benny had heard something too. It was coming from the back of one of the jeeps, an urgent bleeping. She hopped up. In the back seat lay the Warboy device, its screen blazing with a regular pulse of light.

'Into the jeeps!' shouted the Brigadier.

'Leave the Warboy here!' called Benny, shoving it into the mud. 'I don't know how, but that's what's doing this.'

Benton had started one of the jeeps. 'Hop in, miss!'

Benny leapt in as the vehicle lurched forward. Behind her, the remains of Broadsword were jumping on board as the three jeeps sped out of formation, wheels flinging up mud. 'Anybody see Captain Pike?' asked the Brigadier.

174

'His jeep went off in another direction,' called Yates. 'I think he was having communication problems.'

They drove straight past a line of raging Vardans. Benny watched humanoids attempting to raise their weapons.

'Bastards. Tempting, eh?' Doyle trailed the muzzle of his automatic along the line of twitching bodies as they roared past.

'No,' Benny was surprised to find that she was hugging herself. 'Not at all.'

They broke out onto the road. Far behind them, a column of army vehicles was approaching the monument.

'Shall we contact them sir?' asked Benton.

'No.' The Brigadier glanced back at Bernice. 'I think from now on we're on our own.'

The Monk's TARDIS was warming up. Icicles dropped from the roof of a gothic ballroom, its walls carved in intricate scenes of revelry. They crashed into the centre of the dancefloor, splintering into shards which soon began to melt. The pool of water that was forming on the floor was slowly gravitating towards discreet vents that had opened up at the base of the walls.

Ace and Mortimus watched from a table under an overhanging balcony. They were sharing a bottle of wine, drinking out of metal goblets.

The Monk had been staring at the icicles. 'I feel strangely empty,' he told Ace. 'But happy. Oh yes, happy. Perhaps I just don't remember what those positive feelings are like. How are you feeling?'

'Glad it's all over. Tough, though, innit? Hard to do what you've gotta do sometimes.'

The Monk glanced at her, and flicked a quick look at his watch. 'You don't need to worry about anything, or fear anything. You don't need – '

'I wish you'd stop trying to control me,' Ace frowned. 'It isn't working.' She laughed at the sudden fear she saw cross the Monk's features. 'It never has, I just pretended to go along with it. I've had tons of training on how to resist mind control.'

'But then, you – '

'Like I said. I agree. I trust you. I've done all this 'cos I wanted to. Stop being so paranoid.'

Mortimus had got half out of his seat; ready, it seemed, to flee. He settled slowly back down again. 'I should have more faith, I hadn't realized . . . Now that is a wonderful thing. Forgive me, I didn't think I could actually persuade you without use of . . . I thought that eventually perhaps – I thought . . .' He trailed off, and clapped his hands together. 'Thank you. The future is going to be wonderful, I know it is!'

Ace raised her goblet. 'To the future. It's always better than what you've got now, eh?'

'It is indeed! Well, my child, we will soon have the freedom to explore new places and put things right.'

'How soon? What have you got left to do?'

'Well, there are just a few loose ends I have to tie up for the Vardans. Basically, I've just got to handle the invasion for them, then we can be on our way. Shall we bother? Or shall we just leave and see if they can manage on their own?'

Ace smiled. 'I don't think they could manage a piss-up in a brewery.'

'No!' laughed the Monk. 'No, neither do I!'

The three jeeps had been hidden in various parts of an industrial estate near Old Sarum. By eleven o'clock, Broadsword were in civilian clothes, wandering at an unhurried pace through the streets of Salisbury. They'd taken a chance by visiting the flat that Yates had rented in the city. The Brigadier had borrowed some of his clothes, and looked rather awkward in a Shetland sweater and jeans.

'So what's the plan?' Claire Tennant carefully omitted the 'sir' as the team spread out across the street, hanging around in groups that wouldn't be identified as being together.

'I think, Claire, that we should find a quiet pub and have lunch.' The Brigadier glanced at Benny once more.

She'd been silent since they'd got to the city. 'And discuss our options.'

Bernice had her hands stuck deep in her pockets, lost in thought.

The Doctor was gone.

She wanted to see Danny, but there really didn't seem like much point in doing anything. She could feel it, somewhere inside her, a lack of something that she hadn't previously noticed having. She supposed that she ought to hate Ace, and perhaps she would if she saw her again, but all she felt was error. Like she was the last thing left at the end of an enormous chain of mistakes. The sunshine and cheer in this pleasant old city's morning bustle didn't really help.

Benny had suffered loss before, of course, and she could feel the first fingers of that old devil in her mind. It'd get worse, it'd reach some sort of internal score draw, and then it'd get better. She had all that to look forward to, all the ups and downs of grief. Again. Such a long way to go. And she was tired enough already.

Doyle wandered over from a hi-fi shop across the road. 'Something you ought to see,' he muttered.

The Brigadier walked slowly over. In the window of the shop, several televisions were carrying news broadcasts. The pictures flickered between images of destruction.

'Don't look at it for too long,' advised Yates.

'I'll keep my mantra in mind, thank you.' The Brigadier gestured to Benton. 'You've had less exposure than everybody else, Benton. Come and watch a bit of telly.'

Inside the shop, a group of customers had gathered round one of the televisions, listening intently to Kenneth Kendal.

'Following the attack on Her Majesty The Queen, a number of other prominent figures have had attempts made on their lives by the Black Star organization. Some of those attempts have been successful. Junior treasury minister the Right Honourable Sir Louis Barfe was murdered outside his London residence by a gunman in a car. Entertainer and television personality Jimmy Tarbuck was badly hurt in a hit-and-run incident, and the private jet containing pop group Pink Floyd has been lost over the English Channel. The group were on their way to a pop festival in Rome. Black Star have claimed responsibility in all cases. We have reports coming up on several of those incidents . . .'

The Brigadier frowned. He could see the vague flutterings of Vardan interference on the screen. Benton was blinking, too. Lethbridge-Stewart turned away and directed the RSM towards some stereo systems on the other side of the shop.

'Black Star bastards,' somebody was muttering. 'They ought to be strung up.'

'And those punk kids with them, they're all the same. They're bringing the country down between 'em.'

'In several areas of London,' the newsreader continued, 'police are preparing for a third night of violence. Despite pleas for calm from community leaders, rioting erupted in several places over the last two nights. Home Secretary Tony Benn has expressed a desire to meet the rioters and discuss their grievances, but only if the violence ceases.'

There was widespread jeering in the shop. 'Discuss what, how much they're getting off the dole?' An old man with a stick was waving it angrily. 'Old Enoch warned us, didn't he? Rivers of blood, he said. And he was right.'

The Brigadier gritted his teeth. 'Come on, John,' he muttered. 'I think we've heard enough.'

Into the shop breezed Alex Pike, his hands tucked into the pockets of a baseball jacket. 'Hey, Alistair, Johnny! Long time no see!'

The Brigadier slapped Pike on the shoulder and led him out of the shop. 'Come away, Alex,' he told him. 'I wouldn't want you to have your illusions about Britain shattered.'

Ace turned her head. Quickly. She'd just missed something as they walked down the corridor. A flicker of something in the corner of her eye, like somebody had hopped across the space behind them.

It'd be the woman in the red dress again. 'Mortimus . . .'

'Yes, my child?' The Monk was busying with his tie, having changed into his business suit once more.

'This woman keeps appearing in my dreams. And I think that was her mouth that you were pretending to sacrifice me to. Who is she?'

'She's not a woman, for a start. She's a dangerous animal, a means to an end. If you want, I can take steps to keep her out of your mind.'

'Nah, some of it's cool. Who is she, then?'

The Monk strode into the console room, and inspected himself in a tall, gothic-framed mirror. 'It's a long story. Once I've done this little final bit of business, I'll tell you all about it.'

'All right. Where are we?' Ace glanced at the console.

'Back at the Priory Building. I have to catch a taxi to Whitehall. Details, details, but it wouldn't do to appear on their doorstep, now would it?'

'Well if that's all you're up to, I'll stick around. You got a pool?'

'Not as such. The ballroom might still suffice. Remind me to reconfigure one for you. In the meantime, there is a gym. Now, there is one thing that you must promise me.' He turned from the mirror and peered at Ace intently. 'There are some rooms in the TARDIS that contain dangerous things. We can explore them later, and nothing will be left unexplained, but for now . . .'

'Fair enough. I'll just go and have a work-out.'

'Good.' He ruffled her hair. 'I can't say how pleased . . . how happy . . . oh, it's all rubbish in the end, isn't it?' Grinning, he activated the door control. 'I'll be back soon.'

'Have a good one,' Ace called after him. She listened to his footsteps as he wandered out into the real world. Then she waited for exactly a minute.

Then she closed the door and sprinted from the console room.

Benny was writing in her diary, glancing out of the window from time to time. The train had just passed through

Didcot. Broadsword were scattered along various carriages. Opposite her sat Pike, his eyes closed, his hands forming a pyramid. As they waited at Salisbury station, he'd whispered to the Brigadier that his jeep had run into an outrider group of Vardans. The others had been killed, and he'd managed to get away in the confusion.

'Don't do that,' muttered Benny, glancing up.

'Uh, do what?'

'Put your hands in that sort of cathedral shape. The Doctor used to do that.'

'Do you want to talk about it?'

'No.'

'Okay.'

'Only I feel rather lost, and I'd prefer not to be reminded of just how lost that is, if you don't mind.'

'Was he a great friend?'

Benny bit her lip. 'Oh yes. A very great friend. And when we were ... parted, things had been bad for such a long time. We haven't had much of what you'd call quality time, lately.'

'I wouldn't call it that, I never heard that before.'

'Sorry. Wrong era. And it's childish to get so worked up about it. The planet's about to be invaded. Feels odd to be stuck here, really. This is just what the situation was like when I was ...' She paused, and went back to writing in her diary for a moment. Then she looked up again. 'When I was young. I keep trying to think of what the Doctor would do. And I have no idea.'

Pike chose his words carefully. 'He may not be – '

'He is. I know he is. Because she did it. She would have made sure.'

'The Brigadier talks about the Doctor often. And what I got from that, and these are really intense conversations that happened a lot when we were both seeing off our hallucinations, what I got from that was that he's never been known to lose. If there's a way out, the Brig said, he'll find it, like water running downhill.'

'The Brigadier just sees him as another sort of soldier.

Or as a piece of military equipment, like a sentient bazooka.'

Pike smiled wryly. 'You got a thing about soldiers, huh?'

'Yes. My father . . . oh, it's a long story. But that's what Ace is. That's what got the Doctor killed. Trusting a soldier.'

'Well, pardon me for living, ma'am. Hey, on that subject, the guys have been talking about you.'

'The answer is no, but I'd like to hear the question.'

'The question is, what do you call somebody who shoots down a helicopter with a hand-gun and calls a Brigadier "sir"?'

'I'd call her a bloody idiot,' Bernice tapped her diary with her pen. 'That's what I'm calling her right now.'

The Prime Minister sat at a long table, flanked by cabinet ministers and their civil servants. In front of them stood Robert Bertram, waving a sheaf of papers.

'A peaceful and serene event . . .' The Monk slapped the papers with his hand. 'Disrupted. And not just by these Black Star people, but by Brigadier Lethbridge-Stewart and UNIT factions still loyal to him.'

'We've seen the police reports,' the Prime Minister nodded. 'It can't be long before they're found. Everyone's been called out.'

'Indeed. And that's why now is the time for my idea. Civil disturbances are breaking out across the globe, not simply in what might be called the usual places, but seemingly at random. And for the first time, these outbreaks of violence seem linked to the activities of various terrorist organisations: Eta and the Red Brigade, Black Star, the IRA and the PLO. In West Berlin, we've seen crowds of teenagers chanting Baader-Meinhoff propaganda. We are looking, Prime Minister, at the breakdown of rational civilization, and its replacement by the horrors of anarchy.'

'Yes, yes,' a minister spluttered. 'Get to the point, will you? You say you've got something that'll solve our problems here at home? I mean, what with Louis being killed . . .'

'Hear him out, Roy,' the PM told him. 'I have every faith in Mr Bertram's technical abilities.'

'I'll come straight to the point, then. You may have heard that I've spent the last year or so organizing a pop concert, linking various capitals and venues across the world, using my satellite technology.'

'Oh really!' Another minister sucked his pipe in smokeless consternation. 'I think the last thing we need at this moment is a sales pitch.'

'Ah, but that's just the ... what do security people call it? The cover. Here's something I prepared earlier.' Bertram clicked his fingers and two junior civil servants wheeled in a black box, a spiral light spinning on the front.

'What are you going to do?' asked the first minister. 'Saw somebody in half?'

'This is something I've been rushing through laboratory tests. It's a basic pacification device. It beams stable, peaceful alpha waves straight into the aggression centres of the brain. If one were to operate it during the broadcast, a blanket of calm would descend across the globe, lasting for several months. It would be the solution to all our problems.'

'But that's monstrous!' The pipe-sucking MP stood up. 'Are you seriously suggesting that we attempt to interfere with the civil liberties of our entire population? I won't be privy to such a fascistic – '

Bertram hit a button on the top of the box.

The MP sat down, sighing. 'I just think that it's a very bad idea,' he said, opening his hands in a gesture of resignation. 'I wish I could explain to you how much it offends my sense of justice.'

The first minister clapped his hands, laughing. 'You've made Tony into a hippie! Do you think we could call for an all-party committee and turn it on Maggie?'

'The important thing,' Bertram switched off the device, 'is that your right honourable colleague here still holds all his opinions and beliefs. He just expressed them in a much more passive manner. I wouldn't call that mind control, would you?'

The Prime Minister raised an eyebrow. 'I wouldn't call it cricket, either, Mr Bertram. You intend to turn this ray on during this concert of yours?'

'Indeed. It'll be broadcast from my satellite, sweeping the world, with the permission of various foreign powers. Quite a few people will be watching. We've got Crosby, Stills and Nash, Wings, The Rolling Stones... many more.'

The Prime Minister glanced across the table. 'Tony, how do you feel?'

The minister chewed the end of his pipe thoughtfully. 'Quietly angry,' he muttered.

Ace stalked the corridors of the Monk's TARDIS, hunting. Her hands were poised in front of her face, in the posture that could kill a target with a flicker of flechettes. That was force of habit.

'Lead me to you. Show me where you are.'

There had been flashes of red ahead of her, glimpses of something moving ahead, just a corner away.

Finally, she came to a big old wooden door, in an elaborate stone setting. The carvings were magical sigils, runes and Gallifreyan motifs. The battlesuit went mad, telling her that the door was really bad news. Yeah, so? No time to worry. She put a palm to it. The wood was cold, even though the rest of the TARDIS had warmed up. There was no keyhole or visible lock system. If she wanted to get in, she'd have to blow it open. Damn. She took a step back.

'You'd know when, wouldn't you?' she whispered. 'Timing.'

Ace turned and walked quickly away. At least she knew where the place was now. Behind her, she thought she heard the sound of distant cries.

She got back to the console room and wandered to the main doors, which stood open.

Bertram's office lay beyond, the TARDIS disguised as a filing cabinet this time. Hence no desk. She went to the window, and gazed out over London. God, there were fires everywhere, smoke columns rippling across the sunlit sky. Out there, people were getting their heads kicked in on a very large scale.

Mortimus bustled through the door. 'It's on!' he smiled. 'Vardan Aid is scheduled for next Saturday!'

'Is that what you're gonna call it?'

'No, I think that would be a little obvious. I demonstrated the machine to the Cabinet today. Basic Chelonian technology, but they lapped it up. Nobody seemed to make the obvious connection.'

'What's that then?'

The Monk put a hand on either side of Ace's head. 'Soon it will be time to show you my little secret.'

'Yeah,' Ace grinned. 'I love surprises. What is it?'

'Not yet. Please just trust me for a little while longer.'

'No problem. We can trust each other.' Ace took his arm and they walked some way along the corridor. 'Before we leave this dead old place, could I go and say bye to Danny?'

'Why, my dear, we can take him with us if you want.'

'Nah,' Ace shook her head. 'Can't take everybody. I don't like him that much.'

Benny had disembarked at Paddington, and walked quickly away from the soldiers. Yates had run after her, turned her round and asked if she was all right, the tannoy ringing with shouts of platforms and destinations over her head.

Yes, she was fine, and she took the telephone number he wrote on the back of her hand, and didn't look back at the Brigadier or his troopers.

All this noise would soon be gone, in the bigger noise of energy blasts and nukes. And there was nothing to be done. She had, after all, seen it before, pulled across that space between the town and the shelter by her mother's hand.

184

This place is destroyed, time and time again.

She was standing on an escalator when she thought that. The rail rolled against something as she leaned. The gun in her waistband. Well, that could go in the first river.

She took a train to Charing Cross, looking at everything the people did, in their hundreds. Mums and kids, old people, a few beggars. Not so many as in the eighties, the Doctor had said. There was an atmosphere, perhaps, an atmosphere of tension, but maybe that was just normal for this city.

The Doctor had stood with her in Dresden once, as the first noise of bombers came up over the horizon. He'd turned a circle, trailing a finger over the buildings that were going to be flattened into powder, hopping it over the running families and the vulnerable babies.

'This,' he'd said, 'is done by the winning side.'

'So history doesn't dwell on it?'

'History comes to an end here. After this, there's only propaganda. Only manufactured consent.'

From a distant tranny now, Benny heard condemnations clanging out. Bishops and MPs and victims' families asked about what they thought of the murderers, and celebrities saying how they'd be doing benefits and playing their latest singles and putting aside all their profits for charity.

Down the windy tunnels came the news of rioting, and calls for hanging, and policemen murdered in front of their children. 'None of it's safe any more,' somebody in a star T-shirt said. 'You can't walk down the street, and you can't be sure of what's in the water, soon you won't be able to get laid without it killing you.'

The doors of the tube train closed in front of her face and she was squashed against them, leaning at a bad angle, as the darkness flashed by. She was glad to stumble up the steps at Charing Cross into the sunlight. There were posters for Subway Sect and new clubs and ripped-out ransom note letters everywhere.

'Hey!' A Scots boy in make up and rips. 'Aren't you that one out of Plasticine?'

'No,' Benny told him. 'You've got me confused with somebody else.'

'I know it's you. Sod you then, missus.' And he shouldered by.

Benny crossed the road at a run to avoid being run over by a black cab.

Nelson's Column was surrounded by tourists and spiralling flocks of pigeons, the sun shining off the scaffolding around Big Ben in the distance. Benny walked around into the cold shadow side and, not caring if anybody saw her, opened the marble.

Ace had meandered between buses and tubes to Danny's squat. She thumped on the door until a tired-looking Danny tottered downstairs and opened it.

'Oh, hi. Thought you'd vanished. Teatime. You wanna cuppa?'

'Yeah.' She wandered inside, trailing her hand along the flaking wallpaper on the wall. 'Just thought I'd see you again, talk about dreams some more.'

'Last time I saw you,' Danny went into the kitchen and selected the two least dirty mugs, 'you were excited about that strange object dream I had. Now you're down again.'

'Not sure it meant anything. I can't find any doors, Danny. Not one to get at the red woman, and not the other one I'm after, either.'

'What you going on about now?'

'Sorry. I haven't been sleeping much. You're my last chance. I thought maybe the woman in the red dress might have been talking to you.'

'Funny you should say that.' He said it like a sitcom character, with a precise little bit of finger-wagging. 'She was around last night, talking about you. You got an answerphone in my dreams, you have, sorry but Ace ain't in right now, here is Dan's subconscious instead.'

'What did she say?'

'A lot of warble, a lot of guff about how your dreams had become real. There's something in them that'll set her free, apparently. And then the Wombles came in and

started singing "Give Wombling Peace A Chance."
Relevant?'

'The first bit. Maybe the second. I dunno, I'm making
this up as I go along. What do you think it's all about?'

Danny handed her a steaming mug. 'Remember you're
a Womble?'

'Hello?' Benny looked up, frowning. The white corridors
of the TARDIS seemed silent and brooding, the familiar
hum of power muted. But she thought she'd heard something, far away. Distant footsteps.

She took another bite from her all-butter croissant and
turned another corner. Benny didn't quite know why she
was here, what she was doing. She'd just wanted to be
near to the ghost, to see some familiar things. Several
plans had come to mind. One: she could hide here, safe,
as the world was destroyed around her. That hadn't really
been worth thinking about. Two: she could try to pilot the
TARDIS somewhere. Or perhaps she could just flap her
arms and fly off-planet. Three: she could find some device
or weapon or knowledge that might help in the battle
against the Vardans. That had sounded like a Doctory
thing to do. The first step had been a cup of coffee and
the all-butter croissant. Those, Benny thought, were also
Doctory things.

The gun was still with her. That felt a bit wrong, actually.
'I'm turning you into some sort of faith,' she told the
Doctor. 'Listen, I never really understood what your
morals were on a lot of things. I thought that you were a
person, really, and you didn't seem certain about things
sometimes and . . .' She slumped onto the wall, putting
her hand to her chest, the place where she'd been shot. It
still ached sometimes. 'I loved you very much.'

The Brigadier shone his torch along the deserted stretch
of underground tunnel. 'Clear,' he called.

Pike and Benton ran forward into the darkness, crossing
the tunnel from side to side, covering every angle. Doyle
was at the rear of the party. The Broadsword team had

made its way down into an access tunnel near Shoreditch, and had crawled and run through a series of narrow tunnels. At one point they'd slammed themselves against a wall as a tiny GPO automated train sped past, at another they'd bypassed corridors sealed by purple tape. 'Royal escape route,' Yates had smiled.

'Guess we'll have company soon,' Pike had answered. 'Hey, and we didn't bring the caviar.'

Now they were at their objective. A pair of rusted metal doors were kicked open, and Claire Tennant hopped inside, filling the space with her body as she hauled down on the power switch.

That was so that if anybody was in here, she'd be the only one to die. But that was so far back in her training that it wasn't even a thought, just an instinct. She'd transferred from the regular army with the same lack of thought, and it had taken the Brigadier to make her realize why. It was because of a rabbit. Every new private in her regiment had been required to keep one, to feed it and to take care of it until a bond had been formed between rabbit and soldier.

And then they were marched out and ordered to kill their pets. Some with guns, some with hands.

Tennant didn't think that she'd minded at the time. She'd gone to her bunk that night with a feeling of pride, that she was a warrior now, that she'd erased her conscience. But the Brigadier's training had taken them all so deep inside themselves. She'd told him that she hated that moment, the warm life in her hands shivering and halting.

He'd put a hand on her shoulder, and said: 'Then they were bastards, Tennant, to order you to do that. What were they?'

'Bastards, sir.'

'And what are they now?'

'Slags, sir. Regular army slags.'

'And what are you?'

'UNIT, sir. Broadsword, sir. Saving people from monsters.'

'People and rabbits. Carry on, Corporal.'

Dying for him now would be fair exchange.

The generator kicked in and the lights came on, revealing an ancient tube station platform. The line had been removed, and the tunnel blocked at either end. On the platform stood a table, some filing cabinets and a computer bank connected to a monitor. Maps hung along the wall.

'As you can see, I've been busy.' The Brigadier swung the access door open wide and wandered out onto the platform. 'All the data I downloaded is here, and there's rations for fourteen days. Shouldn't need longer than that, should we?'

Ace arrived at Nelson's Column and shuffled between the tourists, finding the key in her pocket. The Monk would want that soon, want to finish it all off. He was waiting for her to offer it to him. Well, he'd get it, after she'd had a last look around.

People in sunshades and garish shorts were sitting on the steps of the monument. Ace climbed up between them, and opened the TARDIS door with her key. The tourists looked up, astonished, as she hopped inside.

She grinned back at them and closed the door.

Benny had found her way to the costume room, wondering about finding some bermudas or something. The chest that Ace had been rummaging through when she found that knife caught her eye, and she opened it up.

A long silver robe, and a turban. Lots of gold coins. This must have been the relic of some sort of arabian adventure. The coins didn't ring a bell, though.

It was while Benny was examining them that she heard the noise. Whistling. She didn't know the tune, but she knew the tone. Jaunty self-satisfaction. The whistle of a soldier, on the way to kill somebody who didn't matter.

A great anger gripped her heart, and all thoughts fled. Benny grabbed her gun and stepped out into the corridor.

She relaxed into a firing posture. She'd only have one shot. Straight through the heart.

Ace turned the corner and threw up her hands.

Blood burst from Benny's wrist, and the gun slapped upward, firing into the ceiling.

Ace was gone.

Benny yelled as she tugged a flechette from the base of her thumb. She was so angry she could barely feel the pain, only a rage that made her sick with the size of it.

Clutching her right hand into a fist, she took the automatic in her left, and rounded the corner close to the wall.

Nobody there.

Where would she go?

Benny licked her lips quickly and ran on the pads of her feet, rounding corners fast and with momentum. She found Ace's room and burst in through the door, covering the bed and the Brett Anderson poster and the kitbag and the chemicals and no Ace.

So she spun out of the door again. There was that other room, of course. The one that Ace had created when she restructured the TARDIS. Nobody had ever found out what was in there.

Something tactical.

Benny scuttled low through the corridors once more, taking the long way round. Ace had had time to prepare a position now, a line of fire. Important not to run straight into it.

She ran along the side of the swimming pool, and up a low flight of steps flanked by pot-plants. She ducked through another door, and caught sight of the new room at the end of the corridor.

Still no sign of Ace.

Benny padded up to the door of the room and saw that it was open a crack. Open for the first time. Ace had said that not even she could get in there. That was it, then. She was inside, waiting for Benny to push open the door, and then she'd fill her with little daggers to end her life.

Tempting. But no.

She ran back to the stairs, hitched up a pot-plant by the

leaves, and flung it roughly at the door, diving aside as she did so.

The door burst open, and Benny snapped up into firing stance, her left arm stretched out to find . . .

Forested hillside. Benny stood in a doorway amongst trees, looking down on a beautiful valley of rustling grasslands. The sun was low in the sky, and a mist was rising. From the land came the distant calling of birds and animals.

The room was a park. No, not a park. This was . . . oh my God.

Heaven. On Earth.

She stepped forward, taken off-guard by the smell of it. Rough mossy wood and gentle pollens. The air tasted of smoke and the rising cold breeze of oncoming night.

If this was meant to be Heaven, then . . . yes, it was a real place. This was Shepherdshay, a couple of kilometres to the west of the valley where . . . where Jan and his people had been camped.

How much of that could fit in a single TARDIS room? It'd be pushing it, surely?

Benny was suddenly afraid of ghosts, for the first time in her life. She carefully closed the door behind her, finding that it was part of a big old oak tree.

'I'm coming to get you,' she whispered. 'Whatever psychotic fantasy you've hidden away in.'

Shivering, she marched off into the forest. Impossible not to think of Hoothi really. They'd been everywhere, in the trees, in the soil. This version seemed to be the original, but it was still easy to think of some soft thing hiding in the bushes, waiting to engulf you.

If Ace had made this place, who knew what dangers it included? Mental scars, all the things that had twisted her so, made flesh.

Benny decided that she'd just kill everything until she'd killed Ace. Big thought, filled your lungs with the force of it. She grasped the gun tighter in her fist.

She came to the edge of the forest almost before she'd realized it. A chalky hillside scarped down and various small trees hung on there, their roots exposed in the white pebbly soil.

Down below was the Valley Of The White Horse. Empty. No camp, no Travellers. No Jan, thank God. But on the opposite hillside was the Horse itself, a white figure cut into the chalk. Its eye sparkled in the low sunlight that scattered through the trees. And up the bank towards it trudged Ace.

Too far to shoot her from here. And too exposed to cross the open ground. Benny moved off towards the path that led around the head of the valley, and had to lose sight of the Horse for a few moments.

She moved cautiously between the trees, gun up, ready to kill the first movement she saw.

Breaking cover cautiously, Benny realized that she was now high above the White Horse. The chalk formed cliff faces here, which the Travellers had fenced off with wire and timber. Those things weren't in this room, it seemed.

No sign of Ace on the slope below. Had she gone back down into the Valley, or had she also hidden in the –

The hand closed on Benny's gun.

She spun round, and the flat of Ace's palm caught her against the chin, sending her flying. Arms out, Benny went straight over the edge of the cliff. Her uninjured hand grabbed a root, and the injured one scrabbled helplessly after it, trying to hold on as her legs twisted in space.

The fall was over eighty feet. On to the cluster of fallen rock above the head of the Horse. It might not kill her. But she couldn't make herself let go.

Ace peered over the precipice. In her hand, she held a glittering silver ball. 'All this doesn't matter much any more,' she told Benny. 'Not now I've got this.'

'Finish it!' screamed Benny. 'Kill me like you killed the Doctor!'

Ace smiled down at her. 'Nah,' she said. 'I'll leave you to it. See if you can make it on your own, eh?' And she turned around and marched off into the forest.

Benny's fingers were already turning white around the root. It'd be a release to let go, a surrendering of pain and horror. But then Ace'd win, and nothing the Doctor meant would have lasted at all. He'd want her to hang on. She had to hang on.

Dad and Mum and Rebecca and the Doctor and all the good and beautiful stuff in the world was going to be lost to – lost to –

Benny hollered it as her fingers slipped from the root.

'Doctor!'

15

Never Mind the Moroks

Benny fell. Two inches.

And then the hand caught hers.

A strong hand. A hand that was etched with ages of pain, but could still be gentle and sure. It was a hand Benny knew very well.

The hand drew Benny up over the edge, until she could stand again.

'You called?' asked the Doctor. He stood there, like when Benny had first met him, in his jacket and paisley scarf, carrying that bizarre question-mark umbrella. On his face was a cunning smile, and his eyes sparkled in the setting sun.

She took a step away from him, back towards the trees, dizzy. 'But . . . you aren't even wounded! How did you – ? Are you alive?'

'Yes. I'm alive. And I'm not wounded. Time for explanations later. There's a planet to save.'

Bernice stopped herself from shaking or embracing him or bursting into tears or something. Carefully, she reached down to the ground and picked up her gun.

The Doctor put his hand on hers. 'Don't. You won't need it.'

'I won't need it, well, that's really good, because I don't think that I want to kill anybody ever again and . . . and – ' The tears started to shake from her throat. Closing her eyes, Benny grabbed the Doctor and held on. 'You git!' she cried into his scarf and comfortable shoulder. 'I thought you were dead! Git git git!'

194

'I'm sorry.' The Doctor held her, his voice full of regret. 'It wasn't a plan this time. Not mine, anyway.'

Benny let the gun fall from her hand. It dropped over the edge of the cliff. 'But what about the Monk? What are we going to do about him?'

The gun bounced back up into Benny's line of sight.

'Literally and metaphorically . . .' The Doctor murmured determinedly. 'He's history.'

It was late afternoon when Ace got back to Priory records. The building was buzzing with excitement, phones ringing and PAs running back and forth in the sunshine.

Ace walked through it with her eyes closed. When she entered the Monk's office, he was on the phone. 'Cliff, Cliff . . . I know Plasticine are on my label, but a peace concert isn't the time or place for these punk rock gestures. Believe me, there's no way I'd put them on the bill.'

'Tell him not to worry.' Ace slumped into a chair and bit her nail. 'I just killed their lead singer.'

'Ah . . .' The Monk frowned. 'I'll, erm, get back to you . . .' He put the phone down. 'You killed Bernice? My child, why?'

'Cos she was annoying.'

The Monk considered. 'I see. How did you do it?'

'Dropped her off a cliff in the TARDIS.'

'Yes. Well, I think it's only natural that young women sharing a confined environment should have these small disagreements. About the Doctor's TARDIS . . . I've been meaning to ask . . .'

Ace threw him the key. 'What do I need it for? I'm with you now, aren't I? You and Jan.'

The Monk caught the key and popped it into his top pocket. 'Jan, yes. We must do something about that soon. I don't intend to leave you in suspense, I promise. As soon as I've finished here, you'll have your Jan. I hope the two of you . . . well, you will stay with me, won't you? I've grown used to your presence, and having young folk in my TARDIS will so improve the place. Jan and I have much in common, from what I've seen. We're both rebels, we both like to act against the grain . . .'

'You were gonna show me this big secret of yours. You got time now?'

'Well, I am in the middle of putting together the bill for the biggest concert in history.' The Monk looked around his office. Then he smiled. 'But this organization virtually runs itself. For you, my dear, anything is possible. Come on through.' He waved a hand over his desk and the side sprang open, revealing a stony tunnel entrance.

They walked down a narrow flight of stone stairs into the console room. The place was starting to smell great, full of sunshine and leafy churchyards. The stone of the walls and columns had a warm feel to it.

'When they talk of revenge,' the Monk opined, rubbing his hands together, 'they never mention how good it feels afterwards. Not only has one actually disposed of an irritant in one's life, but one is free of the burden of revenge itself. It's good to be . . . free.' He shrugged vaguely, as if trying to shake something off. 'Is it still cold in here, or is it just me? This way.' He led Ace through a doorway, and off down a spiral staircase, deep into the darkness at the heart of his TARDIS.

They came to the doorway that Ace had found in her own travels, and the Monk turned his back on her a moment, tapping instructions into his watch. The door sprang open.

With a sense of anticipation, Ace stepped into the room. Cold again, her breath billowed suddenly. The place was as frosty as a refrigeration unit. Dark, too, after the sunlight that had been sparkling through the rest of the TARDIS. This room held its darkness close. It smelt of electricity, an ozone shiver which hung just under the scent of frost. Occult patterns were scrawled on the floor, and the walls were hung with fractal charts, jumbles of thin lines with notations on them. What really caught Ace's eye though was the sphere, a huge glassy thing swinging from a pendulum mounted in the ceiling. It was dark and covered in condensation, as if something warm was inside. From the ceiling and from numerous control surfaces, silver probes were poised against the sphere, ready to be inserted. Like a magician with a woman in a box, Ace thought, sticking in knives.

Something moved. Every instinct and armour reflex made Ace take a step back. Something had moved inside the sphere, as if some giant fish was in there, just fitting. She put a hand to her mouth. A palmprint appeared on the glass, and then was gone. Was the woman actually – ?

'Don't worry, my child, the creature in there isn't remotely human, though it can pretend to be. This is what I pretended to sacrifice you to. This is my unwilling servant Artemis . . . Artemis the Chronovore!'

Major Carpenter punched his chest with his fist and saluted.

The Vardan leader, many light-years away, returned the gesture with a ceremonial flicker of the hand. He could be seen on a viewscreen in the Vardan command ship. 'So . . . the Doctor is dead!'

'The Time Meddler says he's been left to rot on some Godforsaken planet somewhere.'

'Before the contract is completed, find out where. The fleet will obliterate the surface of that world from orbit. It is the only way to be sure.'

'Quite right, sir,' Carpenter muttered. 'But do you think we can trust his word? He is, after all, a Time Lord. He's flabby, lacks discipline.'

The Vardan leader nodded. 'True. But he has done everything that he said he would, thus far. And he has some impressive credits in the past. This is the man, after all, who was technical adviser to both the Moroks and Yartek, leader of the alien Voord.'

'Yes, blast it, and look what happened to them.'

'Because of the Doctor's intervention. That problem is now behind us. And soldier, try harder to ignore the memory patterns that you absorbed from this man Car-

197

penter. It is not fitting that you should talk as a human on board a ship of the fleet. Remember you're a Vardan.'

'Remember you're a Vardan!' Carpenter repeated the coda proudly. 'Yes sir, sorry sir.'

'Is there any word on why our assault at this place humans call Stonehenge was foiled?'

Carpenter pulled a sheaf of papers from his pocket. 'No, sir. There was obviously a standing wave set up. It caught those Vardans who were in their electronic form, and interfered with our control over humans who have been influenced by the Mediasphere. Only Vardans in physical form would stand any chance against such a weapon, and they would be vulnerable to gunfire.'

The Vardan Leader visibly shivered. 'And we have no idea where this terrible effect originated?'

'No sir, we're still working on that.'

'What of locating the humans who got away? Will they succeed in alerting their world to our forthcoming assault?'

'No sir, they've been discredited. Mortimus has the ear of the local politicians, and it seems that various foreign powers have been in touch, interested in the effects of his pacification beam. Violence and social unrest spread easily in such an undisciplined species.'

The leader laughed. 'It is the same everywhere, commander. This small feudal state will be ideal for our bridgehead. International assistance will not be forthcoming to a state in debt to this thing they call . . .' he glanced down at the papers on his desk, 'the International Monetary Fund. Why, the whole planet is in a state of readiness for civil war. Our influence will spread globally within a matter of days.'

'And shall we honour our bargain with the Time Meddler, sir?'

The Vardan Leader considered. 'While he's got the Chronovore,' he decided, 'I think perhaps it's better if we do.'

* * *

198

Ace reached up and put a hand against the sphere. 'So what's a Chronovore?'

'An inhuman beast, my dear. They exist outside of the space-time vortex and feed, as the name implies, on time itself. They're essential to the ecology of the cosmos; they help with structural flaws and snap up the ill-considered trifles of time-faring races. Some say that the universe would begin its collapse without them, easing the stresses and strains of physics as they do. And of course, they are magic personified. The laws do not apply to them. They can do anything.'

'If they can do anything, why's she in there?'

'Ah, I say they can do anything, but they are constrained by certain ... codes of conduct. There are rituals and incantations that one can use. Back in the Dark Time, where none can visit, I dare say that the elder powers – I mean people like the Daemons, the Eternals and the Gods of Ragnarok – wrote all this down. Now we're just left with the pieces, trying to make sense out of them.'

'Isn't it cruel, keeping her in there?'

'I can see why you might think that.' The Monk jumbled his fingers. 'But consider, Artemis lives outside time. To her, the passing of hours is a foreign language. What can such a being make of imprisonment? A vague cause for puzzlement, at worst.'

'And you can control her?'

'Yes, using the rods. I can influence her behaviour, order her to construct an alternative universe, or change this one. The former is easier than the latter. It was with her help that I managed to trace all the differences between the universe that would have been, the one where the Doctor leaves himself notes and instructions and thus defeats the Vardans, and this one, where he does not!' The Monk clapped his hands together and chuckled. 'I was able to remove every foundation to the Doctor's tactics. I have truly outplayed the player of games. Do you think the Daleks will call me the Ka Faraq Gatri now?'

Ace smiled a slow smile. 'Is that what you want?'

The Monk frowned, as the size of the idea struck him. 'No. No. I think that must be very uncomfortable, on second thoughts. Too much of a responsibility. Now, I think we'd best leave. A lot of the equipment in here's very sensitive. Sometimes when I stay too long, having a bit of a gloat, I set off the intrusion detector.'

'The whatsit?'

'Intrusion detector. It detects the presence of any new equipment or signal in the chamber. Anything that might disturb the balance. Let's go and have some tea, shall we?'

Ace followed him from the room. 'Ka Faraq too bloody clever by half,' she whispered, glancing back at the sphere.

The Doctor marched into the console room and hit the door lever.

'You're not going to tell me anything?' Benny waved her hands vaguely. 'Listen, I have been through a lot lately. I have been through more than can be put right with a hug and a tub of Haagen-Dazs. Just because your sense of drama is entertained by sudden rescues and lengthy plot explanations – '

'No. No, it's not about drama.' The Doctor pulled a thin circle of metal from his pocket. 'It's about winning. Winning everything. Have you got a hat?'

'What sort of a hat?'

'Any sort. Something that'll cover your forehead.'

'I can find something.'

'And do you know where I can find the Brigadier?'

'I've got a phone number.' Benny held up the back of her hand. 'Can Vardans travel down telephones?'

'Oh yes.' the Doctor murmured. 'But they don't like it. Ruins their hair.'

Broadsword had unpacked their kit, and were gathered around a planning table that the Brigadier had laid out on the northbound platform. 'Now then, what have we got?' He tapped a map of London with his swagger stick. 'Alien invaders who can move along any waveform, even thought, and can impersonate humans with incredible precision. Now, we would be worried about the identities of our own group here, except that we all escaped from whatever strange effect immobilised the enemy at Stonehenge.'

'Yeah, what was that?' Pike tapped a biro on his teeth. 'I never really figured that one out.'

'No, neither have I,' the Brigadier muttered. 'I can only assume that it was some trick of the Doctor's.'

Benton and Yates glanced at each other. 'Sir,' Benton began, 'Miss Summerfield thought that the Doctor was probably – '

'Nonsense, Mr Benton. If the Doctor was dead, I'm sure that I'd know about it.'

In an office along the platform, a telephone began to ring.

The Brigadier glanced at Yates, a half-smile on his face. 'Go and answer that, would you Yates? If it's not Professor Summerfield, say this is Timothy White's and how can we help them.'

The Brigadier continued his tactical planning for a few moments while Yates was absent. Then the soldier ran back across the platform, a grin of joy on his face. 'Sir!' he called. 'It's – '

Lethbridge-Stewart raised an eyebrow. 'Yes. Put the kettle on, will you Benton?'

16

The Library in the Body

Mortimus had been planning for decades, accumulating information and stealing useful devices, financing his operations by taking on discreet commissions across the universe. It had taken time for him to repair his TARDIS while stranded on that ice planet, and while he was constructing new circuits, he'd plotted. Once he had the necessary knowledge and equipment, he'd taken his TARDIS as far as it would go, out to the edge of the universe. Here there lived things that even Time Lords talked of in whispers, here stretched the great wave of quasars and dark matter in continuous explosion. Ye shall go no further. If you looked back, you'd see the complexities of the structure that contained the galaxies, a tangle of gravitic strings and muscles. If you looked forward, beyond the roar of universal expansion, beyond the background flare of first creation, there was only darkness.

It was said, in the forbidden texts, that there was life even in that darkness. But then those who wrote the forbidden texts were romantics, scared awake at nights by what they had written. Mortimus was not scared by what lay in the void beyond the universe. His quiet hatred extended beyond it, made the vacuum just another distance inside the hand of his ambition.

On the scanner screen of his TARDIS, two mighty collapsars spun, new-formed suns exploding as they burst across their event horizons. The solar debris was blasted away in two great relativistic jets. The blaze of white light that the system gave off was enough, even from the small area of the scanner screen, to pick out the details of the chamber that Mortimus had prepared for this occasion.

It was cold of course, with frost dripping off every surface. On the floor a grand pentangle was drawn, etched out in the blood of five separate intelligent species. The elder books of the Dark Time had specified their races, those that had had their genetic destinies changed by the Capitol. The blood of Minyan, Silurian, Dalek, Human and Mandrel mingled in the ice on the floor of the Monk's timecraft. At the corners of the pentangle stood spheres stolen from the Sisterhood of Karn. They had, typically, forgotten their function.

The Monk pulled his hood over his face to cover his features. He stepped out of the pentangle and took the crystal from a nearby table. It was an oddly shaped thing, a pyramidal spar.

'Artemis!' he shouted. 'I call you! I call you in the name of Rassilon The Ravager! I call you in the name of Omega The Fallen! I call you in the name of the Other, he who completes the Trinity and whose name is forever lost! You must enter the continuum and pay me heed, for I would give you sustenance!'

She appeared straight away, to the Monk's surprise. A simple figure, standing in the corner of the pentacle, a woman in a black dress. She had long black hair and a shining red mouth of immaculate teeth.

'So . . .' she smiled. 'A Time Lord. A Time Lord who has consorted with the Eternals in his time.' She licked her lips. 'You have much time about you and thus little left.'

'I claim protection and grace.' The Monk quickly made the sign of Rassilon. 'You are bound to consume only these histories.'

The woman walked towards him, her bare feet leaving steaming footprints on the icy floor. She stopped at one of the blood lines. 'You know the ceremonies.' She knelt, gracefully, and put a finger to the blood of the Minyan.

The pale figure of a child rose from the corner of the pentagram and spiralled around it, getting older, until when he returned to his corner, he was an old man. There was a blaze of regeneration, and the Minyan circled again, this time as a different youth.

'He will go round thirteen times, widdershins,' the woman smiled wryly. 'He was called Antokh, a minor functionary in Minyan military service. He had eight children, and his most fond memory was of helping with the birth of the first. You killed him at the end of his regenerative cycle, with cloth and poison.' She raised her head slightly and grinned white teeth at the Monk. 'You regret that the poison required to kill a Minyan is rare, and particularly expensive.'

'Well, yes.' The Monk jumbled his fingers. 'But we all have to make sacrifices, don't we?'

Artemis smiled. 'No. What favour would you ask of me?' She touched another blood line with her toe. 'Speak quickly, there are only four of these morsels left.' A Silurian broke from its egg and spun around the pentagram, shedding skin in a blizzard of debris until it crumbled into fossilized dust. 'And some last longer than others.'

'I wish to ask you for . . . guidance,' the Monk smiled benignly. 'I believe that I have lost the path I once followed. I wish to begin a cult devoted utterly to your worship, you beautiful creature!'

'Oh, please . . .' Artemis watched as the Mandrel lumbered around the chamber. 'I do not require worship. All I require is food.' She glanced back to the Monk as the ungainly creature vanished in a puff of Vraxoin. 'And entertainment. It might be entertaining to set you to living your life in reverse. Or to make you a woman. Or a human. Would you enjoy being a human, Time Lord?'

'Oh, no, I doubt it!' blustered the Monk. 'I mean, their lives are so short, aren't they? They're like insects, gone in an instant, no time to think.'

The Dalek whizzed round the chamber shouting threats and exploded. 'Look who's talking,' murmured Artemis, taking a step nearer to the cowering Monk.

'Wait!' he shouted. 'I have much more to offer you!'

'Hush.' Artemis touched the final bloodline. 'How many

times have I been through this ritual? Always the same group of species, never any surprises.'

A handsome young man appeared at one corner of the pentagram and began to slowly walk around the chamber, unchanging. His lustrous dark hair reflected the fire that had erupted in Artemis's eyes. He completed his circuit of the pentagram and, smiling mockingly, began another one.

The Monk raised his head and smiled. 'It seems I do have the power to surprise you.'

Artemis flexed her hands, red nails shining. 'An Eternal!' she whispered. 'You have the blood of an Eternal! How?'

'Gold,' nodded the Monk. 'Some of them are very partial to it. Oh, and I agreed to be the champion of one who calls herself Death. I'm not entirely sure what that implies, but I'm sure it won't be too demanding. The one who's circling you is called Vain Beauty, or Brett as he preferred to be known when I met him. He was playing Russian Roulette in a bar in Paris. He allowed himself to lose, and I helped to clear up some of the mess. We had a chuckle about it afterwards, I can tell you. He's quite keen to learn how all this turns out.'

Artemis hissed, and for a moment the pentagram was a blinding flutter of thunderous wings, a huge strength struggling against the force around her. The TARDIS walls vibrated with a bellow that eventually resolved itself into a human-mouthed cry. 'What do you want?'

'Your service. If you do well, I may let you go.'

'Let me? Let me?!'

'Something of a new concept, I know.' The Monk tapped out a series of instructions on his watch. The roof opened and a great clear globe descended, its surface glistening with liquid.

'You expect me to –'

The Monk hit another control. Lightning jumped from the globe into the pentagram, and Artemis dissolved into a fine grey mist. The mist hung for a second and then

205

vanished inside the globe. A silver probe shot out from the roof into the interior and the globe went pure black.

The Monk took a step forward and, making the Sign of Rassilon nervously, wiped across the Eternal's blood trail with his sandal. The boy bowed and vanished, but the globe remained black. He gave a great sigh of relief, and then clapped his hands together in joy. 'Good! Good! Now the real job can begin! Oh, this is going to be so much fun!'

He ran from the room. Behind him, the interior of the globe flickered like an oncoming storm.

17

Going Underground

The Doctor raised the cup to his lips and sipped. 'Strong and sweet,' he murmured.

Benny, who was sitting on the other side of Broadsword's makeshift ops-cum-tea table, caught his eye and mouthed 'like you', silently. She had been smiling all the way across London. Just to have him gone for a while . . . it was like the lights had gone out on the world. She was wearing a beret that concealed a rather hippie-looking lead band that looped her forehead. She'd had to muck about with a few strands of hair to make the concealment complete, but the Doctor seemed to think it was pretty vital.

She glanced at the Brigadier, who was stirring his own tea. He was looking at the Doctor too, a sort of faraway expression on his face. He was remembering, she realized, all those adventures that they'd had together. He'd thought about what the world would be like without the Doctor, too.

'So, Doctor,' he said, 'what are we going to do?'

'We're going to stop the Vardans and the Monk. We're going to win.'

'The Monk? Was that the fellow at the stones?'

'Yes. He's a Time Lord by the name of Mortimus. He used to be an *agent provocateur* for the High Council. There was some sort of controversy, they betrayed him. He started to meddle as a hobby, change things that shouldn't be changed, just to see what would happen. Very foolish. He actually was a monk, of sorts, an initiate in one of the colleges of scholars in the Capitol. They don't worship as such, or they pretend they don't. They just keep secrets. And sometimes the secrets keep them. Mortimus is a victim, but he's also very dangerous. He's tried to kill me, to make me despair, to distance me from my friends . . .' He glanced up at Bernice. 'I have to stop him.'

'But how do we do that, Doc?' Yates was sipping from a clear mug of herbal tea. 'We don't even know where he is.'

'Yes we do,' the Doctor told him. 'Mortimus is calling himself Robert Bertram.'

There was a general gasp of surprise. Doyle nodded. 'Yeah. I suppose he was the patron that poor old Julie kept on about. Damn him. She kept on about how surprised she was that somebody with so much money could talk so well about the cause.'

'He can talk well about anything he likes. He's a very good liar.'

'And I thought he was such a nice man,' Benny smiled. 'Shows what a good judge of character I am.'

'You went off with me.'

'You promised to show me puppies. I'm still waiting.'

The Brigadier tapped the front page of that morning's *Times*. 'So presumably this peace concert that he's planning has some hidden motive?'

'What?' The Doctor looked up and took the paper. 'Satellite link-ups, concerts all over the world, the Rolling Stones . . . yes, Brigadier, I think this is his final move. How many people would tune into this?'

'Most people, I guess.' Pike had draped his jacket over the back of his seat, and seemed to be avoiding the urge to put his feet up on the table. 'Concert like that, world-wide . . . maybe a billion up?'

'And we've seen how they're using television . . .' the Brigadier muttered.

'A Vardan invasion force, ready to beam into a quarter of the minds on the planet,' concluded the Doctor. 'All we need to know is how. Time to show you something.' He reached into his coat pocket and pulled out a video cassette. 'I got this during my escape – '

'About which there are many things we still don't understand.'

'Later, Brigadier. Can I use your video?'

'Liberty hall, Doctor. I brought down a VCR unit as part of the training package.' The Brigadier stood up and led the gathering across to the other platform of the tube station, where a television and video stood beside a flip chart and an overhead projector. Pike and Benton busied themselves setting it up.

'The generator down here was left intact when the place was decommissioned,' the Brigadier explained. 'I gather there was always some thought to the station becoming a secret establishment.' He wandered over to the television. 'Now, do I have to be careful how I switch this on?'

'I doubt you'd get a signal down here,' the Doctor told him. 'Which is why this place is so useful. You planned well, Brigadier.'

'Oh, I didn't know about the nature of the enemy.' The Brigadier switched the television on, and found the video channel. 'I think it's a human instinct, going underground. You go into the pit, Doctor, and you emerge as a new man.'

'Been there, done that . . .' The Doctor handed the old soldier his video. 'It's still odd to hear you talking like a mystic.'

'A very British mystic. What is this tape, anyway?'

'It's one of my adventures, as recorded by the Monk. I think you'll recognize certain elements in it.'

The pattern on the screen shifted into a mass of flickering lines. Pike looked away, uneasy. 'I'm never gonna watch TV again.'

'You're not missing much,' Benton told him. 'I only ever see the cricket. I think I'd notice if they influenced that.'

'Yes,' Yates agreed. 'England would start beating the Aussies.'

The flickering resolved itself into a picture, the Doctor standing between Benny and Ace.

'So,' the on-screen Doctor said. 'You're having problems with the Vardans, Brigadier.'

'How did you know that, Doctor?' The Brigadier and Benton were standing with a whole squad of UNIT soldiers.

'Because of that!' The Doctor pointed up. Overhead was hovering an advertising balloon, with an advertisement for a new computer game: *Vengeance Of The Vardans.* 'It can't be selling too well, I'm no good at writing games.'

'But I am!' Ace grinned. 'Wicked idea, Professor!'

The Doctor hit the fast-forward button, and they ran about at high-speed, the picture chopping and changing. 'The Monk can visualize and record actual history, or any number of possible other outcomes. That was what was going on in your White Room, Brigadier; an actualization of another planet, probably Varda itself. Ah!'

On the screen, the Doctor was being pursued through a building by humanoid Vardans. He hopped up stairs, set off fire extinguishers, and finally found himself cornered by an open window. Without hesitation, he threw himself backwards and fell, only to bounce off a mattress that was lying on the pavement.

'Well, at least you didn't try that!' Benny muttered.

'I don't quite understand, Doctor,' the Brigadier frowned. 'What are we watching?'

'This is the Monk's private record of how my battle with the Vardans would have gone, did go, does go . . . oh, English grammar doesn't cover it. Without the Monk's intervention, this is what happened.' On screen, the Doctor was looking over Ace's shoulder, clicking his fingers in sudden surprise as he glimpsed himself standing behind Pete Shelley in a photo in the NME. Then there was a scene of the TARDIS landing on the lunar surface, the Doctor leaving a beacon blinking against the harsh landscape.

The Vardans moved in on UNIT, who were firing burst after burst at the crackling creatures as they advanced towards Buckingham Palace. Suddenly the Doctor dashed forward. 'Stop this madness!' he called. 'Or you'll all be captured!'

'What do you mean?' hissed the Vardan leader. 'You have no power, Time Lord!'

'Typical of a Vardan to underestimate me.'

'Yes, as monsters you're rather crap,' added Benny.

The real-world Benny raised an eyebrow. 'Don't get a lot to do in this, do I?'

'No . . .' the Doctor agreed. 'But you get all the best lines.'

On the screen, the Doctor clicked his fingers, and Ace could be seen through the open doors of the TARDIS. She smiled at him and pulled down a big red lever. 'She's still with me, still trusts me,' the Doctor whispered, watching the story unfold. 'That makes a difference.'

With a hiss, the Vardans dissolved in a blur of static and vanished.

'So, you see, I just trapped them in a standing wave between the Earth and the Moon,' the Doctor was telling the assembled forces of UNIT in the bar of the Valiant Trooper. 'I'll take both wave generators away in the TARDIS, and we'll leave the Vardans somewhere where they won't escape like they did last time. Gallifreyan time-loop technology is so unreliable.'

'But,' the on-screen Benny raised a finger. 'There's just one thing I don't understand . . .'

'Oh no!' the real Benny groaned. 'Personally, I'm really glad things didn't go like this.'

'Ssh!' The Doctor smiled, raising a finger to his lips.

On screen, the Doctor took from his pocket a vinyl record. 'All the clues were on here,' he told the assembled audience. 'Plasticine's live debut album. All you have to do is listen carefully.'

Danny and the band lurched into the pub and looked around in puzzlement. 'Hey!' called Danny. 'Did we miss the party?'

The UNIT troopers started to laugh and, hugged by Benny and Ace, the focus zoomed in on the grinning Doctor. The picture faded to black.

'I have never seen such yuckety,' commented Bernice. 'And what about that costume I was wearing? Where have I just been, the leather fetishist's ball?'

'We . . .' Pike threw an arm around Yates's shoulder, 'are disturbed. Where were we?'

'I don't know.' The Doctor tapped his lip with his finger. 'I suppose that you, Captain Yates . . .'

'Just Mike, please, Doc, I'm not a captain any more.'

'Force of habit. I suppose that in that reality you were never called out of retirement. I arrived and saved the day before the Brigadier had to start thinking about such desperate measures. And as for you, Captain Pike . . .' The Doctor turned a finger on Pike. The digit wavered slightly. 'I don't know. I wish I did.'

'Well, one thing's obvious,' Benny opined. 'The world is saved by whatever's on our record. A live recording, presumably from that concert where Bertram appeared. That's why Danny's so famous in the future.'

'But in this universe – ' the Doctor stood up, 'when I listened to the CD, I didn't hear anything. I only recognized that it was Bernice.'

'Well, you could try again – ' Yates began.

'No, no!' The Doctor waved a hand angrily. 'I've listened to it a dozen times. There's nothing there. That's why it was only released on CD, that's why Mortimus has brought CD technology forward ten years, just so that I won't hear whatever I'm supposed to hear!'

'Hey, wait. I've got it,' Benny cut in. 'I play a really significant part in this version, because I've actually got it. It's Danny.'

'What?' The Doctor turned round.

'Danny bootlegs every gig he plays. You might not be able to hear this information on CD, but you'll be able to hear it – '

'On analogue tape!' The Doctor grinned. He reached out and touched Benny's nose. 'What would I do without you?'

'Get lonely,' Benny smiled back. 'And fail terribly.'

212

Claire Tennant emerged from a drain and blinked in the light. The drain was in a backstreet of Shadwell. They were partly hidden by a row of dustbins. 'Clear!' she called, standing up. Distantly, there was a sound of shouting coming from the streets.

The Brigadier hopped out of the sewer after her. 'Been down that particular stretch of sewer before, I shouldn't wonder,' he told Tennant. 'Lot of ops round here during that Yeti business, right down to Tooting Bec. Before your time.'

'Yes, sir.'

The Doctor walked straight up out of the drain, miraculously clean, holding a map in front of him. 'Danny lives in Wapping, according to the address that Benny's got, so from here it'll be quicker if we take the tube.' He wandered to the end of the road, twirling his umbrella like some sort of aerial. Then he glanced around the corner. The shouting grew suddenly louder, and was joined by the clatter of horses. 'Hurry!' he called.

Benny had just been helped out of the hole by Captain Pike. The two of them joined the general charge to the end of the road. As they rounded the corner, they could see what the Doctor was worried about. A group of people, mainly young men, was rushing towards them down the street, a sudden splinter from some nearby commotion. Behind them cantered policemen on horseback. The boys were shouting as they ran, some of them spinning round to throw bottles and bricks.

The Doctor's party sprinted up the street in front of them.

Benny found that she was running beside Danny.

'Hullo!' he grinned. 'This is dull, innit? Fancy a brew?'

'Could I bring some friends?'

'Yeah, Ace was here earlier. We were talking about dreams and stuff.' Danny had found every grimy mug in the house to make coffee for the Brigadier's people.

'Any idea where she's got to?' asked Mike.

'No, mate. Now, this lot are soldiers, right? They sit like

213

soldiers, and they're mob-handed. So what are you doing back with them? They, you realize, are the enemy.'

Yates sighed. 'I don't really know anything any more, Dan. I just want to get back to my cottage.'

'Were you working for them when you were saying all that beautiful stuff the other night?'

'Well, that's a complex question – '

'No it bloody isn't, it bloody isn't!' Danny ran a hand back through his hair. 'You should see what it's getting like out there. There's a revolution starting, people are rising up in the streets...'

'No.' The Doctor looked up from his examination of the tea leaves in his cup. 'They aren't rising. They're being tugged to their feet like puppets. They're being influenced. And amongst all that, you saved me. With an autograph.'

'What are you talking about?'

'It's difficult. Everything I say to you has to be so precise, because if you do the wrong thing, if you speak the wrong line or put a foot off your mark ... how does that feel to you? Being a hero, I mean?'

'I'm no hero. I just want to play in my band, help out in the revolution.'

The Doctor smiled suddenly. 'Danny, do you have a tape of Plasticine's concert at the Chelsea Club?'

'Yeah, of course I do.'

'Then you shall go to the ball.'

'That was all right,' Benny's taped voice called out over the sound of a crowd cheering and stamping its feet. 'This is an old Yes number ... no it isn't, no it isn't, and thank you for your phlegm, sir. This is called Chaos.'

The band struck up another high-speed number, and the Doctor took off Danny's headphones, shaking his head in despair. 'Nothing,' he told the waiting group of soldiers. 'All I can hear is the crowd. Whatever's on there, the signal's buried under all that noise.'

'Well,' suggested the Brigadier, 'is your TARDIS about? You're bound to have some contraption that can pick out quiet sounds, aren't you?'

214

'Your faith in me is touching, Brigadier. And you're right, I could probably knock something together. We must get back to Trafalgar Square.'

'A police box in Trafalgar Square?' Mike Yates smiled. 'They don't have them in London any more, Doc.'

'No,' the Doctor muttered, standing up from the lotus in which he'd been curled next to Danny's hi-fi. 'Prepare yourself for a surprise.'

It was late afternoon by the time they got back to Nelson's Column. Danny had come along too. The Doctor produced the key from his pocket and smiled his secret smile.

'Good Lord, Doctor.' The Brigadier raised an eyebrow. 'You're moving up in the world.'

The Doctor smiled proudly and wandered to the base of the monument, ignoring the tourists. He pulled the key from his pocket, and tried to find the chink in the masonry where his key should have fitted. After a moment he stopped, and lowered his hand.

'What's up?' Benny leaned on his shoulder.

'The TARDIS has gone. He's taken it. Ace must have given him her key.'

'Damn. What are we going to do?'

The Doctor slipped off his hat and pondered, tapping it on his lapel. 'Give him a taste of his own medicine.'

It was early evening when Broadsword arrived in the cabling conduits underneath the Priory Records building. They were following the Brigadier's extensive maps once more, although in his many provisions he hadn't included, much to Benny's distaste, a set of boiler suits and wellies.

The conduits were full of bunched and insulated cables. The Brigadier tapped on the metal plate beside him. 'About here, Benton.'

'Right, sir.' Benton had a thermic lance unit strapped to his back. He began to cut away a section of the wall.

'I hesitate to say it, Doctor,' the Brigadier continued, 'but I don't think we've been followed since we arrived in London. These Vardans don't seem up to much, not in the field of intelligence at any rate.'

'They don't have to be, Brigadier. They can hear your thoughts, tune in to everything you say. They don't practice intelligence because they are intelligence.'

'And they can travel down anything electronic, like these cables here?'

'Yes.'

'Tricky. So why haven't they found us?'

'Why indeed?'

Benton completed his cutting job and, with Yates' help, pulled the metal inwards, opening up a door. The Doctor popped his head through the gap. 'Ah. Ventilation ducts. Where would we be without them?'

The smooth metal ducting led upwards, light slanting through a series of ventilator grilles. Far below, a powerful fan roared in the darkness.

'Suckers,' and the Brigadier held out his hand.

'My thoughts exactly.' Benny gave him a set of sucker pads, which the Brigadier attached to his hands and knees. 'How many of these have you got?'

'Four sets.' The Brigadier slapped one pad to the wall, and it stuck. He pulled it away again. 'Myself, the Doctor and Captain Pike will climb the shaft using three of them.'

Benny nodded. 'I'll take the fourth.'

'No, Professor Summerfield – '

'I know what you're going to say, it's too dangerous, etcetera. That's a load of – '

'Indeed. No, I was actually going to say that we need somebody here with the last set in case we get into difficulties. I see no reason why that person shouldn't be you.' He craned his head out of the gap, and slapped the first cup onto the inside of the shaft. 'If you wish, that is.'

The Doctor, Pike and the Brigadier made their way up the interior of the shaft, the updraft plucking at their clothing. The Doctor had folded his hat away into his pocket and left his umbrella with the others.

'Can anybody hear us in here?' Pike asked the Doctor over the sound of the fan.

'I doubt it. The system will be muffled.'

'That's good. If I give a really loud scream, nobody's gonna hear.'

'Nothing to scream about, is there Pike?' The Brigadier glanced down.

'I'm a soldier sir, not a rock star. I don't like to get physically involved with fans.'

The Brigadier raised an eyebrow. 'Stupid boy . . .' he smiled.

'You've been waiting to say that since I got posted here, huh?'

'I don't know what you're talking about, Captain.'

The Doctor had reached the ventilator grille that he'd pin-pointed when examining a schematic of the building. 'Here.' He raised his shoulder and took the sonic screw-driver out of his pocket, holding it between his teeth. He tapped it on the wall to activate the pre-settings, and started to pass it over the end of the first screw. The screw began to push itself out of the wall on the other side.

'Glad to see you've still got that little gadget,' the Brigadier opined.

The fourth screw popped out of the grating and the Doctor hopped out into Robert Bertram's office. 'It's a replacement,' he explained. 'I only had time to make a new one very recently.'

The two soldiers climbed out into the office. 'Pike, put your ear to the door,' the Brigadier ordered. 'We don't know how long we've got before this Monk fellow gets back.'

'We need to find some play-back equipment.' The Doctor started to open the metal cabinets along the walls of the room.

The Brigadier had gone to the picture window and was staring out over the city. Flames were flickering down by the river, and columns of smoke were everywhere. The tiny lights of police cars and ambulances sped through the murk. From somewhere came the distant thump of mortar fire. 'My God . . .' he whispered.

'Come on, Brigadier!' The Doctor was pulling out drawers ferociously, scattering equipment on the floor. 'The Monk's fond of technology, he surrounds himself with gadgetry.'

'Yes, of course.' The Brigadier went to the Monk's desk, and pressed down on the answerphone's play-back button.

'Hello?' Ace's voice piped up. 'Hey, I knew I could get your personal line if I tried. Listen, I'm in trouble and you're the only one who can help me. Meet me at the Bull and Staff, twenty-one hundred, okay? Please? Cheers.'

'Sounds to me like your young lady's defected, Doctor.'

The Doctor glanced up. 'Nah, mate, I'm just pretending,' he murmured in a perfect imitation of Ace's accent.

The Brigadier looked between the Time Lord and the desk. 'You mean that was – ?'

'Yes. Try to keep up, Brigadier. Now – ' The Doctor hopped up from the drawer where he'd been crouched, and tapped his fingers together, approaching the desk. 'I'd hoped that I'd find what I was after in the office. But if it's here, it'll be in the desk. He wouldn't keep future technology where people could see it.'

'In the desk?'

'The desk is a TARDIS, bigger on the inside than the outside. You know.' The Doctor suddenly grinned. 'It's structure's being disrupted, because of a signal I sent out from my TARDIS. And he's put my TARDIS inside his. So . . . will this work?'

The Brigadier looked at the Doctor in concern. 'What are you planning to do?'

'Forced entry, Brigadier.' The little Time Lord put his palms on either side of the desk. He ran his fingers over the surface. 'Where's the door? Ah.' He hopped round to the side. 'This wouldn't be possible if Mortimus hadn't been foolish enough to put a disrupting signal right inside the structure of his craft. But that's always been his problem. Hubris. That's the trouble with omnipotency. Makes you think you can do anything.' He put his ear to the

218

wood and listened, giving the desk a series of sharp taps. Finally he closed his eyes and raised his hand. He struck the wood, burst straight through it, and hauled out a red lever, which he jerked back. Purple liquid burst from the side of the desk, and the splintered wood groaned open, white light shining across the carpet. 'Come on in.'

'Last time I was inside one of these things – ' The Brigadier protested.

'You found yourself in Cromer. I know.'

Pike stared around the console room of the Monk's TARDIS. 'Okay,' he muttered. 'Let me get this straight. All this fits into that little desk?'

'Yes. That's the best thing about Gallifreyan technology. It's tidy.' The Doctor was inspecting the console. 'Hmm. Confinement systems. So he's keeping it in the ship somewhere. Ah, here we are.' The Doctor hit a button, and from the stone flooring an elegantly carved pillar shot up. Atop it were rather more modern controls and instruments. 'This is where he put together his basic CD technology before he landed on Earth. He'll have wanted to listen, to double-check that the information I need isn't on the CD ... So he'll have sensitive editing and monitoring equipment.' The Doctor found a bulky CD system amongst the jumble of items on the work surface of the podium. 'He's got a disc in here. Let's have a look.'

Pike, who had been staring at the elegant gothic ceiling in wonderment, turned his head, startled. 'No! Don't – '

The Doctor had hit the play button.

With a shriek of escaping energy, a crackling shape formed, blazing out of one speaker on the base of the podium.

The Vardan that had been stored on CD took a moment to gain its bearings. Then the lightning that played back and forth inside it crackled with new purpose.

'Kill!' it screamed. It lunged towards the Doctor.

18

The Revolution Will Be Televised

The Doctor stumbled backwards from the hissing bundle of energy, raising his hands to protect his face.

'Captain Pike,' the Brigadier yelled over his shoulder. 'Try to – '

But Pike was gone, gone in a sudden blaze of light that leapt forward and shone straight into the attacking Vardan. The two light sources flared together, and the two humans threw up their arms to stop themselves being blinded by the white light that flooded the room.

And then, soundlessly, they were gone.

'Pike!' the Brigadier exclaimed. 'He's a – '

'Vardan, yes.' The Doctor turned back to the editing podium. 'I thought so. That's why he didn't appear in the Monk's video.'

'But why? How – ?'

'Later, Brigadier.'

Lethbridge-Stewart put his hands on his hips. 'I'm beginning to think that nobody is what they seem.'

The Doctor looked up briefly. 'Nobody is.'

Two pulsating beams of radio waves hit the ionosphere over Europe, collided, and bounced down into Radio Luxembourg. They buzzed across the stations, making every voice that spoke in the medium wave warble and hiss. They sped east and hit the modulated pounding of Soviet radar installations, soaring and dipping close to that continuous background thumping.

In the dreams of children and animals, two young men were fighting that night, dashing across television screens and cloudy skies, their bodies blazing with light. The oily surface of the Mediasphere projection rolled and spat with bursts of light. It was only a matter of time, Pike knew, before a Vardan observer saw their conflict and intervened.

Pike rolled with the Vardan sentry at the edge of the Reichenbach Falls, being Sherlock Holmes. 'You'll never take this planet, Moriarty!' he shouted.

'Hah!' his opponent replied, shoving him closer to the edge. 'The humans want us to! They love being manipulated, they believe their fictions like they're the truth!' He dug his hands into Pike's neck. 'You are a traitor, and I will kill you in the name of the Vardan High Command.'

'Your army are the traitors. You only believe in dog eat dog, in every man for himself. That isn't a philosophy at all, you cur, it's the absence of one. But if you want to see if someone can fight not to be a soldier . . . then come on!'

With a jerk of muscles, they fell into the waterfall.

They reappeared in front of the controls of Jet Morgan's spaceship. Pike delivered a straight left to the jaw, sending his alien attacker flying.

'What will your family make of this?' The alien staggered to his feet. 'A Vardan who is ashamed of his own people?'

'My family – ' Pike grabbed the Vardan's head and slammed it against the wall. 'Are all dead. Some of them because of you!'

Nightshade grabbed the monstrosity that had once been an astronaut, and lurched with him towards the blazing arc of electricity that burned in his laboratory. 'You'll never conquer this planet!' he yelled. 'The people here can be gentle, kind to the weak. And kindness is a strength!' With a final heave, he threw the alien creature into the path of the electricity, and it dissolved into a burst of static.

Lightning broke a clear sky over England.

And a diffuse cloud of light flickered down across the landscape, sadly seeking home.

* * *

The Doctor flicked his finger across the controls on the editing podium. The crowd noise had long since been edited out of Danny's tape. Now just Bernice's voice could be heard. 'Look at the band, don't look at me.'

In the background, there was something else, a tiny noise.

The Doctor adjusted controls and Benny's voice faded out, the tiny noise grew from a whisper to a thin, crackly voice.

'Good grief!' the Brigadier exclaimed. 'That's Carpenter!'

'Backstage at the concert,' the Doctor nodded. 'Talking over his plans with Bertram. That's another weakness of the Vardans. They're very loquacious.' He continued to play with the sound, sharpening it until it was right on the edge of coherency.

The Brigadier had been pacing around the console. Suddenly he saw something in the corner and wandered over to it. 'Doctor . . .' he smiled. 'Is this yours, by any chance?'

In the palm of his hand sat a miniature police box.

'The dear old thing!' The Doctor took it from him. 'I thought it'd attract attention to itself somehow . . .'

The monitor on the tracking antenna at UNIT HQ suddenly went off the scale. But there was nobody to see it.

Captain Pike stood in the middle of the drill hall, hugging himself fiercely. 'Damn,' he sighed. 'And I was having such a good day.'

There was a noise from somewhere in the building. Pike froze, then scampered to the door. He put his ear to it, and jumped away.

Too late. Ace burst in, her fist flying up to cover Pike. 'Thought I'd already checked this place out,' she told him. 'Where did you come from?'

'Oh . . .' Pike backed away, his hands up. 'I'm just travelling light.'

The Doctor and the Brigadier clambered back into the

222

shaft beside Bernice and Broadsword. Benton set about replacing the panel. 'Mission accomplished,' the Brigadier told his troops. 'Let's move out.'

'Where's Alex?' Benny looked between them, horrified.

The Doctor put a hand on her shoulder. 'We met a Vardan, he fought it off.'

'And it killed him?'

'Not exactly. He was a Vardan himself.'

'That's ridiculous!' Mike Yates spoke up. 'We've been talking about his childhood, about his parents . . .'

'The memories of the original Alex Pike. I was fooled myself. But he did try to help us. He must have been shielding all of you from the Vardans' sensors. From now on, you have to concentrate continually, at least until I can find some more lead.'

The Brigadier glanced between his troops. 'All right, remember the routine? Sergeant Benton do not touch me . . .'

While repeating the words from the old military song, Benton emptied the rounds from his pistol and handed them to the Doctor. ''Scuse me, sir, but I can't take all that abuse. Soon as you melt this lot down the better.'

Pike put down his hands. 'Listen, I don't know what you're planning to do here, and I don't really care. I just want to pick up my stuff and go.'

'Why?' Ace kept her hand pointed in his direction. 'You deserting, or what?'

'Oh, I did that a long time ago. When my little brother got left out on a rock. Didn't seem fair to me, but he had a weird leg, and they said "We've got a free market here, *laissez faire*, if he lives he gets to be in the army". Thing is, thing that really gets me . . . they don't leave all of us out on the rocks when we're kids, do they? The healthy ones . . . they just kind of assume we'd survive it.'

'What are you on about? They don't leave babies out to die in the States, do they?'

'No, but they do on Varda.'

'You're a – ?! Oh no . . .' Ace took a step back and aimed.

'Go on, kill me, I got nothing else to do. Why are you here, anyway?'

Ace lowered her hand. 'Why should I tell you?'

'Cos we're both on the same side.'

'You mean we're both traitors?'

Pike shrugged. 'If you wanna put it like that.'

They wandered through the darkened country house. 'Where do you think everybody's gone?' Pike asked.

'Out blowing things up, stirring things.' Ace still had half an eye on Pike, in case he made a sudden move. 'Everything Black Star didn't do, UNIT did, I reckon. Between them they've been very good at keeping people scared. Why do you keep up that accent, anyway?'

'I like it. I like being Alex Pike, he was a good guy. Another Vardan killed him, in the back of a jeep in the desert. He transferred his memories to me. Intimate stuff. When all this was first planned, Vardan High Command decided to put a couple of guys in every High Frontier unit on Earth: UNIT, the Soviet Vodyanoi, the Chinese Foreign Guard. I was supposed to find out what the USAF had down at Edwards. My people were really into it.'

'Your people?'

'Vardan Popular Front. We don't like what's going on in the Vardan military, we just want to explore the Media-sphere, not use it to get into people's heads. And we want an end to the way we abuse our own race, not letting the weaker ones live, killing off the genetic aberrations. We live by discipline, right? Well, too much discipline's a hell of a thing for a beautiful planet like Varda. Everything got worse since we got screwed by the Sontarans. We're gonna change it.'

'So why do you want to go back home?'

'Cos my cover's blown. Your guys now know I'm an alien monster, and the High Command will realize that their man on the CD was roasted by another Vardan.'

'Their man on CD?'

'It's not important. They'll already be wondering why I haven't shopped Broadsword to them. So what are you looking for?'

'A woman in a red dress.'

'Yeah, I get like that sometimes.'

Ace laughed. 'She's in my dreams, she keeps following me around. Hey, stop nodding. She's a Chronovore called Artemis.'

'I think at this point it would be good if I informed you that I can jam Vardan tracking systems. You can think what you want here, they won't hear you.'

'You mean they could hear me before? Damn!'

'Well, listen, if you've been thinking bad thoughts, they would have picked up on it and iced you.'

Ace frowned. 'Yeah. Well, maybe I just confuse them. Artemis is imprisoned in the Monk's TARDIS. I have to free her.'

'Why?'

'Cos she's really lonely and hurt. She needs me. It's the only thing I'm certain about any more.'

Pike struck a pose. 'And the only thing that keeps me sure is my love for a Chronovore. Don't dream it, be it. That could almost be my slogan, right?'

Ace found herself laughing again. 'You're really cool for an alien invader, you know that? We have to find the White Room. That's where I last saw her. Troll this way.'

Pike waited for a moment as Ace set off. 'You and me,' he called, 'I think we're an explosive combination!'

The door of the White Room was open.

'Yeah,' Pike nodded. 'They'll have just left the place like this, no further use for it. No imagination. Do you know, we used to have something like democracy until that deal with the Sontarans went wrong? We've still got a parliament, but it's just a bunch of whackos trying to hold the strings together.'

'Like everywhere else, right? Last time I went in there, I met Artemis. I can't get to her in the Monk's TARDIS, so this is my last chance.' Ace pulled the silver sphere she'd found on the eye of the White Horse out of her pocket. 'I have to get this to her. How do I switch the room on?'

'Ah . . .' Pike opened a panel on the side of the wall and ran a finger down a series of controls. 'This is not user-friendly. Erm, sorry, wait a minute – ' To Ace's amazement he vanished into a blur of light, then reappeared. 'You get problems with using controls, stuff like that. It's easier to go inside and just do it. Good for getting out of ropes, too. It embarrasses me, though.'

The room whirred into life, the plain white interior transforming into a verdant expanse of alien forest.

'Why?' asked Ace, moving cautiously into the room.

'Well, imagine if you were a champion pool player, and you gave it all up to become a priest. Wouldn't you feel a bit self-conscious about playing again?'

Ace smiled. 'Maybe. You're not ashamed of being a Vardan, are you?'

'No, that's not it. It's just that I'd like to be one thing or the other, not trapped between the two. I had a brother . . . well, Pike had a brother . . . hell no, I had a brother who liked dressing up as a woman, right?'

'Never saw the attraction in that,' Ace grinned.

'Well, Thomas kept on worrying about it, even went to some shrink who told him to stop. That made Pike . . . made me really angry. I told him that he should just be what he was, and do it well. But, like, while I'm telling this story, you can hear me getting into difficulties. Alex Pike is a role I really enjoy, you know?'

'Because,' Ace turned to him and touched his lapel, 'Alex Pike isn't a traitor?'

'Yeah, maybe. You get to be a traitor by believing really hard in one thing, and then you find that what you're doing and what you're believing are different. So what do you believe in?'

'Oh, I dunno. Bacon sandwiches.'

'Not with you, sister. Alex is a vegetarian.'

'I used to believe in some kind of justice, that everything was gonna work out even in the end. Good and evil, right?

226

And the Doctor used to sort of sum that up. But then he started to do crap things, messed up my head. So I went away, but that wasn't cool. You know battle, don't you?'

'Yeah.'

'There's no justice in that, either. Not in hugging some tree while your mates, and these blokes you met a day ago, they quickly get to be the only kind of mate you're ever gonna have, get sliced up around you. I was kind of wallowing, just seeing how far down you could get. The orders you're given, the things you're expected to believe . . . I've seen teams of mercenaries just about holding back their laughter when the officers start to wind up the regular units, telling those kids that what they're fighting for is true and right and good. That's why I liked Silurian Earth, great theme park that was. Fighting for the survival of your species. Pretty basic. Pretty easy to believe in that. 'Cept the Doctor muddled that up, too. And for a tiny minute before that, I'd been thinking that everything was gonna be okay again. Me and him and justice.'

'But?'

'Bernice. Bernice bloody Summerfield. Fake this and fake that. She was gonna be a soldier, but she copped off the troop-ship. She didn't want to go, the poor baby. And now she looks down at me 'cos she's still got all these illusions that you can go through life like a hero. She still thinks the Doctor's a hero, despite everything.'

'I guess she's the Doctor's companion now?'

'Yeah. And I'm just a passenger, like the song they were singing in the jeeps. La la la frigging la.'

They'd come to a familiar fork in the path. The two owls stood on a branch, looking balefully down at them.

'Life is hard and then you die. So what are you doing now?'

Ace shook her head, like she was surprised at how far she'd come. Finally she looked up at Pike and sighed. 'Getting my own back.'

The Doctor had his feet up on the ops table, looking

227

round at the cluster of UNIT troops. All of them had a lead loop around their brows.

'We look,' Benny opined, 'like a touring production of Hair.'

'I hope he's not going to tell us to get our kit off,' Benton muttered.

'There'll be no need for that,' the Doctor told him. 'The Vardans can't penetrate lead, it's their Achilles' Heel.'

'Achilles' Heel, calf and most of the leg,' Benny added.

'So, now I've listened to what Carpenter and Mortimus said to each other, I know what I have to do. I took a moment to adjust the Monk's chameleon circuit on the way out, so he shouldn't guess that I've had access to the information. The concert's tomorrow. I know what the Vardans' plan is, and I know how to stop it.'

Benny frowned at his tone of voice. It was like he was ticking mental boxes, trying to convince himself that he'd got everything worked out.

'I don't suppose you're going to tell us?' the Brigadier asked.

'No. Now, Brigadier, do you know how to break into the BBC?'

'Start as a teaboy and work your way up?' suggested Yates. A moment later he added: 'Sorry.'

Ace and Pike had reached the cottage where Artemis had been chained. 'The Monk can't know about this bit of her projection,' Ace explained. 'It's her way of reaching out to me. There are certain things she can't say, so she's worked around it, put the information in my dreams, ages ago. In that room I made when I restructured the TARDIS. In with ... all the other stuff that was locked up.'

'I've heard legends about Chronovores. Aren't they really dangerous to mess with?'

'Yeah. Maybe. Who cares?' Ace went to the cottage door and opened it. The two of them made their way upstairs, and Ace gently pushed open the door to Artemis's room.

And there she was, still. The beautiful woman in the red dress, chained loosely to her bed. 'Kinky,' Pike whispered, to a disapproving look from Ace.

Artemis raised her head slightly. 'You have returned,' she smiled. 'Have you found what you need to free me?'

Ace showed her the sphere. 'Yeah. Cheers for appearing in Danny's dreams too. Wouldn't have figured it out without him. How come you can do that?'

'He sought me out while he slept, wanted to contact me. I am something he needs, a destroying angel. And I, living outside time, do things to my advantage all across the timestream, with the benefit of infinite hindsight.' Artemis's voice was deep and dark, each syllable plucked from the air like fruit off a tree.

Ace's voice took on a wondering quality and Pike suddenly had a vision of her as a little girl, trying to find her way home. 'Can you tell me about the future?'

'You may ask, but I cannot answer.'

'Damn. Part of the deal, right? Okay, so what do I do with this thing?'

'It is a temporal baffle, a primitive early Gallifreyan device. You created it when you rebuilt the Doctor's TARDIS. It will wreck the control systems of the Time Lord called . . .' she relished the name, 'Mortimus. It will free me. Press hard on the surface.'

Ace did so. The sphere illuminated with a regular pulsating light.

Artemis shifted, moving against her chains for the first time. 'It will take some hours to succeed. The fields containing me will become weaker and weaker, until I can free myself. Then . . . we shall have a reckoning.'

Pike sat on the edge of the bed. 'Hey, Granny, what big teeth you've got.'

The Chronovore ran her tongue across her gleaming incisors. 'All the better,' she told him, 'to eat a Time Lord with.'

19

BBC Blitz

'So, whatchermean we're playing this gig?' Kit tweaked at the lead band around his forehead. 'This is the biggest gig in the world, we're not gonna be invited. And why am I dressed up like a bleedin' hippy?'

Plasticine had reformed in Danny's kitchen, Cob already playing paradiddles with the cutlery. It was early morning, and only the promise of international television exposure had been enough to gather them all from their beds.

'Look who's talking,' Danny grinned. 'I've got to hide this under something, or we'll be bottled off.'

Benny spread out a plan in front of them. 'At two o'clock this afternoon, the British leg of Bertram's Live Peace concert kicks off with Paul McCartney and Wings live from Television Centre. Or that's what they think.'

'So what are we going to do?' Danny asked. 'Shoot 'em?'

'Actually . . .' Benny smiled.

At twelve hundred hours precisely, Corporal Claire Tennant threw a grappling iron over the wall surrounding the Blue Peter Garden. She hoisted herself up, glanced around and jumped down the other side. She whistled a complex series of notes, and over the wall behind her came the rest of the Brigadier's troops, all in civvies, plus a ruffled-looking Plasticine. Danny had his hair hidden by a mob cap, shades obscuring his eyes. Kit was wearing a moth-eaten old suit jacket and a ripped T-shirt with the slogan 'Hurt People' spray-painted on it.

'Well,' he'd told Danny. 'I'm makin' an effort, ennei?'

'Hurt people?' Danny had replied. 'What, you mean emotionally?'

'Physically, pal. If we're gonna be on TV, I'm getting right behind this punk business. Look at you, you oughta be carrying a bag with "swag" written on it.'

The soldiers and the band crept past the Blue Peter pond. 'Hey!' whispered Danny, glancing at the fish. 'Anarchy! Anybody got a spray can?'

'Not now,' Bernice muttered. She had tried to reconcile the needs of combat and performance with a pair of leather trousers and a vest, but she couldn't get over the feeling that she was squeaking as she walked.

There was a pair of double doors that led into Television Centre proper, green-painted and with no commissionaire, only a gardener pushing a barrow. Broadsword and Plasticine walked straight past him and, out of the brilliant sunlight, found themselves in a dull corridor. 'The security at the front of the building will be tight,' the Brigadier told his troops. 'And we might get stopped on our way through the corridors, so – ' He handed out a series of laminated badges. 'The Doctor made these last night. Apparently they're copies of one he acquired when he was a guest on Nationwide during that General Carrington business. Ordnance – ' he patted the kitbag slung over his shoulder, 'is not to be shown until I give the order. Clear?'

'Yeah, well, mate, I think we should have guns too!' Danny exclaimed. 'If this is the revolution proper, then we ought to be prepared.'

'This is not the revolution proper – ' The Brigadier's voice dropped to a whisper as a woman with a clipboard passed by. 'This is a minor military action intended to restore public order.'

'Then why are we taking part?' Danny spread his arms. 'Why are we helping a bunch of pigs with some weird plan I don't understand?'

'Because – ' Cob pointed out, 'we're going to get global TV coverage. Then we can have all the anarchy we want.'

Danny thought about it for a moment. 'Okay,' he decided.

Robert Bertram was walking around the various sets in the Top Of The Pops studio, ticking things off on a clipboard he carried. 'Oh, Major Carpenter!' he called to the UNIT man who was busy briefing his men on the various positions they were to take up around the building. 'Can I have a word?'

Carpenter frowned and walked over. 'What is it, Mortimus?'

'Robert, please!' The Time Lord drew him aside. 'I was just wondering if you've seen my young companion this morning, or indeed if you can – ' he bent his head closer, 'sense her.'

Carpenter concentrated, communicating with other humanoid Vardans across the globe. 'No,' he concluded. 'We've lost her completely. She's either off-planet, in one of your TARDIS capsules, or – '

'Please don't say it. I've grown very fond of her. She called me last night, sounding alarmed, and didn't appear at our appointed rendezvous. I'm most concerned.'

'You're showing unusual interest in a human, aren't you? What is she to you?'

The Monk paused, considering. 'She reminds me of myself,' he concluded. 'Still, what you say about the TARDIS is true, and I hadn't thought of it. Perhaps she's somewhere in my craft, or in . . .' He searched the pockets of his suit. 'Oh, now where did I put that . . .?'

'What's the situation with the Government?' Carpenter asked. 'Have they been persuaded to use your pacification ray?'

'Well, after an entire evening of being exposed to your particular brand of television, they finally came round to our way of thinking. Though even now, some of them are uncertain. Do you know, I think they must have quite some integrity. Odd, for politicians.'

Carpenter raised an eyebrow. 'Unique. So, from fourteen hundred hours onwards, the plan will go ahead. There is no Doctor, to hinder our glorious conquest?'

'Indeed not. He's safely locked away. Believe me, I've thought of everything.'

'You'd better have,' Carpenter smiled. 'I've seen the large pile of gold that we're paying you.'

'Oh, I'm not in this for the money,' the Monk exclaimed. 'This is my art!'

'Fine. Then we'll take the gold back to – '

'No, no, I'll accept it. As a . . . gesture of appreciation.'

Through the studio doors strode a BBC producer, busily flicking through props sheets and looking around in pride. Five different themed sets had been built, each of them representing a different pantomime. Pan's People were in make-up, the electricians were busy, and Paul McCartney had just finished his sound check. Everything was going to plan.

He strode up to Robert Bertram and happily handed him a copy of the finished schedule. 'I'm surprised and delighted,' he told him. 'You've got everybody you asked for.'

'I have great powers of persuasion.'

'Why did you choose panto as a theme?'

'Well, it's family entertainment, isn't it? Family values, Mum and Dad and the children sitting at home watching something wholesome and jolly.' The Monk rubbed his hands together in glee.

'So, no hanky-panky? I'll tell Benny Hill to be careful with the links on the American leg. We've got a whole panel of operators set up, ready to take pledges for the Peace Foundation. And the satellite link-ups have been checked out. Each act here will get about half an hour, and then we'll go by satellite to catch the parallel concerts going on in San Francisco, Rome and Melbourne. Personally I'm looking forward to the Stones finishing it all off at midnight. I'm sure the audience is going to stay tuned.'

Bertram patted him on the shoulder. 'If they turn over, they'll miss so much.'

* * *

Ace and Pike watched as Artemis struggled against her bonds. The chains were actually stretching, the metal glowing red-hot.

'She'll set fire to the bed,' Pike whispered. 'Are you sure about this?'

'Completely,' Ace nodded. 'Only thing I am sure about.'

Broadsword were mingling with a crowd of teenagers in an entrance hallway, trying to look like pop fans.

'Yeah,' Kit was telling a girl in platforms and serious eye make-up, 'I really like Jethro Tull too. What's yer phone number?'

The doors at the end of the hallway opened and a floor manager, earpiece and mike in place, called out to the crowd. 'Okay kids, we'll be ready in a sec. No bottles, no food and no metal objects.' He pointed to a security man, who was holding a metal detector.

The Brigadier patted his kitbag. 'Plastic,' he told Benny.

'Just as well. Have you tested those things?'

'Oh yes, Miss Summerfield. We tested them on a platoon of Spetsnaz troops on the wrong side of the Berlin wall, if I recall.'

The doors were opened, and a group of security men carefully let the crowd in. Metal detectors were passed over Broadsword's kitbags with no trouble, and the whole audience were allowed to file into the studio. The soldiers weren't quite prepared for the teenage rush to the front, and managed to get the third row of seats.

'You can tell he's doing this on the cheap,' Benny opined during the warm-up act, a comedian called Kenny Lynch who seemed to have some odd ideas concerning racial matters. 'At least Geldof managed to get Wembley Stadium.'

'What, Bobby Geldof?' Doyle asked. 'When did he ever amount to anything?'

'Never mind. Oh look, something's happening on the Robin Hood stage.'

The house lights went down, and the crowd began to chant and stamp their feet. The heat was already beginning to build, a studio not being the most air-conditioned of places at the best of times. Above each stage a huge video screen had been set up, with a logo depicting the Earth in the palm of a hand.

'Three . . . two . . . one . . . go studio, we're live.' The producer waved a hand decisively. 'And cue Bob!'

A single spotlight illuminated one of the pantomime stages, and out onto it strode Robert Bertram, clad in a simple monk's habit. The crowd applauded. He turned and beamed to the cameras. 'Ladies, gentlemen, and all of you children at home, welcome to Live Peace. I'm Robert Bertram, this is my dream. A dream that could change the lives of a great many people across the globe. We're talking here to an international audience of over a billion people. Throughout the day, you'll see details of who to call in your area to pledge any sum, no matter how small, to the Peace Foundation, an organization devoted to finding new solutions to the problems currently affecting our cities. But you don't want to listen to a boring old man like me, do you?'

The crowd howled.

'No,' the Monk turned, raising his hand in welcome. 'You want . . . Paul McCartney and Wings!' The curtains drew back and the Monk scampered off-stage.

The audience jumped to their feet. Broadsword stood up too, quickly checking the items that the Brigadier had passed along the line at knee level.

Paul, Linda, Denny and the rest of the boys were clad in Lincoln Green, standing before a backdrop of trees and bushes. The applause was thunderous.

'How you doing?' asked Paul, good-naturedly, giving the crowd a thumbs-up signal. 'This is called – '

Backstage, Major Carpenter took a signalling device from his pocket. The Monk put a hand on his shoulder. 'Now!' he whispered. 'The final move!' Together, they pressed the button.

In their spacecraft on the lunar surface, a line of uniformed Vardans punched their chests in salute. As one, they became blazes of light and faded into an aerial that descended from the ceiling. From out of the oily globe of the Mediasphere monitor a steady stream of lights followed them, thousands of Vardans transmitting themselves up into the antennae that stood on the upper surfaces of the Vardan ships. Their electronic forms leapt across space and intercepted the Priory communications satellite, gathering inside the batteries and circuitry of the orbiting form, communicating on a subatomic level, sharing the impending moment of final triumph.

The Brigadier jumped to his feet. 'Chap with Wings, five rounds rapid!'

Broadsword snapped into firing stance, and spattered the stage with darts from their plastic dartguns. The band fell, knocked cold. The audience screamed and panicked, knocking over chairs and clambering over each other in a desperate dash for the exits.

Carpenter pulled a walkie-talkie from his belt. 'All units! Emergency in the studio area! Move in!'

The Monk shook his head. 'Pitiful. What do they hope to achieve?'

Benny grabbed Danny's hand and hauled him through the crowd. The rest of the band struggled up onto the stage behind them and prised instruments out of the unconscious musicians' hands.

Benny grabbed a mike. 'We're Plasticine!' she shouted. 'And this is a song about freedom of speech and action. It's called Dissent Is Good.'

Kit, Cob and Danny glanced at each other and struck up a high, keening tone with a powerful, driving drumbeat and bassline.

Many miles above the planet Earth, a finger flicked out and hit the play button on an old ghetto blaster. The reverberating rhythm, the same noise that Plasticine were creating, blared out. The TARDIS was parked next to the Priory communications satellite. Thick cables connected the two vessels.

* * *

Major Carpenter reeled as he ran down a side corridor, his head dissolving into a plume of light and fire. After a moment he recovered his concentration, and made his head reform into humanoid shape. Around the corner sprinted a group of UNIT soldiers. 'Follow me!' he shouted to them. 'For the glory of Varda!'

The initial wave of Vardan assault troops sped at light-speed into Earth's atmosphere. Then they richocheted back to the satellite. Disorientated, the aliens felt their internal structure begin to spread out across the length of the beam.

Up in the gallery the producer was staring, horrified, at Plasticine. 'Stop that noise!' he shouted. 'Cut the satellite link!'

'I wouldn't if I were you,' Mike Yates grabbed the hand reaching towards the power button, and flashed a pass. 'UNIT. We're here to save the world. There might be a firefight in a minute, but – '

'In that case, we'll be going, if you don't mind. Our contract doesn't – '

'But the outside of the building will be under attack from hundreds of invading aliens.'

The producer glanced at his crew. 'I think that I have been persuaded to stay.'

Mortimus was hurrying down a darkened corridor, looking over his shoulder at intervals. Tapping on his watch had been no good; something was interfering with his control of the satellite. 'Well, they won't get away with this,' he muttered. 'All I have to do is get up there and change the frequency . . .' He opened a props cupboard ahead of him, diving inside.

He ran straight to his console and activated the scanner. High above the Earth, a tight beam ran between the communications satellite and the uplink in the studio. Beside the satellite, the icon of a TARDIS blinked.

The Monk stared.

'No. It isn't him . . . it can't be him. He's dead.' He pulled his laser gun from his sleeve. 'It's some child from the Academy, some jealous outsider . . . or a Shayde.' He started punching co-ordinates into the console.

There was a regular beating on the studio doors. Broadsword had barricaded them. The place was deserted now, apart from Plasticine playing the harmonic pattern they'd established, over and over again.

The Brigadier settled himself behind a barricade, glancing at the flimsy dartgun he held in irritation. 'Is the satellite link intact?' he asked.

'Yes, sir!' called Mike Yates from the control booth. 'We're not broadcasting to the world any more, but we're still hooked up.'

'Good . . .' Doyle had hidden the unconscious rock stars behind the barricades. The rest of Broadsword were poised to repel the Vardans when they broke through. At least they knew that the guns would work on the aliens, if Pike was anything to go by.

'Doors won't hold much longer, sir,' called Benton, who was stacking chairs into rows.

Kit and Danny were playing with intense concentration, the steady beat of the wave vibration increasing in speed every moment. Benny could only watch them in desperation.

'How much longer?' Kit shouted. 'The buggers'll be through 'ere in a minute!'

Benny glanced at her watch. 'Another ten minutes or so, the Doctor said,' she called.

'Good way to go, eh, my brothers?' called Danny. 'Dying on stage, that'll be a first!'

The Monk's TARDIS materialized inside the darkened console room of another such craft. Mortimus stepped out, his gun poised in front of him. His breath billowed in the sudden cold. That was strange. This TARDIS was as cold as his had been. 'Where are you?' he shouted, his voice on the edge of disintegration. 'Who are you?'

'Who indeed?' A shape was moving in the darkness. 'Who am I?'

The Monk snapped off a shot. A bolt of light reduced a roundel to liquid. The figure had stepped out of the way. 'Show yourself!' the Monk screamed. 'If it's you, Magnus, if it's the gold you want –'

Laughter echoed around the console room. A whisper rounded the corners of the Monk's TARDIS. 'I'm imprisoning the Vardans in a standing wave-formation. Between Earth and the satellite. I'm reducing it in length until they're trapped in the satellite itself. I tried something similar at Stonehenge, but I only had a moment at your controls. I didn't realize I needed a particular waveform. A particular series of chords. I got the idea from that conversation you had with Major Carpenter, in the wings at the first Plasticine concert. A conversation that I finally overheard. Do you remember what he said to you?'

The Monk lowered his gun a fraction, an expression of exasperation on his face. 'So it is you. He said: "some of this so-called music reminds me of the sonic weapons we used in the Vardan Civil War". The talkative fool. But I knew you'd overhear that on the LP, that's why I made sure it was only on CD!'

The voice came from another part of the room. 'You think you're a player of games. You can't even answer basic questions. Who am I? I can understand how you might be confused. I'm not sure myself, any more. Am I Ka Faraq Gatri, the Destroyer of Worlds? Am I somebody who could extinguish a universe with a flick of my finger?'

The Monk was silent, his ears pricked up for any clue as to where the voice was coming from.

'You've pushed me so far, Mortimus... You have pushed me... so far. You've taken me to the brink of despair, taken my friends, my companion. Why didn't you take my life? What stopped you?'

'Doctor? Is it really you?'

'Is it me? Or is it you? You wanted me to feel exactly what you felt. You wanted me to freeze in the darkness.

239

Freeze. You think that I've never felt that way. You think that I live in the sunlight. And you were jealous of that?' A sudden, half-choked laugh broke from the darkness. 'You're jealous of what I am?'

The Monk spun and fired again. The blast sliced straight through something, rags of burnt material spinning off into the darkness. There was a moment of silence, the noise of the blast ringing through the empty corridors of the TARDIS.

When the voice returned, it had an almost reverential edge of wonder to it. 'This place used to be home. Used to be a place that, if you were scared, you could come back to and be safe. And you destroyed it. You lost its heart in a tar pit. You did similar things to me. How far back do we go, you and I, Mortimus? Were you influencing me when I destroyed Skaro? When I fell into my own pit? When I hurt Ace . . . when I hurt her so badly?'

The Monk straightened, a knifey smile dawning on his face. 'You'd like to think that, wouldn't you? You'd like me to take on all your sins? I'm sorry, Doctor. That was you. All the time.'

There was another moment of silence. Then: 'I know. I shouldn't have hoped. That's my problem, you see, I tend to see things in black and white. There is a part of me, Mortimus, that would like to see you suffer for all you've done. But what could I do to you? What punishment could be enough for the agonies you've inflicted on me? What revenge would be enough to make up for Earth, for Ace . . . for the children?'

Mortimus laughed. 'We're exactly the same, then! We're both just time meddlers, only you like to think you're superior! Is that why you don't like to give your companions choices, Doctor, because you're afraid they'll see what you really are?' His eyes narrowed on the movement in the darkness. 'Because when they know what you are, they'll leave you?'

There was silence.

Then a roar.

The Monk turned too late, his gun slammed upwards

by a small body that forced him up against the door of his TARDIS. The weapon spun from his hand, and he gasped at what he saw.

The Doctor had a laser-burn hole in the middle of his pullover. But the flesh beneath was intact. 'What are you?' the Monk gabbled. 'What are you going to do to me?'

'This!' the Doctor roared, his accent spitting the word in incoherent rage.

From his jacket, he jerked out a vicious-looking knife. The one Ace had used on him.

'You won't . . . you can't . . .'

The Doctor plunged the knife into the Monk's chest.

Carpenter stared at the UNIT troopers with him. Some were reeling, some were clutching at their heads in confusion, a few had blazed into their true Vardan form, only to vanish with a jerk of lightning motion. He could feel it himself, the strange tug away from this physical form, the current that was threatening to sweep him off his feet, that was getting stronger every second.

'We're being drawn into the beam! And we were so close!' he bellowed. 'Smash the door! Smash it down, and the glorious Vardan army can still triumph!'

The troopers swung the table they were using as a battering ram back, and slammed it into the door with one desperate effort.

The door burst open.

Blood spurted from the wound.

The Monk fell to his knees, reeling, scrabbling at his chest. But why was there no pain? He put his fingers to the place of impact, and found . . . no wound. Only a red liquid.

The Doctor stood up, calm again. He put his finger on the end of the blade and pushed it back into the hilt with a little squeak of a spring. A spurt of theatrical gore sprang from the weapon. 'They say history repeats itself, Mortimus. The first time as tragedy, the second time as farce. This time, it's panto.'

Mortimus looked up at him, aghast. 'But that means that she . . . that she . . .'

'Yes.' The Doctor glared down at him with contempt. 'She made her choice.' He threw aside the theatrical weapon. 'Checkmate.'

Claire Tennant watched, appalled, as the Vardan troops burst into the room, their weapons swinging towards the band on-stage. Broadsword fired a salvo of darts and a few of them fell, but there were too many of them, they were going to –

The Brigadier stood up. 'Halt!' he bellowed.

Carpenter swung round, staring at his troops. Some of them had actually stopped, were blinking at this human in confusion. 'No, we must – '

'Attention!' the Brigadier shouted.

Kit, his eyes wide open, watched as the Vardans came to attention, haltingly, clumsily, like little boys pretending to be soldiers. The piece he was playing seemed to be coming to a climax, one long note that sustained . . . sustained . . . not long now . . .

Carpenter reeled as darts splattered across his uniform. Snarling, he swung his gun up at the Brigadier. 'In the name of the glorious – '

'Sir!' Tennant yelled, 'he's – '

'Shoulder-arms!' bellowed the Brigadier.

The bullets caught him across the chest and shoulder, spinning him backwards and over into the chairs.

A loop of blood slapped across Tennant.

Carpenter turned to the stage.

Danny hit a final, ringing chord.

Doyle leapt at Carpenter.

The air solidified.

Carpenter's smile froze into a rictus of anger.

Then he was a blaze of light.

Then he was gone.

The music stopped. Doyle hit the wall where Carpenter had been.

Danny dropped his hand, staring at the callouses on his fingers. 'This machine . . .' he whispered, 'kills fascists.'

Within the satellite, the entire Vardan army bounced back and forth in a narrow wave-form, buzzing and screeching with frustration.

Across the globe, people staggered as a clasping hand let go of their minds. Families watching their televisions slumped and groaned, clutching their heads. Everywhere, violence and disturbance eased.

Benny and Yates dashed over to where the Brigadier lay. He was being cradled in Tennant's arms. His face was absolutely white, a thin trail of blood at the corner of his lip. A few of the recovering UNIT men stumbled over too. Most of those that had burst through the door had been Vardan imposters, but a few human originals remained. They surrounded their commander, forming an agonized circle around him.

The Brigadier reached up and took Mike Yates' hand. He seemed to pause a moment, gathering the strength to say the words. 'Are the children safe, Captain Yates?'

Yates took the hand and pressed it to his cheek. 'Yes sir. We won.'

'Very good. Carry on.'

And then he died.

The Doctor's head jerked, suddenly, like he'd been slapped across the face. 'Something terrible . . .' he whispered. 'No. No, it can't happen. Not now.'

Shaking, the Monk regained his feet. 'What's the matter, Doctor? Are you hurt? Are you injured?' He tapped a control on his watch, and grinned. 'What did you say a moment ago? Checkmate? I think you're the one who's lost. Because you're the villain, not me. You!' He hit a button and an image appeared on the screen: the Brigadier lying in a pool of blood, soldiers standing around him. 'You caused that to happen.'

The Doctor stared at the screen. 'Alistair.'

'You know that I have control over a Chronovore. That's how I led you through all those merry games. I have power over the universe itself.'

The Doctor's voice was distant. 'Yes. I know.'

The Monk spread his arms wide. 'So you see, I can just reverse this little victory of yours. All you've caused me is irritation, and yes, some pain. But I can make a universe where all of your interference never occurred. I can wipe the slate clean, wipe it all clean with Ace too. But perhaps I won't have to go to all that trouble. Perhaps we can come to . . . an arrangement.'

The Doctor looked at him sadly, and was silent.

'Let us level the playing field,' the Monk continued, pacing as he thought. 'Release the Vardan invasion force, and I'll have the Brigadier brought back to life. Simple as that.'

The Doctor waited for a full minute before speaking. When he did, his voice was absolutely level. 'No. He'd think that was far too high a price to pay for his life. He's dead. Let him rest in peace.'

'Let him pay the price for your errors?'

The Doctor raised his hands in exasperation. 'Erase all this then, start again! I'll defeat you next time. I'll always find a way to defeat you!' His voice rose to a shout, and Mortimus took a step backwards. Something inside the Doctor had found a strange freedom. 'How many times, Mortimus? How long will it take you to realize that this . . . game . . . is futile?!'

'I could simply cause you never to be born.'

'There'll be others.'

'I could blackmail you with the life or torture of every companion you ever had.'

'They'll bear it.'

'I could show you every aspect of your personal pain.'

'Then do it! Do it!' The words tumbled from the Doctor's mouth. 'But don't tell me that you're somehow better than me. Ace never betrayed me. She betrayed you. Call your Chronovore. Get it over with.' He stared Mortimus straight in the eye. 'Repeat these games time after time, she'll never stay with you, you'll never be able to win. Whatever you do, I have my TARDIS. I have my companions, I have my name. I am the Doctor . . . and you're not!'

Mortimus' face creased into a roar of pure hatred. He hit the buttons on his watch furiously. 'This game is over!' he screamed. 'I'll make her my companion! I'll make her love me!'

The chains snapped.

Artemis sat up and flexed her fingers. She smiled a wicked smile at Ace and Pike.

'Thank you . . .' she murmured. 'Please . . . join me for dinner.'

She snapped her fingers.

And the universe stopped.

20

Broken Heart

The Doctor and the Monk stood in blank space.

'Oh no . . .' The Monk jabbed frantically at his watch. 'This shouldn't have happened. What's going on?'

The Doctor stared at the whiteness ahead of them. From it, an opulent black staircase was unfolding. 'Quiet . . .' he muttered. 'Your beast has got loose.'

A foot clad in a shiny black shoe appeared on the top stair, and then another. Artemis, clad in a glittering black bodysuit and a crown of thorns and diamonds, stepped elegantly down towards them, her red nails outstretched in what might have been a gesture of welcome. The air around the blades at the end of her fingers crackled as individual molecules disintegrated. A great wash of ozone air flowed down the stairs with her.

'So . . .' she said, her voice like velvet. 'There you are, Mortimus . . .'

The Monk fell to his knees. 'Mercy, I beg of you! Mercy! I'll stop, I'll go into a retreat and spend my days in contemplation. Torture me, condemn me to a life of pain and despair, but – '

Artemis made a gesture, and the Monk didn't have a mouth. 'Really . . .' she asked, 'why do you think that I would be so . . . merciful?'

In the middle of all this, somehow quiet in the face of the storm, the Doctor had been thinking about his old friend. Alistair had once cut a rose from his garden, in a future that now would never happen, a future where Ace had been young and hopeful. He'd pinned it to the Doctor's lapel.

'What is it?' the Doctor had asked.

'Hope And Glory,' the Brigadier had told him. 'Now there'll be part of that TARDIS of yours that is forever England.'

So narrow-minded. English as treason, and totally incapable of it. And now Mortimus had cut him off, before he was due, denied him that late and peaceful death in bed. Maybe he would have preferred it this way.

He ought to let the Monk suffer.

But he knew what the Brigadier would have said about unnecessary suffering.

The Doctor stepped forward, putting himself between Artemis and the Monk. He looked up at the Chronovore, a rather silly-looking and scruffy little man gazing up at the power of a goddess.

'Stop,' he said.

Artemis stared at him. 'Stop?'

'I know. He's the man who tormented me. He's my enemy, but –'

'Never mind that!' Artemis flicked a nail, and the three of them were standing on the Embankment, the Thames flowing below them. 'Never say "stop" to a Chronovore, Doctor! It . . . annoys us.' Pedestrians were stood still, frozen in a moment, and the sunlight had a golden, echoing quality. 'Individual photons,' Artemis said, noticing the Time Lord's interest. 'Halted. We can only see because I think we should. The year is nineteen hundred and seventy six, by this world's calender. All sorts of new things are beginning. This place is waking from a long winter . . . and it is heading into a terrible autumn. But in this brief summer, there is such beauty.'

'Artemis,' the Doctor began, 'you are very powerful, and this planet is fragile –'

'I've been imprisoned so long, fed on a minor trail of chronons from some distant collapsar. I am hungry and surrounded by new life . . .' The Chronovore pointed at a man in shirt-sleeves, and he vanished into a flutter of dust. The grains spread through the sunlight for a moment, silver on gold, and then they were sucked away into nothing. 'And you tell me that I shouldn't eat? Really. Such sweet and tiny lives, these humans have. Barely a morsel.'

The Monk's eyes were bulging above his smooth face.

'There's no reason for you to do this,' the Doctor said carefully, controlling his urge to leap forward and argue. 'You could go back to the vortex, satisfy your hunger – '

'Yes, I could do that.' Artemis disintegrated another frozen passer-by, a girl in chains and boots. 'But why take the trouble? You do know that these humans will die anyway, don't you? There's no point in getting upset about it.'

The Doctor clenched his fists together by his sides. 'You have such intelligence, such knowledge. Can't you accept that we have different standards from you? Please . . . don't feed here.'

'I'm just exploring, I won't eat the planet or anything. Probably. Perhaps I should eat both of you Time Lords. You're much better fare, if I may say so. And you irk me, every time I meet you. Not like that wonderful girl who rescued me.' The Doctor began to speak, but Artemis held up a hand. 'No. Don't interrupt me. Time Lords seem to think they own time, which is like . . .' She looked around, licking her lips, eyes rolling, as if searching all language for a metaphor. 'Like the fish in that river, who think they own water. But at least those fish can claim ignorance, Gallifreyan, at least – ' she spun around, eyes burning with sudden inexplicable violence. 'At least they have never heard of fishermen!' She slapped the air with her hand, and the Monk's cheek had a hook through it, piercing the flesh twice. The wound looked old, the flesh grown scabbed around the metal.

The Monk's face contorted in a silent scream.

'I know he imprisoned you. But you don't have to be cruel. You could show compassion, prove that you use your power with wisdom – ' The Doctor stopped. 'Or you could just stop using your power, take the universe as you find it. Be surprised.'

'No, no, no . . .' Artemis raised her hands impatiently.

'These are just words. Mortimus' pain is only beginning. It is a strain, Doctor, keeping together what mortals call a personality. The concept is alien to me, because it is a thing of time. Any decisions I make will simply be made. You cannot persuade ... the hurricane, or sway the ... rain. And these metaphors, this language you use, is irritating in itself. I want to feast here, so I will.' She raised her hands to the sky, her face cracking with a vast, all-consuming grin. 'I'll eat all this and then both of you.'

The Doctor raised a finger. 'Artemis, listen to my words, grant me leave to speak.'

Artemis ground her teeth together. Ungraciously, she mimed the most offhand of curtsies. 'Then I grant you a moment, state your case.' She glanced up. 'Unless you've got a Containment Unit. Then, rules or no rules, you're supper.'

The Doctor jumbled his fingers, pondering. Finally, he said. 'Show me the moment in the TARDIS just now. The moment when I was shot.'

Artemis moved her head, and the three of them were standing in the darkness of the console room. The Monk snapped off a shot, a brilliant laser burst flickering across the room.

'Stop,' the Doctor told Artemis. 'Slow it down.'

In brilliant, strobing light, the Monk brought his gun up and fired. The beam stretched across the room and touched something on the other side. The Doctor. Illuminated for a brief moment, he threw up his hands. The beam caught him straight in the chest. His expression changed from pain to amazement, and he dived aside once more.

The scene came to an end, and they were in the void again.

'Now that,' the Chronovore raised a finger to her chin, 'is interesting.'

The Doctor pulled vaguely at the circular burn mark at the centre of his pullover. 'Yes. I should be dead. As far as Mortimus knew, that was a killing charge, correct?'

The Monk nodded mutely, making affirmative noises.

'So there are three ways that it could have happened. I could have gone back in time to set it up, in that way of mine . . . put a blank cartridge in the pistol, something like that . . .'

Artemis shook her head slowly. 'That is impossible. I have decided to eat you.'

'Or perhaps Mortimus here arranged it, as some subtle part of his plan.'

Mortimus shook his head frantically. Artemis gestured again, and his mouth reappeared. The hook vanished at the same moment. 'No, no, nothing to do with me.'

'Then there's only one possibility left.' The Doctor smiled. 'Artemis, you rescued me yourself.'

Artemis raised an eyebrow. 'And why should I do that?'

'Ah, because you're merciful and wise.'

The Chronovore paused. 'That much is true. Very well, there seems no other explanation. I'll do that now.' She concentrated for a moment. 'There, I saved you from the blast. There's symmetry to that, since it was my power that allowed the reptile Morka to kill you.'

'And thank you also for not harming Earth.'

'I . . . did that?'

'Of course. What would be the point in saving my life and then crushing my spirit? That would be foolish. Pointless. You're wise, remember, not fickle.'

The Chronovore paused, a smile playing on her features. 'I seem to have acted . . . most mercifully.'

'Because you are merciful, that's the nature of your personality here, as you're discovering.' The Doctor slapped a fist into his palm triumphantly. 'And that's why you returned the Brigadier to life!'

Artemis twitched her eyebrow, and Lethbridge-Stewart spun once more under the impact of Carpenter's shells. The Doctor winced.

'And why did I do that?' she asked.

The Doctor walked a slow circle around the Monk, thinking. 'Because . . . killing the Brigadier was another action of this traitor here. This unworthy gaoler who tormented both you and I . . .'

'Doctor – ' the Monk muttered.

'Shut up. His actions are obviously not something that . . .' he caught sight of the look in Artemis' eye, 'you . . . could . . . tolerate?'

Artemis threw her head back and burst out laughing.

'Good,' the Doctor smiled. 'We can be amusing, us mortals. If you'll just – '

Artemis was shaking her head. 'No, no, you've gone much too far. The first two premises I can accept, there is evidence that I have done these things, in physics and in my nature. But the last? No, I have no reason. What is the death of a mortal to me?'

The Doctor stared at her desperately. 'But you must, I know him in the future, I know how he's supposed to die – '

'That isn't enough. The future is now changed, Oh – ' Artemis pricked up her ears, listening. 'My dear rescuer is calling. Wait,' She waved her hand.

Ace and Pike appeared beside the two Time Lords.

'My dear . . .' Artemis stroked Ace's hair. 'Thank you so much, I wasn't going to neglect you, I just wanted to finish off my business with these two.'

Ace stared at the Doctor. 'Flip. You got out.'

'Sorry.' The Doctor lowered his hands to his sides, his face impassive.

Ace seemed about to say something to him, but changed her mind. She turned to Artemis. 'You said I'd get a wish,' she said. 'I've thought about it, and I know what it's gonna be.'

'I'm sure I can guess,' the Chronovore smiled. 'You want what this charlatan here promised you. You want to go and live happily ever after with your Jan.'

'I'm not a charlatan,' Mortimus said. He walked up to Ace, a pained expression on his face, searching for any sign of the bond that had existed between them. 'My child, I would have given you exactly what you wanted, you know I would.'

'Yeah . . .' Ace nodded. 'Yeah, I know. But the thing is, I was looking at Jan when he died, right at him. There

251

was no fade-out, no sudden teleportation bit, no gimmicks. I saw him die.' Her voice had risen a notch, like something was about to explode out of her. 'Which means he's dead. He's dead. He's really, finally, dead.'

'That's not the way it works – '

'It is for me. Don't tempt me.' She grabbed the Monk by his collar. 'How do you sleep at night, knowing that you've given people all these options, all this false hope? How do you live with yourself?'

The Monk met her angry gaze. 'You were happy with me.'

'No I wasn't! I was just going along with you, trying to find out how to free Artemis, trying to find out what your plan was, to see what I could do to stop it!'

'That's not true.' Mortimus' expression froze. 'You know that isn't true.'

Ace let go, and turned away. 'Yes it is. You gotta be certain about some things.'

Mortimus sat down, with some dignity, and put his head in his hands. He started to rock back and forth silently. After a moment, the Doctor reached out and put a hand on his shoulder. 'Hush,' he said.

'So . . .' Artemis smiled. 'This wish of yours.'

'We saw what happened to the Brigadier,' Ace told her.

'Yeah,' Pike nodded. 'Great TV you got in that cottage, better than cable.'

'So . . .' Ace turned to the Doctor. 'You and he are old mates. D'you want me to use my wish to save him?'

The Doctor looked at her for a moment, and saw something in her face that he hadn't even realized he'd missed. He saw seven hundred and fifty, going on seventeen. He smiled, and shook his head slowly. 'No. Get Jan back. Go home. Be happy. That's only justice, after what I did to you. You lost your lover, I lost my best friend.'

Ace bit her lip. 'But you'd say that just to make me feel guilty. You know just what buttons to press. You always – '

The Doctor took her hand. 'Stop.'

Ace saw the look on his face, and squared her shoulders. 'All right. All right. I'm gonna end this now.' She turned back to the Chronovore. 'This is my wish. That creep Carpenter doesn't shoot the Brigadier. I'm there. I grab the gun. I save him.'

Artemis stared at her. 'That a mortal could be so . . . clever!' she spat.

'Cheers,' Ace grinned.

Pike raised a finger. 'Now, wait a minute, this isn't good for me, guys, this'll leave me in the – '

Artemis waved her hand petulantly.

Carpenter reeled as darts splattered across his uniform. Snarling, he swung his gun up at the Brigadier. 'In the name of the glorious – '

'Sir!' Tennant yelled, 'he's – '

'Shoulder-arms!' bellowed the Brigadier.

Ace burst through the door, and a cluster of flechettes sent the weapon flying from Carpenter's hands.

He glared at her. 'Vardan Army – ' he spat.

And he vanished in a blur of light.

Danny dropped his hand, staring at the callouses on his fingers. 'This machine . . .' he whispered, 'kills fascists.'

'Great line,' Ace told him.

'I thought so,' he grinned back.

The Brigadier helped Ace to her feet. 'You must be Ace. Glad you could make it to the party.'

'Wouldn't have missed it,' Ace sighed, 'for the world.'

The Doctor and the Monk had appeared back in the Doctor's TARDIS. The Monk sat, defeated, at the Doctor's feet. 'She betrayed me . . .' he whispered. 'And you . . . you saved me!'

'Ace saved you.' The Doctor helped him up. 'By choosing to stop Carpenter in that particular way, she made sure that she wasn't in a position to release Artemis in the first place. She obviously thinks a great deal of you.'

'Perhaps . . .' Mortimus felt the line of his chin, where the hook had penetrated his flesh.

The Doctor sighed. The anger he'd felt towards the Monk had vanished. All that was left was a great tiredness.

'We have a lot in common, Mortimus. Never mind the Vardans, this game's over. We don't have to play another one. Let's talk, communicate. We shouldn't be enemies . . .'

'No . . .' The Monk leant on the corner of his TARDIS, apparently considering. 'Tell me, where would Artemis be now?'

'She's still imprisoned in there.' The Doctor tapped the shell of the Monk's craft, and frowned. 'Probably.'

'In that case . . . I'll be seeing you again!' The Monk shoved the Doctor aside and dived into his ship, slamming the door behind him.

As the TARDIS dematerialized, above the rending and groaning of space-time, an insane, girlish laughter could be heard. As the final phantom of the craft died away, the laughter mingled with a long, agonized scream.

'Probably not,' whispered the Doctor.

21

Pure Soap Opera, I May Cry

On a brilliant summer's afternoon, the forces of Broadsword, Plasticine, Doyle, the Brigadier, the Doctor and his companions gathered in the bar of the Valiant Trooper.

Benny raised a finger. 'One, two, three, and – '

'There's just one thing I don't understand!' chorused the band.

'Yes . . .' The Doctor took a long sip from his glass of brandy. 'I think it's time I filled in the gaps. But first, Brigadier, I gather you've resolved your differences with the authorities.'

'Indeed I have.' Lethbridge-Stewart was sipping from his pint, looking dapper, as always, in civvies. 'There were several Vardans working at Cabinet Office level. When they vanished, it was quite an easy matter to convince old Shirley that she'd made a mistake. All UNIT personnel have now been returned to operative status. Mind you, we're having to arrange counselling for some of the more advanced cases of mind-control.'

Ace had been sitting next to the Doctor all afternoon, just looking at him. Every now and then she would shake her head, as if she couldn't quite believe that they'd all got through this alive. Or maybe it was just that she couldn't believe the choice that she'd made.

Now she looked up. 'Blimey! Look who's here!'

Captain Alex Pike was standing in the doorway, his hands held high. 'Okay, okay, don't shoot me.'

The Doctor tapped a barstool seat with his palm. 'Come and sit down. I'm surprised to see you. I was planning to rescue you today. I thought that you'd be with the rest of

255

the Vardans, trapped on board the satellite, now that Ace didn't release Artemis.' He noticed the Brigadier and Benton looking at each other in puzzlement. 'Time things,' he told them. 'Don't worry about it.'

Pike sat down on the appointed stool. 'I don't know why you say she released that thing. It was me, I did all that stuff. I let Artemis go.'

Ace slapped her forehead. 'Aw no . . . and I thought that I'd got it all worked out!'

'Strange thing is,' Pike continued, 'she was laughing all over her face when she broke her chains. She told me to tell you some stuff Doctor . . . Let's see . . . she's gonna leave the world alone, and let all the things that were already done remain done, because she thinks that's what Ace would want. But she couldn't let Mortimus get away with it. Could I have some of that?' He took a sip of the Doctor's brandy. 'Thank you. Make any sense to you?'

'Oh yes.'

Pike turned to Ace. 'And hey, you must be Ace?'

'Yeah . . .'

'Well, she said to look in the TARDIS, whatever that is. Something good's inside.'

The Doctor met Ace's gaze. 'I'll see you later, if you – '

Ace shook her head. The two of them still had to have words. 'Nah, I'm enjoying this, I'll check it out later.'

'Captain Pike.' The Brigadier reached over the table and shook the Vardan's hand. 'You did us a great service. I hope you'll stay on as,' he raised an eyebrow, 'alien liaison officer?'

'Ah, no . . .' Pike grinned. 'No ET, no comment. I gotta get back to Varda, if the Doctor'll help. With the military marooned up in the satellite, I got a revolution to organize.'

Danny made a fist salute. 'Alien anarchy. Right on.'

'Yes.' The Doctor took a tiny device from his pocket. 'I realigned the satellite's tracking antenna. It's now pointed straight at the Vardan solar system, which is some five thousand light years away.' He pressed a button. 'They're off, in a tight beam, at light speed. You've got a five-thousand-year start to make your homeworld a better place.'

'So . . .' Benny leaned on the Doctor's shoulder. 'Come on then, tell us the plot. Do you want to go from the top, or are you going to need a flip chart, overhead projector, clay models, things like that?'

'No. Well, where to begin?' The Doctor gazed brightly around the eager faces at the table. He loved telling a story, particularly one of his own. 'Mortimus had given his pacification ray to the Vardans, and they'd been using it for months, beamed from the satellite on its negative setting, stirring up hatred and violence. I was caught in a particularly awful example of that, on an underground train. In a climate of uncertainty like that, people shield their minds against new ideas like they curl up their bodies when they're caught in a storm. They get all hunched and tense. It's a lot easier for the Vardans to climb inside, because they can tell their host that they've got a purpose now, that what their media tells them is true. They start to get silly ideas about hanging people, things like that.'

'Ere!' muttered Kit. 'What's so silly about that?'

Danny dug him in the ribs.

'So the three of us arrived, and all had our own ideas about what to do. I went to UNIT, and found it in sorry shape.'

'Ahem!' the Brigadier coughed. 'We'll be shipshape within the year, Doctor, you needn't worry about that.'

'I won't. Benny got to join Plasticine, because Danny Pain is going to be a hero of the far future – '

'Am I?' Danny looked up. 'Shouldn't it be starting now, then? Where are the parades, where's the cash?'

'Heroism grows,' Benny told him. 'I get the feeling that you'll be commemorated for now in those underground magazines of yours. When Earth starts to accept the existence of aliens, you'll become a bit of a legend. After you've been dead a long time, of course.'

'Cheers. Just what I need. The thing is, why? What did I do?'

'In a moment,' the Doctor told him. 'If I start putting

in brackets and things, I'll get lost. And we're getting to the good bit. A bit about a player of games, a manipulator who saw the chance to win and took it. Ace,' he turned to his companion, and put a finger on her nose, 'I should have trusted you all along. You beat me at my own game.'

'Yeah, well.' Ace looked down into her drink. 'Saw the chance. Took it. Mortimus was really into the idea of me being his companion. He thought he was controlling me, and when I realized he wasn't, then I knew I could do something useful.'

'Artemis protected you,' Pike said. 'That was the bit I'd forgotten. She said that she'd managed to shield you from everything.'

The Brigadier frowned at Ace. 'I suppose that this undercover assignment of yours included taking pot-shots at Her Majesty?'

Ace shrugged. 'Only a flesh wound. She'll get over it.' She took a swig from her glass. 'I put a couple of shells in some MI5 men too, one of them 'cos he was gonna shoot Danny. Mortimus believed me when I said I was trying to kill Benny. I just don't understand how he could be so vulnerable. I mean, trusting me to finish the Professor off . . .'

'He was lonely,' the Doctor said. 'If you're left on an ice world, you get lonely. He couldn't be a dragon without his Johnny Piper.'

Ace didn't meet his gaze. She wasn't ready to. 'I knew there was gonna be something important in that locked room, but there was another door, one in the Monk's TARDIS, that I never found. One that would lead to where you were locked up.'

'Ah, but I didn't need that.' The Doctor smiled. 'And this is where you come in, Danny. You and your valuable autograph.'

'Yeah?' Danny grinned. 'Go on.'

'It was written on a bit of the Monk's TARDIS, a bit of the desk – '

'The desk!' Mike Yates spilt a little of his pint. 'Doctor,

the desk vanished from the . . . I'm sorry, I was going to mention it, but – '

'It's all right, Mike. The Monk's TARDIS was unstable. Bits dropped off, but they were still connected to the whole. When I was put in the isolation tank, it took me a minute or so to learn how to breathe that oxygenated liquid. Nasty. Bitter.' The Doctor took a long sip of brandy. 'And hard on the lungs. I decided I wasn't staying there long. Shut off from external stimuli as I was, I could feel the presence of a TARDIS. A quick search of my pockets revealed the piece of Priory notepaper, one of the detached doors of the Monk's TARDIS. A bit of damp origami, a bit of wriggling, and I slipped straight through the paper and into one of the lower chambers of the main craft.'

'I didn't understand a word of that,' Danny murmured. 'But it sounded great.'

'Spitting out oxygenated liquid, I ran straight to his console room. Since Priory ran Skywatch, and that was how Black Star continually knew what UNIT were up to, I knew there was going to be a satellite link down to the Warboy. I used it to set up a narrow sonic beam that managed to halt the Vardans at Stonehenge.'

'Yeah,' Pike nodded. 'Hurt like hell. I freaked out under a jeep.'

'Well . . .' The Doctor looked abashed. 'I didn't know you were a Vardan then. Anyway, I left straight away after that, pausing only to steal one particular video. Then I headed back to my own TARDIS for a change of clothes.'

'Well, there's still a few things that I don't understand,' Doyle interjected. 'Like what happened at Stonehenge? Didn't she,' he gestured to Ace, 'stab you? And what was that thing in the sky?'

'In answer to the latter, that was the image of Artemis the Chronovore. The Monk had fooled me, made me think that he was insane enough to release the creature and offer it a sacrifice. I should have realized that there was no need when he had such fine control over her. He could use her for such precise tasks as emptying people out of various buildings on Salisbury Plain. Very neat. Very nasty.'

Bernice had been watching the way the conversation was going. The bowed heads, the concentration. In amongst all this plot, she thought, a few important things were going to be missed. Ace was looking away often, her face adopting a distant expression. In a while, she'd be thinking that she'd made the wrong decision, that nothing had changed.

Something had to be said.

'So,' said Benny. 'Why did you think that Mortimus was that insane?'

The Doctor stopped. 'I wasn't really thinking. He ... distracted me.'

'What, by securing Ace to a rock? If you got distracted every time one of your chums got tied up, we'd all be in the soup.'

'I don't know, I – '

'I suspect,' Benny continued mercilessly, 'that you were actually rather relieved to see her in that situation. Because that meant – '

'It meant that Mortimus had betrayed her. Yes. That's true.' He turned to Ace, suddenly fumbling and tripping over his words. Behind him, the Brigadier tactfully started taking orders for another round. 'I rushed in, like a fool. I was full of sudden joy. I was so shocked when you stabbed me, I expected the blade to be real.'

'Why?' Ace couldn't look at him. 'Did you think you deserved it?'

'Yes.'

'Well, you didn't. I never wanted to hurt you, I just wanted you to know what it felt like, being manipulated. That's why I whispered to you.'

'Yes. "Scream, I'll save you later". That could almost be my slogan.'

'Too right. For a minute there, you were my companion. And I was the Professor.'

'How did it feel?'

260

'Great. As a part-time job.' She finally looked at the Time Lord. 'Pressure must get to you, all those plans going at once. Ever had a coronary?'

'Two hearts.'

'Both made of stone.'

'No. Stone would have broken your blade.'

'Aladdin, right?'

'I was the villain. Aladdin stole that pretend knife and used it to free the genie from the bottle.'

Benny was amazed. 'So you were in panto? When?'

'UNIT staff Christmas party, 1973. Captain Yates was Widow Twankey.' The Brigadier placed a new pint of bitter in Benny's hand. 'And Jo was Aladdin.'

Benny turned back to Ace. The Doctor had started to talk to Danny now, leaving them alone. 'What was that thing you were fetching in the valley?'

'Something to free Artemis. On the eye of the White Horse, where I'd made it when I recreated bits of the TARDIS out of my memories. Danny saved the world again, there. Artemis came to him in his dreams, and told him stuff when she couldn't get through to me.'

'Thanks for the bouncy floor.'

'I thought that everything I did was being watched,' Ace sighed. 'So I couldn't tell you. But the bouncy floor must always have been there. It must be kind of how I remember Heaven.'

'You mean you remember the ground being all sort of soft and welcoming and pneumatic?' Benny smiled archly. 'How strange.'

'Maybe we could go back to that Academy of yours one day and check out the soil conditions,' Ace deadpanned.

Benny took a deep breath. 'I brought down a helicopter at Stonehenge, you know. Shot the pilot.'

'Head or chest shot?'

'Head. I didn't enjoy it in the least.'

'Nobody does.'

'But I did feel a really awful sort of comradeship with the people I was fighting alongside. I called him,' she inclined her head at the Brigadier, 'sir. In the end, I suppose I was just doing what I had to do to stay alive.'

'Same here. I don't really want to be a soldier, right?' That had come out quickly, in a rush. 'But I am one, now. And I don't think you stop being one. Hey, does Danny remind you of Jan?'

Benny laughed, a little taken aback by the sudden conspiratorial air Ace had adopted. 'A bit. Not a lot. And no matter what he may have told you, we –'

'Nah, neither did we.' Ace reached out and adjusted Benny's hairband a fraction. 'Pain, isn't it?'

'Sort of . . .'

'So, what are you going to do now?' the Doctor was asking Yates and Doyle.

'Well, Black Star is over,' Doyle told him. 'We haven't got the resources to recover, like UNIT have. So me and this good old traitor Michael have decided to set up something new together. A little co-operative food shop, none of these additives that make you a junkie, and a booksellers. We'll have a printing press too, if they don't come along and smash it up too often. We're going to go and spread the word.'

'Doctor,' Yates leaned forward. 'You know the future. Are things going to get easier, now that the Vardans have gone? Or are greed and money going to win out over humanity?'

The Doctor looked past Yates, into the middle distance. On the pavement in front of the pub sat a man with no home, basking in the sunlight. The difficult smile on his face was that of somebody who knew that winter would come.

'It'll get worse,' the Doctor told Yates. 'But one day, perhaps, it'll get better.'

That afternoon had melted into a balmy evening, and Benny had agreed to fulfil Plasticine's last gigging commitment, bottom of the bill at the Roundhouse.

'Killing our manager . . .' Danny was running from wall

262

to wall in the dressing room, bouncing off things. 'How credible can you get? What we need to do now is – '

'Find another lead singer, for a start,' Cob interjected. 'There's this guy called Sidney who's hanging about, calls himself Hymie. He's trying to be in everybody's band.'

'What's he sound like?' Kit asked.

'Dunno. Looks great, though.'

Benny swirled into the room in a full silver ballgown, carrying a little wand with a star on the end. 'Well?' she asked. 'Ahead of my time or what? I have become a New Romantic.'

Kit turned to Cob. 'Give this Sid bloke a call.'

Bernice walked onto stage, and shouted back at the crowd who shouted at her. 'We're Plasticine, and we've just saved the world. What did you do today?'

At the back of the hall stood the Doctor and the Brigadier. 'I must admit, it all sounds the same to me,' the soldier opined. 'But then, I suppose it's not made for my old ears, is it?'

'No.' The Doctor looked at him questioningly. 'How are you feeling?'

'Feeling? Fine, Doctor, absolutely fine.' Lethbridge-Stewart stuck his fingers in his ears as Danny hit the first of his three chords. 'Although I won't be if I stay here long. Fancy a walk?'

They made their way out of the building and into the early dusk. The sun had just set over the railway yards and terraced houses, and lights were springing up as families finished tea and switched on the television.

'Funny, you asking how I feel,' the Brigadier began. 'Haven't quite shrugged off the Vardan mind-control, I think. I wanted to watch the news this evening, just to catch up on how the public's taking the official explanations, you know.'

'What are the official explanations?' the Doctor asked.

'Bob Bertram was a crook, halted in the world's biggest fraud attempt by the forces of British Intelligence and the BBC. It's very nearly true, you know. That so-called charity he'd set up was based in Switzerland for reasons other than European unity.'

'He never could resist stealing pennies. Couldn't you tell them the truth?'

The Brigadier smiled. 'No. National panic, all that. Besides, they'd never believe it. You start to tell people the truth, Doctor, and they'll crucify you.'

'But that's what this is all about, isn't it? What did you see on the news?'

'There were a lot of reports about the aftermath of the Black Star actions, and how they seemed to have stopped. They'd found this little boy, about eleven, who'd been hit by a stray piece of shrapnel. They visited his hospital bed. Fair enough, human interest and all that. And then they had a word with his parents. They asked them what they thought of the terrorists. Some strong language was used, which is understandable. But then they asked a police inspector the same question. And then they started to ask it to people who'd seen the Big Ben explosion.' Lethbridge-Stewart paused, folding his hands behind his back. 'And I was thinking, all the time: is this really news? I know that killing people isn't a decent way to conduct one's business. I don't need some journalist telling me what to think, over and over again. And as I thought that, Doctor, I had what I can only describe as a hallucination. I thought I saw a little Vardan there again, in the corner of the screen. And he was pointing right at me. Laughing.' The Brigadier straightened up and took a deep breath, staring at the hundreds of illuminated households across the railway tracks. 'Now why do you suppose that he was laughing?'

The Doctor stepped round to face his old friend, his face a picture of agonized concern. 'I'm sure he wasn't laughing at you. I'm sorry. This is my last rewrite.' He reached up and touched Lethbridge-Stewart's brow. 'Forget.'

The Brigadier rubbed his forehead, and stared down at the Doctor. 'Well, it was good to see you again, Mr, ah . . . yes. Anyway, must be going. Things to do. Planning to see

Doris tonight. Might take a bit of a holiday. Who knows, might chuck it all in and retire. Been hard these last few months. Give my love to . . .' he waved his hand vaguely, as if struggling to remember names. 'The children.'

The Doctor inclined his head, smiled sadly and watched the Brigadier as he marched off towards the glowing city. Then he turned and walked back to the door of the venue. So, things would progress as he knew them. The Brigadier would retire before his time, take up a teaching post without ever really knowing why. That was good, in the end. The old soldier stood for things that wouldn't matter a damn in the next decade.

Claire Tennant was leaning on the wall beside the entrance, staring up at the stars through London's light pollution. She was wearing her big trousers again. 'I've been looking up at the night sky ever since I was a child,' she told the Time Lord. 'Sometimes I wish I could meet somebody who's been there and not have to shoot at them.'

The Doctor took off his hat, and pulled a white rabbit from it. He handed it to her. 'You've just achieved your ambition,' he told her. 'Take care of him.'

'What's he called?'

'Alistair.' The Doctor frowned at her. 'Didn't he ever tell you?'

Deep inside the Doctor's TARDIS, Ace stood in front of a door. She'd come here when the party had split up, not wanting to go and see the band. The attraction of Artemis' final gift had proved too strong.

'Okay . . .' she whispered. 'Let's see.'

She opened the door a notch. Low autumn sunshine and the heady smells of grassland and forest wafted out.

Clenching her fists, she went inside.

Heaven was still heaven. The forests swayed and sighed along the slopes of the Valley of the White Horse. Ace stepped through the trees, pained and longing and very scared. She felt seventeen.

She came to the edge of the undergrowth and didn't

look, closed her eyes and just took a deep breath of what might have been.

The breath included wood smoke. She made herself look.

Underneath the White Horse, along the valley, there was a camp and a circle of standing stones. Beside a fire, a group of people were sitting.

At this distance, she couldn't see any faces.

She watched for what must have been an hour, until the sun dropped below the horizon and the first torches were lit in the valley.

Beside her, two owls settled on a branch.

'No,' Ace told them. 'I'd never come out.'

And she turned and walked back to the door.

Epilogue

The Future

1993. The Doctor, Ace and Benny wandered through the sprawling site of the Glastonbury Festival of Performing Arts. Distant music echoed from the stages, people walked by in paint and dreadlocks, and the smell of hot food mingled with aromatic summer breezes in the cool dusk.

'Neat idea!' Ace was looking around in delight. Benny had noted that she hadn't been wearing her mirrorshades and armour lately. In the brilliant light of the torches that illuminated the tent stalls, she looked young for her years. A young woman off to see a band in a fractal T-shirt. 'But why here, Professor?'

'Ah,' the Doctor was striding purposefully along, his umbrella needling the churned-up ground of the market area. 'Did you know there's a mobile library that calls into Glastonbury for three hours every Wednesday afternoon?'

'Not going there, are we?'

'No.' They'd stayed in 1976 for a few days after Plasticine's farewell gig. At the end of the performance, Benny announced that she was leaving the band, and invited auditions from the audience. A few skeletal lads had leapt up on-stage. A couple of them had been good. They, of course, had been discounted immediately.

Alex Pike had been given a trip in the TARDIS. He'd stepped out into the Vardan jungle, the real Vardan jungle, staring at Ace in puzzlement. 'You know,' he said. 'I keep thinking I've met you before.'

'In your dreams,' Ace told him. He'd shrugged and run off into the undergrowth, heading for the distant spires

267

of an alien city. The last they saw of him was a cheery wave as he disappeared between the trees.

'A brave and efficient Vardan . . .' Benny had murmured. 'I do believe I'm about to see an elephant fly.'

Now, Benny raised a finger to ask a question. 'What were you going to do with Mortimus, anyway?'

'Let him go,' the Doctor told her. 'I thought that he'd learnt his lesson. Like I'd learnt mine. Peace. It's the only way. Unfortunately, Artemis doesn't really think in those terms.' He was about to say something else when a little bundle of energy and plaited hair barged into his kneecaps.

The girl was about five, and she'd been crying. 'I'm lost!' she shouted at the Doctor. 'I'm Amy, and I'm lost!'

Ace picked her up. 'Not any more, you're not,' she told her. 'This is the Doctor. He finds lost children . . . and he beats up monsters!'

'There aren't any monsters!' Amy told Ace.

'Oh yes there are.' The Doctor fluttered his hand and produced a bag of chocolate buttons. 'Which is why I'm only going to give you these if you promise that next time you're lost, you talk to a policeman, or a nice lady like Ace.'

The little girl nodded seriously, staring up at the Doctor with big eyes. She took the buttons eagerly, forgetting that she'd been crying.

Benny held out a hand. 'Can I have a chocolate button, please?' The girl reluctantly gave one to her. 'What's your second name, Amy?'

'Paripski!' Amy told her proudly. 'My Dad's famous!'

'You mean your Dad's a famous rock star?' Benny took Amy from Ace. 'Come on then, we might find him near the smaller stage, mightn't we?'

Amy nodded. 'That's what I got lost from.'

Benny winked over her shoulder. 'Back in a minute. Stay there, okay?'

Ace and the Doctor found themselves alone together for the first time. They looked at each other, a bit awkwardly.

'Cute kid,' Ace said.

'Yes. Full of potential energy. I wonder what she'll grow up to be?'

'Don't you know?'

'No. I thought I'd give up trying to find out things in advance. Give up trying to be a monster's nightmare. I'm looking forward to being surprised.'

Ace grinned. 'Didn't I surprise you?'

'Your faith surprised me.' The Doctor turned away. 'You sacrificed everything for me. And I thought I'd finally lost you.'

'Never. You'd have let your friend die for me.'

'I thought that would be fair. Fair for all my sins.'

'That sounds like Danny. He did something wrong, and he gave himself the luxury of wallowing in it, of living in the past. I just got fed up with you and me sacrificing ourselves, of all that guilt and resentment. I got my choice, right? Thanks to Artemis, I finally got to choose. And I chose to go and find out what the future's gonna be like. In Spacefleet, they taught you not to get involved. Not to make it personal. I always thought they were talking rubbish. I was sure.' Ace took a deep breath of the glorious Glastonbury air. 'Thanks for teaching me I was right.'

The Doctor turned and embraced her. They held each other for a long time. 'The warrior,' he mumbled into her shoulder, 'becomes the healer.'

'Do you mind that I'm a soldier?'

'Some of my best friends are soldiers.'

'Hey!' Benny called. 'Look at this for a coincidence!'

Amy was being carried by Danny Pain. He was seventeen years older, a healthy and well-fed man in dreadlocks and multicoloured overalls. 'Doctor! Ace!' he called, and dashed forward, grabbing them both in a bear hug. 'You're not older! You're not even a year older!'

'Looking good yourself!' Ace clambered out of the rather awkward three-way cuddle. 'Is Amy yours?'

'Danny Paripski's my real name. I never told you that? Yeah, Amy's my daughter, and she's got two brothers and two sisters.'

269

'He seems,' Benny told them, 'to have overcome his fears.'

'I met this woman,' Danny looked at his boots. 'Over from Aussie, she was, called Helen. We hit it off, joined the travellers, had lots of babies.'

'What happened to the woman?' Ace asked carefully. 'You know – '

'I haven't seen her,' Danny didn't meet her eyes. 'But I've heard that she's okay, that she got healed. In the end I just thought that I'd better get on with it. Talking of which, Doctor, we need you here now, some of the laws they're introducing . . .'

The Doctor shook his head. 'Local difficulties. You can beat them on your own. So you're famous now?'

'Well, in a way,' Danny was grinning at them all in astonishment, his arm curled around Benny. 'Plasticine couldn't find another deal when Priory went into liquidation, not even with all these other singers that we tried out. We cut one single with Stephen Hall on lead, over at EMI, but they just got fed up with us and never gave us a long-term contract. Things were tough for a while. I struggled through the eighties. Then all these kids into ambient dub started dropping my name in the music press. Ozric Tentacles went on and on about me stopping the invasion. That's sort of an urban legend now. I got together with The Orb and put down some tracks that wouldn't do the Vardans any good. They kept asking if I'd ever been on a spaceship. I'm a bit of a guru. I'm guesting with Back To The Planet in a few minutes.' He looked at Benny with a sudden grin. 'We could do a Plasticine reunion! Cobby's here too, and Kit's popped down from the smoke. He's in management now. The crowd'll go wild!'

Benny glanced down at her bermudas and trainers. 'Oh, what the hell . . . it won't rip open the fabric of the space-time continuum, will it?'

The Doctor grinned. 'Go on. Your fifteen minutes has become half an hour.'

Benny scampered off with Danny, little Amy skipping between them.

'Very like Jan now,' Ace whispered to the Doctor. 'I was right about that, at least. There's no justice.'

'No.' The Doctor ruffled her hair. 'There's just us.'

'You and Jan and Danny. You're all similar people.'

'Really? Do you think I should go crusty?'

'Wait until your next incarnation,' Ace advised him. 'I like you the way you are.'

The next morning, the three friends walked, arm in arm, back through the Greenfield area. The washed-out morning sunlight was scattering reflections across the expanse of tents and cars on the hills around the festival site. They'd spent the night in Danny's camp, listening to a sound system, baking spuds and drinking home-made beer.

'And Kit's just this yuppie nightmare!' Ace was laughing. 'He hadn't changed at all. He asked me if I slept on my front, I said no, so he asked if I minded if somebody else did!'

'And did you mind?' Benny asked innocently.

'Yeah. Which is more than I can say for you – '

'I was in the arms of Bacchus . . .'

'Strange name for a Scotsman.'

'He was with that woman Lucy. I only wanted access to her alcohol.'

They had arrived back at the TARDIS, which was disguised as a tarot reader's tent. A painting of the Hanged Man was propped outside. The Doctor fumbled in his pockets, producing the key and a small hammer. 'Wait a moment,' he told his two companions.

He opened the tent flap and went inside. A moment later there came a concussion, a bang and a screech of wrenching equipment.

The stall shimmered, twisted, and reformed into the familiar shape of a police telephone box, circa 1963. The Doctor opened the door and threw the hammer over his shoulder. A cloud of smoke wafted out behind him. 'It's the chameleon circuit,' he told them. 'I'm afraid it's broken again.'

'I approve.' Benny said. 'But do you at least know where we're going?'

'No. I've let the controls set themselves. We could finish up anywhere, in any time or place, facing who knows what.'

Ace took Benny's arm. 'There might be monsters. D'you think we should go with him?'

Benny considered. 'If there are monsters, he'll want to fight them.'

'Yeah, but he'll beat them. They'll probably fall into their own traps. This is the Doctor, right? I think we can trust him.'

The Doctor held open the door of the TARDIS, and Benny and Ace stepped inside. He looked up at the old shape his time and space machine had once more assumed.

'Yes,' he decided. 'It's old-fashioned, Eccentric, even. But after all these years, I think it's me.' He patted the bulk of the TARDIS, and then stepped inside, closing the door.

There came a strange wheezing, groaning sound, and the blue box faded from the fields of the festival.

The Doctor and his friends were off on another adventure.

Long ago in an English summer.

WHO ARE YOU?
Help us to find out what you want.
No stamp needed – free postage!

Name _____

Address _____

Town/County _____

Postcode _____

Home Tel No. _____

About Doctor Who Books

How did you acquire this book?
Buy ☐ Borrow ☐
Swap ☐

How often do you buy Doctor Who books?
1 or more every month ☐ 3 months ☐
6 months ☐ 12 months ☐

Roughly how many Doctor Who books have you read in total?

_____

Would you like to receive a list of all past and forthcoming Doctor Who titles?
Yes ☐ No ☐

Would you like to be able to order the Doctor Who books you want by post?
Yes ☐ No ☐

Doctor Who Exclusives
We are intending to publish exclusive Doctor Who editions which may not be available from booksellers and available only by post.

Would you like to be mailed information about exclusive books?
Yes ☐ No ☐

About You

What other books do you read?

Other character-led books (which characters?) _____

Science Fiction	☐	Thriller/Adventure	☐
Horror	☐		

Non-fiction subject areas (please specify) _____

Male	☐	Female	☐

Age:

Under 18	☐	18–24	☐
25–34	☐	35+	☐

Married	☐	Single	☐
Divorced/Separated	☐		

Occupation _____

Household income:

Under £12,000	☐	£13,000–£20,000	☐
£20,000+	☐		

Credit Cards held:

Yes	☐	No	☐

Bank Cheque guarantee card:

Yes	☐	No	☐

Is your home:

Owned	☐	Rented	☐

What are your leisure interests? _____

Thank you for completing this questionnaire. Please tear it out carefully and return to: **Doctor Who Books, FREEPOST, London, W10 5BR** (no stamp required)